K.C. MILLS

INNO CENT INTENT

BLACK
ODYSSEY
MEDIA

WWW.BLACKODYSSEY.NET

Published by
BLACK ODYSSEY MEDIA

www.blackodyssey.net
Email: info@blackodyssey.net

Library of Congress Control Number: 2023919158

First Trade Paperback Printing: July 2024
ISBN: 978-1-957950-16-7
ISBN: 978-1-957950-17-4 (e-book)

10 9 8 7 6 5 4 3 2 1

Manufactured in the United States of America

Distributed by Kensington Publishing Corp.

Dear Reader,

I want to thank you immensely for supporting Black Odyssey Media authors, and our ongoing efforts to spotlight more minority storytellers. The scariest and most challenging task for many writers is getting the story, or characters, out of our heads and onto the page. Having admitted that, with every manuscript that Kreceda and I acquire, we believe that it took talent, discipline, and remarkable courage to construct that story, flesh out those characters, and prepare it for the world. Debut or seasoned, our authors are the real heroes and heroines in OUR story. And for them, we are eternally grateful.

Whether you are new to K.C. Mills or Black Odyssey Media, we hope that you are here to stay. We also welcome your feedback and kindly ask that you leave a review. For upcoming releases, announcements, submission guidelines, etc., please be sure to visit our website at www.blackodyssey.net or scan the QR code below. We can also be found on social media using @iamblackodyssey. Until next time, take care and enjoy the journey!

Joyfully,

Shawanda Williams

Shawanda "N'Tyse" Williams
Founder/Publisher

EMOTIONAL MISTAKES

SEPTEMBER 5, 2024
10:30 P.M.

There's only you, Cass. No one but you.

Those words played over and over again in Cassidy's mind. As much as she wanted to believe them, her instincts dispelled the lie and hovered like a dark cloud, looming with betrayal. The possibility of her worst fears was crawling up her spine. After all, she had spent the better part of her life being a human lie detector. Dr. Cassidy Evans, bestselling author, accomplished criminal psychologist, and forensic profiler, was the best at her job. With certainty. If that were truly the case, why couldn't she say with *certainty* that her husband, the man to whom she'd pledged her life with vows of love and loyalty, who'd pledged his love to her, wasn't betraying those vows?

I would know.

I should know.

But I don't.

The car in front of her turned left, so she turned left. The brake lights illuminated, cutting through the darkness as the vehicle slowed, then paused at the parking garage entrance. Cassidy watched while an arm extended from the car. She recognized the expensive fabric of the track jacket that covered that arm and swallowed thickly as a white plastic card was waved in front of a sensor. Seconds later, the gate lifted, and the late model BMW glided into the parking garage. Cassidy gripped her steering wheel, sucked in a cleansing breath, and advanced toward that same entrance. She had no access card available, so she pressed the button, removed the parking ticket, and slowly crept in, swiping her head left and right trying to locate the vehicle she was following.

On the second level, she found a spot tucked in the corner and kept her eyes on the tall, lean figure who moved through the garage with his phone to his ear, smiling in the way that would normally cause her stomach to flutter. Today, that smile had nausea crawling within.

She quickly got out of her vehicle and hurried behind him but maintained enough of a distance to go unnoticed, grateful that he was lost in the conversation he was deeply engaged in. He had no clue that he was being followed, which meant he spoke freely, and Cassidy's chest grew tighter.

"I'm on my way. I told you I would be here. I keep my promises, sweetheart."

That was the last thing Cassidy heard before he entered the metal car. She paused and watched the numbers above the steel doors illuminate with the up arrow as soon as the doors separated them. She moved toward the elevator, her foot bouncing as she watched the numbers crawl. L for lobby, 1, 2, and then 3. Third floor. He was on the third floor. The number on the display paused briefly before descending, and the metal doors in front of Cassidy slowly peeled open. The car was empty. She struggled with stepping inside, hands misting over, heart racing, pulse thrumming rapidly in her neck. This one moment could change her life. Cassidy wasn't sure she was ready to have her world turned upside down, so she stepped away. On the way back to her car, she removed her phone and dialed, holding her breath until she heard the automated voice.

Please leave a message . . .

Cassidy dialed several more times, back-to-back, and each time got the same result. On the last call, she decided to leave a message. What was there to lose? He was a liar, a cheater. Maybe he would leave *his sweetheart whose promises he kept* and come home to explain and beg for forgiveness that Cassidy wouldn't give.

"I can't believe that you would do this to *me*. To *us*. This ruins everything—*everything*, Niles. I'll make you regret this. You're going to regret fucking me over. I promise you'll regret this."

After ending the call and sliding into the driver's seat, Cassidy's fingers burned from her tight grip on her phone. Her heart ached. Tears were falling, and there wasn't a damn thing she could do about it.

"How could you?" she whispered.

There's only you, Cass. No one but you.

Cassidy's logical mind knew that she should leave. Nothing good would come from confronting the situation this way. She had far too much to lose. Her career, her reputation. She would become a headline and not the type she had been proud of in the past. But still, she couldn't bring herself to leave. Cassidy needed answers, so she did the worst thing possible, the one decision that would change her life forever . . .

She stayed.

1.

"**C**assidy? Is that you?"

After the night she'd had, the last thing that Cassidy wanted was to deal with anyone. She'd only left the house because the walls seemed to be closing in on her. She hadn't arrived home until well after three in the morning, removed her clothes, showered, and then crawled into bed. At lunchtime, she felt anxious and decided getting out of the house would be the best option. Fresh air could do her some good, and lunch at one of her favorite places felt like a smart option. But now, not so much.

"It is . . ." She forced a smile and tucked a few loose tendrils of hair behind her ear. The blunt-cut bob she'd talked herself into was cute but not very functional when she wanted to throw in a ponytail for a low-maintenance day. "Greg, how are you?"

Cassidy watched cautiously as her old friend and colleague, Detective Gregory Harper, approached. He was dressed in his norm—slacks, a starched and pressed button-up shirt with a sports coat, and loafers. Neat but not very stylish.

"Great, actually. Just stepped out to grab a bite to eat. Mind if I join you?"

Yes.

God, yes, I mind.

"No, not at all." She silently cursed herself for not requesting to be seated inside, which offered a bit more privacy. The outdoor area was filled with small, metal, high tables, and you could sit wherever you liked. It also offered fresh air and a perfect view of the outdoor shopping center where the restaurant was located. Cassidy had planned to grab a bite and, hopefully, be distracted for a while people-watching. It had become a thing for her years ago. People-watching was a bit of a treat and a challenge for someone constantly analyzing others' behaviors. Cassidy had hoped for a distraction but not that of an old colleague.

"You sure . . ." When her eyes lifted to Greg, she noticed the pinched look of concern and quickly forced another smile.

"I'm sure. It's been a while. I'd love to catch up." She flicked her wrist, motioning for him to sit across from her. The table only had room for two high-back stools, one of which she currently occupied.

"So, how are things? It feels like forever since I've seen you. With all the hype and success you have now, I'm actually shocked to see you out here alone."

Cassidy smiled softly. She was a bit of a celebrity, but only to those who were privy to the world she lived in. Criminal psychologists were a far cry from other celebrities such as athletes, musicians, and other entertainers. Cassidy didn't need to travel with security or hide behind low-sitting hats and oversized sunglasses. She could hide in plain sight for the most part. However, she did occasionally get recognized, primarily by others in her field or college students who studied her work, intending to follow in Cassidy's footsteps.

"I'm no one important."

Greg offered a genuine smile. "Your book has been trending. Hit number one on the New York Times Bestseller List. I purchased a copy *or two* myself. I'd call that important. Not to mention all the traveling and speaking engagements. You're a big deal, Cass."

"To some, maybe," she offered humbly before arching a brow. "You read my book?"

Greg smiled bashfully. "Well, no, but I've worked enough cases with you to know it's nothing but the good stuff, and don't downplay your success, Cass—more than just *some*. Because of you, the world is a safer place. The cases you've helped solve, a few of my own actually . . ." He paused and winked. "And the knowledge you're offering those that are coming behind you . . . You're more than important. You're *necessary*. It hurt a little when you decided to stay behind the scenes and no longer showed up on crime scenes. We miss you."

"I miss you guys too, but I had to step back. It got to be a little much." She hesitated. "It weighs on you, you know?"

Gregory nodded with understanding. "I do. Every day is a constant struggle between finding the good in things when the evil, poisonous ways of people always surround you. Can't say I blame you for stepping away. Also can't say I was happy about it, but I understand." He offered another genuine smile.

"So, I guess I should not only congratulate you on your new career path but on your personal life as well. Word on the street is that you're married now."

She cringed slightly before lowering her eyes to the modest diamond on her finger. "I am."

"Well, congratulations. Didn't see that coming. I'm pretty sure you told me more than a few times that marriage wasn't for people like us."

Cassidy laughed lightly, although her chest pinched just a little. "I did, and I still feel that way. We see and experience so much that it's hard to block that out and trust enough to let our guard down."

"But you did," he offered quietly before adding, "Or, at least, I think you did."

Cassidy frowned. "What's that supposed to mean?"

Gregory pointed to her hand. "You're wearing that fancy ring, and I've heard the rumors but can't say for certain anyone has ever seen the guy."

Relaxing a bit, Cassidy nodded. "We keep our lives private. It works better that way for both of us. With my past, dealing with and working the type of cases I did, and now the book? Things can get a little crazy. We wanted as much of a normal life as possible."

"Makes sense. So what does he do? I'm curious to know what type of man got and kept your attention long enough to get you to say I do."

Grinning, Cassidy glanced at her ring again before her eyes met Greg's. "He's a PI. More on the private sector end. He travels a lot, locating missing persons. Some who have simply lost their way, and others who don't want to be found but have loved ones who need to know they're alive. Another reason for keeping our lives private. Anonymity is necessary for him to keep a low profile for work and all."

It wasn't until that very moment that Cassidy realized there might be other reasons her husband insisted on keeping their lives hidden away from prying eyes. She lifted the glass of wine she'd been sipping and swallowed a few hefty gulps, hoping Greg didn't notice the shift in her mood. He was a detective, after all. Capturing the little things was his job, and he was damn good at it.

"Makes sense. Can't have your name and face attached to someone of your caliber if you're trying to fly under the radar."

Or if you're cheating on your wife.

"Welcome to Roman's Grill. Can I take your drink order?"

Cassidy lifted her eyes to the server that joined them. She already had her meal: chicken Caesar salad, fresh Italian bread, and a glass of wine. While Greg placed his order for an imported beer and pastrami sandwich, she busied herself watching the people passing by.

Once his food arrived, the two ate, and the conversion shifted away from Cassidy's personal life to the recent cases Greg had been working. He wouldn't dare miss the opportunity to pick the brain of an old colleague about things that could possibly give a different perspective.

When they finished their meal, and the server placed the leather binder holding the bill on the table, Greg quickly handed over his card to cover the meal. Cassidy had appreciated the distraction and temporary escape from her life, so she argued that she would pay, but Greg eventually won the battle.

"Well, thanks so much for this. I enjoyed catching up. I almost miss that life. It feels like an eternity separates then and now instead of a few years. The lectures and book signings aren't as exciting as being out there and having firsthand experience with the case files I used for teaching purposes."

"And it's also not as mentally taxing. Trust me, you've got the better deal. Be grateful you escaped before it totally weighed down on you. I have my good and bad days, mostly bad, though."

"You're right, but I still miss it."

Greg nodded and held up a hand just as a call came through. "Let me take this real quick." Before she could give her parting words, knowing it was time to get back to her life, Greg accepted the call. Cassidy thought leaving without saying goodbye would be rude, so she waited.

"How many? Where? Our guys already there?" He lifted his eyes to Cassidy, who assumed it was a work-related call, which was confirmed moments later.

"I'm not far from there now. I'm on my way," Gregory rattled off and then ended the conversation.

"Work?"

"Yeah. Shooting in an apartment building not far from here, one of those fancy high-rises. Housekeeper came in and found the body. Never-ending cycle," he muttered, shoving his hands into his pockets.

"Seems that way."

"I'm gonna head out. It was good seeing you, Cass. Glad you're doing well."

"Same. I really do miss you guys, you know."

Greg nodded and then smiled. "You wanna head over there with me. You know, for old time's sake. Remind yourself why you shouldn't miss this *too* much."

Cassidy smiled and shook her head. "No, thank you. I'll leave that to the experts."

"Which you are. Might do you some good to get back out there. Shake up the fancy, mundane life you're living these days."

She laughed lightly. "Or it might do you some good to have another set of eyes on your crime scene."

"Yeah, that too. What do you say?"

"I, uhhh . . ." Cassidy frowned, thinking about the prospect. She hadn't been in the field in years and hadn't planned on going back to it, but the thought of going home to sit and overthink the situation she recently found herself in with her husband was a little far less intriguing. She would have to deal with her life at some point, but for now, she decided to take the out.

"Oh hell, why not."

"*That's* what I'm talking about. Let's go. You can ride with me, and I'll bring you back later to get your car."

"Sounds good."

◆─────❧─────◆

As Detective Harper pulled in front of the building where the shooting was reported, Cassidy's heart rate galloped. How much of a coincidence was it that there had been a murder in the same building where she'd been the night before?

She thought carefully about declining the offer to go inside after her mind spiraled toward all the things she hadn't considered the night before. The cameras, possible witnesses, her cell phone pinging off a nearby tower. What if it was her husband who had been murdered?

Relax.

There was no way those things would matter. At best, the world would find out that her husband was a lying, cheating asshole because he was most certainly alive. The universe wouldn't be so cruel. As hurt and angry as she was, she wouldn't wish death on the man who broke her heart. This was all just one big coincidence. One that meant she would have to burden herself with the hassle of marriage counseling or divorce.

If he cheated, could I forgive him?

No. Absolutely not.

"Cass, you okay?" The frown on Greg's face had her climbing out of the dark hole her thoughts had sunk into.

"Yes, I'm fine."

She wasn't fine. Her mind was sprinting in a million different directions, but something deep within, that small voice that she wanted to ignore but couldn't, was clawing at the back of her brain, pushing in a way that meant she was going through with this.

"Good, let's go."

Cassidy exited the car and followed Greg through the massive glass doors to enter the building, through the lobby, and then to the elevator. She remained quiet as they stepped inside, only for her heart to race again once he punched the third floor. Her mind flashed back to the night prior.

Just a coincidence.

Once they reached the third floor, Cassidy's past came flooding back. It had been years since she'd found herself submerged in a situation like the current one, but not much had changed. Truthfully, only the faces and the location.

A uniformed officer met them outside the apartment as they neared the crime scene. While they both slipped on the protective booties and latex gloves that were handed over, an officer brought Gregory up to speed on what they'd discovered thus far. Once properly suited to avoid compromising the crime scene, Cassidy slowly scanned her surroundings. She took in the lingering residents and the handful of people working the scene, moving in and out of the apartment. Nothing seemed out of place. Just a typical crime scene. It wasn't until the uniformed officer extended a gloved hand toward Gregory that Cassidy brought her focus back to them.

The officer held an opened leather wallet, which exposed a driver's license from another state. "Guy's name is Jerrod Williams. The apartment is his based on what little we have so far. Found a stack of mail on the counter. Utility bills, credit card statements, and cable bills. They match the name on the license."

"You speak to any of the neighbors yet?"

"A few. Said they don't know much about him. One did say he's been here for at least a year. She's seen him coming and going, mostly with women. Maybe that's what got him killed. Someone didn't like being one of many."

Cassidy frowned at the way the officer made light of a man losing his life but kept her thoughts to herself.

"Maybe. They done in there?" Greg glanced around and motioned to the open door with a nod.

"Still collecting evidence and getting photos. The MEs are tending to the body, though. Should have this wrapped up soon. You can go on in."

Greg nodded and glanced at Cassidy when he noticed the uniform staring curtly. After checking the guy's badge, he decided to make an introduction. "Officer Carter, this is Cassidy Evans, criminal psychologist and forensic profiler."

The officer nodded, and his expression tensed. "This doesn't seem like the type of case that needs a profiler."

"I'm here in an unofficial capacity. Just tagging along with an old friend."

Carter glanced at Greg. They had been to a few crime scenes together, and Carter knew of Greg and his record. Stand-up guy who followed the rules, but he still questioned bringing in a civilian, which Cassidy would be if she weren't there in an official capacity.

"You sure that's a good idea?"

Greg glanced at the guy and tilted his head to the side. "My crime scene. My call. I'm giving her clearance."

Carter shrugged and stepped away, giving them more access. "Your call, Detective. Not my business."

"You sure this is a good idea?" Cassidy questioned.

"You've done this a million times before. You know the protocol."

"Stay out of the way, and don't touch anything."

Greg nodded with a smile. "Come on, let's go."

———— ❧ ————

As soon as they entered the apartment, nostalgia set in. Uniforms were moving about bagging items, taking photos, and whispering amongst themselves. No one paid much attention to anything besides what they were working on.

"Where's the body?" Greg asked. A female uniformed officer pointed to her left as she took in Greg and Cassidy.

"Bedroom."

They made their way down the hall, pausing just outside the room where they noticed the ME leaning over the body. The bed blocked their view from the doorway, so it wasn't until Greg completely entered the room and Cassidy followed that she had a clear visual of the body. Once she did, her world tumbled.

"Oh God. Oh God …" Cassidy threw a hand over her mouth, feeling a wave of nausea rushing through her system. She had worked enough crime scenes where the rancid smell and bloated features of a body settling into rigor mortis shouldn't have been so overwhelming. However, this current body brought out a very different reaction. She buckled over, slamming her eyes shut, and began gasping erratically. After a moment, she attempted to blink away the visual of the body she had just caught a glimpse of. Male, on his back. One arm bent across the chest, hand resting on the blood-soaked jacket that covered his upper body. The same jacket he'd worn the night before.

"Ma'am, are you okay?" someone asked. The voice sounded muffled, and Cassidy couldn't tell which direction it came from. Her mind had gone hazy, but she managed to pull herself together long enough to take one last look at the body. She had to be sure.

Is it really him?

The minute her eyes landed on the body splayed on the floor between the bed and floor-to-ceiling windows, resting in a pool of blood, something in Cassidy snapped, and she stumbled backward before jetting out of the room and the apartment. Once she reached the hallway, her hand pressed flat against the wall, and she buckled over again, gasping for air.

He's dead.

Someone shot him.

He's dead.

"Oh God," she whispered just before she felt a hand on her back, which caused her to jerk away from whoever it belonged to.

"Cass, what's going on? You okay?"

"Name," she rushed out, lifting her eyes to Greg to find him staring at her with concern and confusion. She threw an arm across her stomach and asked again when he didn't respond. "Name. What's the name of the victim?"

Gregory took a step forward, lowering his voice after glancing over his shoulder and realizing they had an audience. "Cass, what the hell is going on? You're pale as shit and acting crazy. You've seen more than enough bodies in far worse condition than that one in there to be able to handle a simple gunshot." It took a minute for him to make sense of what was happening. "Shit, do you know him? You know the victim, don't you?"

"Name," she whispered again, ignoring Greg's accusations.

"Cass . . ."

"Name?" she barked with a little more force. "What's his fucking name?"

"Whose name? The victim?" Greg's brows were pinched in frustration. Cassidy nodded, so he quickly handed over the requested information. "Jerrod Williams."

She shook her head slowly, throwing her hand over her mouth once more before she managed to swallow down another wave of nausea. "That can't be right. Can't be. They're mistaken."

"I've seen his identification. Picture matched the victim. What do you mean it can't be right? Do you know him?"

Her eyes navigated past Greg to the apartment door before they found his once more. She swallowed thickly, not believing what she was about to admit. "That can't be right because that man in there is my husband, and his name is Niles Anderson, *not* Jerrod Williams."

2.

FIRST FORTY-EIGHT

"What were you thinking?"

Detective Harper's jaw clenched as he stood in Allen Jones's office, his captain, being berated for simple missteps. One that anyone could have made, but after fifteen years in homicide as a decorated detective, he shouldn't have those types of missteps.

"You know who she is—"

"Of course, I know who she is. I've worked side-by-side with her plenty of times, just like you. She's good at her job, the best, actually. But today, she was a fucking civilian and had no business being on *your* crime scene. Do you know how bad this looks for the department?"

"I do." There wasn't much Harper could say to defend his actions, so he didn't bother. It was a rookie mistake one couldn't have foreseen. And there was no going back.

"Damn it, Harper," Captain Jones growled, shaking his head.

Detective Nathanial Davis kept quiet while his new captain and his colleague went back and forth about the details that led to the three of them ending up in an office together. He was already processing how he would approach the case he would be taking

19

over but needed to wait until the official announcement. He was impatient and wished the two of them would move this along.

"You know what this means, don't you?"

Davis's eyes moved slowly between Detective Harper and their captain.

"What what means?"

"You bringing Evans to the crime scene where her husband was found murdered?"

Davis caught the exact moment when Detective Harper understood what was happening. His eyes traveled across the room to Davis, who remained quiet while Harper's face tensed and flushed red. "You're not taking me off the case—"

"I am," Captain Jones replied with a huff and then raked a hand down his face and over his head. "You didn't leave me much of a choice."

"I get why you think that's necessary, but I can be impartial, and more than anything, I can investigate in a way that will ensure justice is served. It's her husband, for Christ's sake." Detective Harper threw his hands up exasperatedly.

"You're too close to the situation, and you've already potentially compromised the case. You don't need to be a part of this." Nathanial's tone was even, diplomatic when he finally spoke up. Both Captain Jones and Detective Harper listened to the newbie. The captain remained quiet. He was the one who'd made the call and filled Detective Davis in before calling them both into the office. Detective Harper's reaction was explosive.

"Of course, I'm close to the case. She's one of us—"

"No, actually, she's not, and you're proving why you don't need to be a part of this investigation. She hasn't been ruled out as a suspect. You two share a personal relationship that might cloud your judgment and—"

"She didn't kill her husband," Harper growled. "And you're damn right; she and I have a personal relationship—as does everyone else in this precinct . . ."

"Not everyone," Detective Davis noted, which further infuriated Harper.

"I've worked side-by-side with Cassidy. She's part of why our precinct has been so successful in solving tough cases over the years. We owe her this."

"Possibly, but we also can't be sure she's not involved. We have to protect ourselves. Cover our own asses, which means not trying to cover hers. Wouldn't you agree, Captain?" Detective Davis didn't bother looking at their captain. He kept his focus on Harper to deliver the final blow. "You, of all people, should understand."

Harper cringed with the silent reminder that he'd almost botched a very important case for the same reason. He had a prior relationship with the senator's son. They had been old college fraternity brothers. Their familiarity came into question during a sexual assault case where the senator's son was the suspect. He was innocent, and Harper wanted justice for his old college chum but could have compromised the investigation's validity by not recusing himself from the case due to their friendship.

"This isn't the same," he gritted through clenched teeth.

"Close enough," Davis chimed in, still relaxed and void of emotions. He rarely got riled up, which often helped him become a better detective.

"You stay the fuck out of this," Harper warned.

Davis stepped away from the door, closing the space between him and his colleague. Harper was angry, but Davis didn't care. If Harper decided to get physical, Davis could surely defend himself. He was younger, more fit, and a skilled boxer from years of training before joining the force.

"Like it or not, the case is mine. You're too emotional, anyway. Emotions mean mistakes, but regardless, the decision has been made. Captain's orders. Not mine."

"You cocky son of a bitch." Harper stepped forward but relaxed his posture after hearing his name called. When his eyes landed on their captain, he reeled in his anger.

"He's right, Harper. Like it or not, the case is his, and you will stay as far away from this as possible. Considering who she is, we can't afford to mess this up, nor do we need the bad press that will be attached to it if we do. Things are quiet right now, but that won't last long if Cassidy's name gets attached to Williams's. Stay out of it. If I find out otherwise, you'll see me. Understood?"

"Yeah."

Harper kept his eyes trained on Davis, scowling for a moment longer before his eyes moved past him, delivering one last glare at their captain. Davis didn't react other than to follow the path that Harper took, leaving the office until he was out of his line of sight. His focus then moved to their captain.

"I'll get started right away."

"You do that, but please understand, he's right about one thing. She's one of us. Don't fuck this up, Davis." Davis offered a nod before turning to leave, stopping at the door when he heard the captain's voice once more.

"Davis . . ."

"Yeah . . ."

"You've only been here a year. Technically, you're still new. The guys around here are a family. You might want to try not to make enemies. Messing with Harper will get you just that. A bunch of enemies."

Davis glanced over his shoulder, expression neutral but with amusement in his eyes. He wasn't moved by the threat. He was his own man and a bit of a loner. He didn't need friends in the department or to be considered anyone's *family*. His only responsibility was to do his job, which he did efficiently and without bias. Still, he offered the confirmation that he knew his captain wanted.

"Noted. I'll keep that in mind."

With that, he walked away prepared to do what he did best: solve the case.

※

"What do we have?" Detective Davis stood over the body of his newly acquired victim, Jerrod Williams, arms akimbo. His face was relaxed, expression schooled, aside from the intense stare he used when looking over the body and then the ME when she began to deliver the preliminary results.

"Three shots to the chest. One was lodged in the heart, which caused him to bleed out. I bagged up the bullets so you can take them with you." She nodded with her forehead to the table beside Davis and continued. "He died shortly after. No signs of a struggle. No lacerations or bruising that wasn't from the gunshots. The guy was in perfect health. Body is amazing."

Davis shot her a hard stare, and she grinned and shrugged. This was his first time working with the current ME. She was younger, early thirties at most, and not yet affected by the steady flow of dead bodies she handled daily. Or at least he could only assume based on her inappropriate comment about the current victim.

"So, based on what you have so far, someone, potentially an invited guest, shot him due to the lack of struggle?"

"Based on my initial overview, yes, but that would be determined by you, Detective. If there wasn't any forced entry at the scene, then I'd say this wasn't the work of an intruder. He didn't fight back. Based on the angle and trajectory, the first shot appears to be the one that took him down. The second and third were basically overkill. His heart was already bleeding out by the time the last two shots were delivered. Crime of passion, maybe."

He snorted at the amusing banter she delivered. "My job, not yours, but thanks for the input. I'll need a copy of that report."

"Of course. I'll send it over once I've signed off on it. Is there anything else I can help you with, Detective?" He wasn't thrilled with the flirty smile she offered, but he wasn't surprised by it either. He had become immune to the attention and whispers at this point in his career.

Davis wasn't oblivious to how others—women, especially— viewed him. At six-three, his lean, athletic frame reflected the time he spent at the gym boxing to let off steam. His medium brown skin with red undertones was passed down from his mother, and his square jaw, deep chocolate eyes, and full lips were from his father. The two, at times, passed as siblings versus father and son. Or at least, they had before his father was killed. Nathanial Davis was a very handsome and fit man who women appreciated.

"Thanks," he muttered on his way out.

An hour later, Davis was walking back into the precinct, met with a few unwelcome stares from other detectives. Stares he smirked at and then ignored. He bypassed his desk and headed straight for the break room to get a bottle of water, only to be cornered by the reason for all the dirty looks he received from his colleagues.

"Here."

Harper tossed the thick case file on the counter near where Davis was standing.

Davis's eyes lowered to the folder as he untwisted the cap to his water bottle and took a drink, swallowing slowly. A smug grin crossed his face seconds before he spoke.

"What's this, a peace offering? Olive branch, maybe?"

"Fuck you, Davis. I don't need to extend shit to you, most certainly not a peace offering."

"As the leader around here, I would assume you'd want to lead by example. Picking fights with the newbie isn't a responsible move." Like always, Davis's demeanor was relaxed and unbothered. He cared very little about the opinions of his peers—especially not Harper's. Harper was a decent enough guy but had a God complex that often guided him to command the respect that hadn't been earned or given in return. Davis wasn't the type to fall in line.

"Since you know the order of things around here, seems to me like you would make smarter decisions about how you deal with things. Might make your time here less confrontational."

The heated glare Harper delivered brought back the smugness of Davis's smile. "I don't give a shit how any of you feel about me. You do your job, and I'll do mine. When the job involves us crossing over and working side-by-side, I'll show the respect I'm given. That's how I see things, and that's not changing for you or anyone else here."

Davis didn't give a damn about being liked. He was more concerned with being respected. People liked you based on their feelings or emotions. Being respected was founded on indisputable facts about how one operated and carried themselves. Character was far more important to Davis than personality.

"No one survives this type of job without allies, but you know that, don't you? There are whispers about why you transferred here, Davis."

Harper held his stare, feeling accomplished for returning the same gut punch that Davis had delivered to him hours earlier. They both had pasts. Davis only chuckled lightly, lifting the file and holding it up with one hand while gripping the half-empty bottle of water with the other.

"Thanks for this." He walked away, pausing a few steps outside the break room. He could feel the heat from Harper's stare but didn't bother to face him when he spoke again.

"And just so we're clear, you and no one else here knows shit about me. Might want to get a grip on the *whispering* thing. That's not a good look for grown-ass men. More of a characteristic for gossiping teen girls."

He walked away without a retort from Harper. Davis didn't care if he pissed off the precinct's golden boy. Harper's approval or allegiance wasn't necessary for him to survive. As long as Davis did his job efficiently, then they could all fuck off.

At his desk, Davis moved carefully through the evidence he currently had: crime scene photos, bagged evidence, and DNA analysis. The only DNA found on the scene belonged to the victim and the cleaning lady who'd found the body. There was nothing significant about the crime scene either. No forced entry, which either meant they'd caught him as he was entering or he knew the assailant and had allowed them entry into the apartment. The latter was likely the case, considering there were no signs of a struggle. Nothing was overturned or out of place—no damage to any furniture other than the blood stain that pooled around the victim's body. The bullets had been lodged in the victim and removed by the ME.

"Too clean," he mumbled to himself. Which then had him considering the obvious. Cassidy Evans very well could have done this. She could have had access to the apartment. He flipped through the witness statements, stopping at the one given by the cleaning lady.

Amira Sanchez.

Female, midtwenties, cleaned the place weekly.

Amira mentioned she used an access code to enter the apartment. Williams provided the code after hiring the service.

He scanned further and noticed that she mentioned he traveled a lot, but she had no clue what he did for a living. They didn't interact much. He wasn't there often when she serviced the unit, but he was kind, friendly, and pleasant each time they communicated. *A good man.* Her exact words.

Interesting, Davis thought. *Good men rarely got murdered in cold blood the way that Williams had.* Amira, however, wasn't the shooter. She had a solid alibi, considering she'd spent the evening at dinner with her boyfriend, after which they had drinks at a bar, not leaving until a little after three a.m.

A good man.

Williams might have been a good man, which Davis doubted, but he also had secrets. His identification didn't match who he was supposed to be. The New York license was valid, not a fake, and the credit cards he kept in his wallet matched the identity on the license. He had plenty of personal items around the apartment, signifying that he spent enough time there, but as Jerrod Williams and not Niles Anderson, Cassidy Evans's legal husband.

"What are you hiding, Anderson or Williams, or whoever the fuck you really are?"

Davis drummed his fingers on the photos of the body before leaning back in his chair, lifting one leg to rest an ankle on the opposite thigh.

"Once I figure out who you are, then I can start to figure out who killed you."

3.

*D*r. *Cassidy Evans.* Her name meant something. She wasn't exactly a world-renowned celebrity, but her name held value. It had taken a long time for Cassidy to reach the point where she was proud of the woman she had become, but she had indeed arrived.

As a child, she lived with parents who shouldn't have been allowed to procreate. They weren't abusive or cruel. Jana Oliver and Donald Reynolds were simply careless and irresponsible. Inserting a kid into the lives of two people who loathed responsibility didn't make for a happy, nurturing home life. There were flashes of memories where Cassidy could recall her rough start with Jana and Donald. Only a few, and she rarely revisited the time she spent with her parents. Most children, even those from broken homes, had good memories to balance the bad. Not Cassidy. The flashes from the time she spent with her parents were of hard times. Being left alone, hungry to the point of pain, dirty, and neglected. Cassidy never had the proper care that children required. There were no hugs, smiles, or encouraging words, only mutters about how she slowed them down, got in the way, and cost them money they didn't have.

The most prevalent memory was when Cassidy was eight years old. Her mother marched her to the neighbor's house, which stood directly across from the shotgun home her parents had rented.

Every structure in the neighborhood was run-down—paint peeling, rotted wood, and barely standing—but Cassidy loved to visit her neighbor, Ms. Clara. *Clara Evans.* Her house wasn't the best with its old, worn furniture and creaky wooden floors, but it always smelled like cinnamon and vanilla. The place was also spotless, and Ms. Clara always had food and treats. Those fresh-out-of-the-oven chocolate chip cookies were the best, warm and gooey.

The day Jana stood on the porch with Cassidy and shoved her toward Ms. Clara for the last time, Cassidy didn't know it then, but it was the best decision her mother, or possibly both parents, had ever made. She wasn't sure how her father felt. He didn't bother saying goodbye and instead, sat impatiently in their old, ratty Honda, tapping the horn while Jana severed ties with their child.

"Her stuff's in the house. Door's open. Get what you need, but you better hurry. Rent's three months behind. Landlord will be showing up soon," Jana said in a rush of words.

Cassidy's eyes bounced between Jana and Ms. Clara, trying to figure out what was going on. She'd stayed with Ms. Clara enough times to know their usual routine, but this time felt different. Maybe it was her instincts or the hushed conversation the two women had, but Cassidy knew. She knew that her parents were leaving her behind, and instead of being sad, she felt relieved. Her mind kept circling back to the scent of vanilla and cinnamon. She would much rather have something pleasing than the smell of stale air and garbage.

That was the last time Cassidy saw her parents. Years later, she realized Ms. Clara was a retired social worker. She'd offered to take Cassidy in when she found out Jana and Donald were leaving. The child had been neglected, deprived of basic needs, and the worst, love. She had always wanted a child of her own, but it never happened. *Until Cassidy.* Things were eventually made official through the government. An abandoned Black child didn't make much of a wave. No one really cared about her well-being and having someone willing to accept the responsibility of caring for the child meant one less case file they had to deal with. When Ms. Clara asked to foster Cassidy, the request was approved, and adoption eventually followed. Cassidy Oliver became Cassidy Evans. That was the end of Cassidy's old life and the turning point where she began to have good memories.

Ms. Clara passed when Cassidy was eighteen. Died in her sleep, but she left Cassidy the best gift possible, as if she hadn't already done enough. What little money she saved was placed in a trust for Cassidy. The funds were sufficient to pay tuition at a junior college, and thus, she began her formal education. Cassidy once looked up her parents and located Jana in a county jail for credit card fraud. She never found her father but hadn't invested much time in searching. He could have been dead for all she knew. Neither of them had ever tracked Cassidy down over the years. If they didn't care, why should she? Her name had been officially changed to Evans, but they could have located her if they truly wanted to. They hadn't.

The early, short time she'd spent with her parents began Cassidy's lack of trust in people. Cassidy's parents let her down. They weren't who they proclaimed to be. *Frauds*. They stole the identities of others, living off their hard-earned money, and then moving on. Now, Cassidy was experiencing the same thing years after she'd felt secure enough to trust and love.

Jerrod Williams.

Her husband was a fraud. She let him in, and he let her down. Cassidy stood in her kitchen, staring out into the living room. Their home was a spacious one-level modern construct. Clean lines, multiple rows of paneled glass, and a mix of imported marble and bamboo wood floors that had been customized with the ability to warm in the colder months. This was her dream home.

She held a glass of wine, Riesling, one of her favorites. The glass was half-empty or full, depending on how you looked at it.

Right now, Cassidy's life had been flipped upside down multiple times, so she viewed it as half-empty. What was the point in seeing the good in things?

Or people.

"What the hell am I supposed to do now?" she whispered lowly to the ghost of herself that now existed.

Because she had worked so closely with APD early on in her career, Cassidy had experienced enough profiling situations to know what was expected. Grieving family members, lost intentions, and uncertain futures. The cases she had worked on in the past gave her multiple blueprints of what to expect and how she should feel. Grief and loss were universal, after all, right? However, none of those scenarios seemed to fit her mood correctly.

She couldn't grieve her husband's death, at least not yet, because the dead body she'd seen carried her husband's face but not the man's name. The victim wasn't Niles Anderson. It was Jerrod Williams.

My husband wasn't murdered. A stranger was.

That was what she kept telling herself, but regardless, Cassidy's rational mind understood this new reality she found herself in. Her life had been a façade. Her husband had been dishonest, and *she* had been played. Niles Anderson was no better than the parents who had left her behind. He was a fraud, just like them. Cassidy swallowed a healthy gulp of wine and stared blankly at an unfocused view of her pristine home. Her fingers gripped the glass of wine until she felt a pinch of pain and lowered her eyes to it.

Okay, first round: anger.

She couldn't mourn the loss of her husband, but she very much could be infuriated by his lies.

Cassidy slammed the glass on the counter and stormed into their bedroom. She paused several steps inside the neatly kept space as if trying to decide what she was doing. With a deep breath, she found a brief moment of clarity, then moved to the closet. The massive, two-sided walk-in separated their lives.

His and Hers.

How ironic.

The symbolism caused a slight twinge of pain in her chest as she began digging through her husband's belongings. She yanked open drawers one by one, tossing around neatly stacked layers of socks, briefs, and T-shirts. All the expensive labels that he loved so much.

Nothing.

Next, she pushed through the racks of clothes that were perfectly organized by functionality and color. Suits, slacks, pressed shirts. Jeans, sweaters, tracksuits. Nothing seemed odd or presented as a red flag, so Cassidy began digging through the pockets and came up empty. She tossed around jewelry, pulled watches from the custom cases, and tossed them on the shelves to ensure nothing was hidden or tucked away.

Nothing.

Everything made sense and was a perfect representation of the man she knew. But that was the problem. She didn't know him at all. Tears welled in her eyes, and a few managed to slither down her cheek. However, they weren't sorrowful tears. They were hot and angry because Cassidy was furious with him, with herself.

How the hell could I have missed this?

How was I so blind to what was happening in plain sight?

Cassidy was at a loss, and instead of searching further, she decided more wine was the best option at present. Eventually, the answers she needed would surely come, but for now, wine . . .

Hours passed, and daylight was traded for the dark cover of the evening. The sky blazed orange with hints of red from the sun sinking into the horizon. Cassidy sat in her living room, tucked in the corner of the comfy linen-covered, feather-down, cushioned sofa. It cradled her body in a warm and welcoming way. Luxury and comfort were important to Cassidy. She needed the familiarity of being safe and protected. She deserved a good life after years of tirelessly working to make something of herself. Cassidy's thoughts drifted to her husband. He had once been that familiarity and comfort . . . or had he? Had she imagined their happy life? What he'd meant to her? What she meant to him?

The sound of the doorbell and the soft chime of a notification that someone had been picked up on the camera that offered a nice view of their well-manicured lawn had Cassidy frowning in the dimly lit living room. She hadn't bothered turning on lights and, instead, chose to sit peacefully alone under the cloak of darkness. Well, not completely alone. She'd had the company of two bottles of wine, both of which were now empty.

Lifting her phone, she pulled up the security app and tapped the front camera to get a better visual of her unexpected visitor. There was a man casually dressed in a button-up, sleeves rolled to the elbows, slacks, and loafers. He had a stern expression etched on his handsome face, accentuated by a strong, square jaw shaded with a dark sheen of hair. He was tall, at least six feet. Niles had been six-two. Cassidy guessed this man was the same. His build was very similar to Niles's also. Broad shoulders, long, lean body, trim waist. The type of figure that allowed for clothes to fit nicely, complementing his physique. But this wasn't Niles.

Niles is dead.

No, Jerrod Williams is dead.

Lost in her thoughts, Cassidy was startled when the doorbell chimed again. The low melody wasn't typical of most doorbells by design. It wasn't intrusive, almost soothing in a sense. Exhaling a huff of exhaustion, she unfolded her body from the sofa. Her feet pressed softly against the ash-gray wooden floors until she extended to her full height and crossed the room to the door.

"Yes . . ." Her voice carried enough to get her visitor's attention. His back was facing the door, and he briefly glanced over his shoulder before fully turning. Cassidy glowered as he took her in through the glass panels and wrought iron metal that made up her entryway. After a brief moment, he offered a subtle smile. It wasn't exactly a smile, but his features relaxed slightly.

"Ms. Evans? *Cassidy Evans.*" His deep tenor was muffled by the glass separating them. He then pointed to the badge affixed at his waist. "Detective Nathanial Davis. If it's okay, I was hoping to ask you a few questions."

She had expected someone to show up eventually—a detective, but not *this* detective. Greg was there when the body was discovered. This was his case. Her defenses quickly heightened.

Greg's too close to me to be impartial. They would have removed him.

"Yes, sure." She twisted the lock, pulling the door open, but kept it positioned as a protective barrier.

"My apologies for showing up unannounced, but I felt it might help to get a few preliminary questions out of the way."

"No problem." She kept her tone neutral and made sure to deliver eye contact. "Please, come in."

"This won't take long. Figured we could talk out here. Didn't want to intrude."

He's asserting his professionalism. Being extra cautious.

Cassidy stepped onto the porch, bringing the door with her. She left it slightly cracked and then folded her arms over her chest, rocking gently on her heels.

"I'm sorry for your loss, Ms. Evans. This can't be easy. Losing someone you love and under the current circumstances."

Finding out that my husband was a fraud.

"No, it's not easy." She kept her responses short and sweet with the understanding that the detective would analyze every detail: her reaction, her words, her level of emotions.

Spouses are the first suspects.

"Your husband was found the morning of September 6th. Based on the timeline, he was killed between the hours of midnight and two a.m. That means he didn't come home. Did your husband often stay out all night?"

She softly shook her head. "No, he didn't. He traveled a lot, but he was home at night when he wasn't traveling."

"Were you concerned when he didn't show?"

A flash of the night in question, following Niles into the parking garage, traveled through Cassidy's mind.

"Yes, of course."

"But you didn't report him missing?"

Cassidy angled her head slightly to the right, keeping her expression controlled. "You're here, so that means you've done your research, Detective. You know who I am, my past, and my relationship with the APD."

"I do."

"Then you also know that I'm aware that it's pointless to report someone missing before the forty-eight-hour window of their absence."

He nodded slowly. "I am. Considering your relationship with APD, however, it seems you should have been granted some concessions."

"Possibly, but I don't often live my life calling in favors."

"Not even when it concerns the well-being of someone you love?"

She straightened her posture. "No, Detective."

He's trying to see if I cared that Niles was murdered.

"Understood. I appreciate your time, Ms. Evans—"

"Cassidy," she corrected.

"Cassidy." This time, he offered a genuine smile, so she decided to pry for details.

"Do you have any leads yet, Detective?"

"No, not at the moment, but I'm hoping that will change soon. I'll review the footage from the cameras on-site at The Atrium today. There might be something there."

"Great. Is that all?"

"Yes, that's all. I appreciate your time, *Ms. Evans*."

His inflection on her name was intentional. He wanted hard boundaries.

He also wants me to be unsure of where he stands. Ha, I know the game, Detective.

Cassidy understood the ins and outs of the first point of contact with cases like these. She was still a suspect and being treated as such.

"You're very welcome, Detective—anything I can do to assist. You understand how much I would like closure. My husband was murdered."

No, he wasn't. Jerrod Williams was murdered.

"Then, at least, we're on the same page. I'll be in touch."

He didn't once reference the false identity or discuss the obvious. If Cassidy's husband was home every night, then how did the apartment he kept across town come into play? The detective also didn't mention any red flags that signaled trouble in their marriage. Cassidy understood his line of questions was intentional. Detective Davis wanted to provide the semblance of trust that he was an ally.

I don't trust you any more than you trust me, Detective.

Davis tipped his head before turning to leave. Cassidy remained in place, watching until the detective's body disappeared inside the unmarked SUV, and he backed out of the driveway. Things were about to get complicated; all she could do was brace for the fallout.

4.

Left, right, left.

   Jab, jab, body blow.

   Uppercut, jab, jab.

Davis remained in a zone while tucked away in the corner of the gym. His fists pounded a heavy bag with a trained force and precision, creating a steady rhythm that pulsed in his ears. Several days a week, he was up by five and at the gym half an hour later for an intense workout. Boxing allowed him the freedom to release stress and stay in shape. There had been a period when he'd considered investing the time and entering into professional boxing. He was good. A natural was what the trainers used to say, but neither of them had a clue about what it took to stay in it for the long haul. The small gym he spent time in as a teen and young adult was a ratty, old place with great potential. That was all they had ever been, but Davis didn't care. He showed up whenever he could and welcomed anything they had to offer. He was a fighter. He had to be, or life would have taken him under.

   Might as well use your fists 'cause you ain't got the smarts to do anything else.

   Cross, jab, cross.

   Useless, just like your mama.

37

Uppercut, uppercut, jab.

Davis huffed at the memory and gritted his teeth even harder. His father was an asshole. He had shortcomings and used his words to take his frustrations with life out on his wife and son. Davis had always been a bright kid. When his grades slipped, it wasn't because he lacked intelligence. It was because he was bored. Once his teachers discovered the issue, they'd set up a conference with his parents to suggest he be moved up a grade and placed in the gifted program to keep him busy and on track.

Jab, jab, cross.

You ain't smart, Nate. Them teachers want to embarrass you. Put you in class with all those smart kids just to make you look stupid. That's why they're pushing you so hard. They know you can't keep up. You're gonna fail, and they're gonna laugh in your face when you do.

Uppercut, uppercut, cross.

Davis hadn't understood why his father hated him so much back then. Most parents would have been proud that their kid was smart. Not Malcolm Davis. His insecurities wouldn't allow him to be proud of his son. Instead, he resented Nathanial and did everything he could to break him down. As a product of his environment, Malcolm Davis dropped out of school at age thirteen. He'd never done well in school, but not for lack of trying. He just wasn't the smartest and didn't have the support he needed from his teachers and parents to do the work.

Davis and his father were like night and day, which drove a wedge between them. As an adult, Davis realized that his father refused to be proud of him because he was everything his father could and would never be. How ironic was it that Malcolm's life was ended by a uniformed officer who caught him robbing a local convenience store.

Malcolm fired at the cop, and the cop fired back, delivering a fatal shot. Two years later, Davis applied for the academy. He told himself that it wasn't about his father, and at the time, it wasn't, but in the years since, he realized the correlation. Malcolm often expressed his views about the legal system and his dislike for any formal justice. As a career criminal, Davis's father deemed the authorities enemies. He hated cops and everything they stood for. Criminals and cops were like oil and water. And Davis had become the one thing his father hated the most. A silent "fuck you" to the man he'd never respected.

Davis pounded out several more combinations without pausing between them and then stepped away from the heavy bag, exhaling his exhaustion. His arms, chest, and back muscles were burning from being overexerted, and his body was drenched with sweat. His sleeveless Dri-Fit shirt was soaked through and clung to his body like a second skin.

With his workout complete, it was time to get to work. Davis left the open space of the gym, appreciating that only a handful of people were there. It was one of the reasons he chose early-morning or late-night visits. He was less likely to have to entertain useless conversations with strangers.

After he showered and dressed in slacks and a button-up, Davis left the gym. He tossed the duffle bag containing his workout attire into the trunk and settled behind the steering wheel to mentally run through his day. One perk of being assigned the case with Jerrod Williams was that the captain had decided all his focus needed to be on that one case. Having just closed out the murder of a hotel attendant, which ended in a conviction thanks to his skilled detective work, Davis didn't have any other pending cases. That meant he was completely dedicated to solving the murder of Cassidy Evans's husband—whoever that may be. *Niles Anderson or Jerrod Williams.*

Pressing the button to power on the vehicle, Davis settled into the space of contemplative thought while he navigated through the city. His mind scoured over what he knew thus far about the murder of Williams.

Eventually, he circled back to his impromptu visit with Cassidy the evening before. She appeared distraught but well put together. Her behavior felt controlled and reserved, which made sense considering her background. Cassidy was a psychologist who'd spent years working as a profiler.

I bet she profiled me the minute she stepped out of her house.

Davis scoffed at the thought. He revisited their discussion. Cassidy's insistence that she wouldn't have reported her husband missing until after the forty-eight-hour window seemed plausible. She credited it to understanding protocol, but Davis felt it was bullshit.

Something wasn't right between husband and wife.

Evans's husband had an alternate life. One she wasn't aware of since she was bold enough to show up at an apartment that her husband kept under a false identity the morning after he was murdered.

That would indeed be bold or intentional. She knew the system. She understood what detectives would look for and how behaviors would be translated. She could have very well known every detail of Williams's life and played the unassuming wife.

Or she honestly had no clue who her husband was.

Both scenarios were possibilities. It was now up to Davis to find the truth. For now, his focus was on Cassidy Evans. She would either lead him to her as the killer or prove that she wasn't.

He had no idea just yet of the outcome, and part of that uncertainty was the woman herself. Cassidy was beautiful, midforties, intelligent, and accomplished. She took care of herself, which meant her age wasn't visible in her features: soft brown eyes, cupid's bow lips, and smooth, brown skin. Cassidy could easily fit into a space where a career driven by looks would be suitable.

Model. Actress. That contradiction of intelligence and beauty only added to her intriguing mystique. Had this been a different space and time, Davis could see himself wanting to know more about Cassidy Evans, but for personal reasons, not deciding if she was capable of killing her husband. Unfortunately, this was where they were.

Hours later, the precinct was buzzing. Everyone seemingly lost in their own worlds, moving through files, interviewing suspects, or clicking through the internet. Some were bouncing ideas off one another about cases they were working, something Davis never did. Davis sat at his desk, closed off from everything around him until he received the email he had been waiting on all morning. After making a few phone calls, he'd managed to get security footage sent over without much fuss. The building owner wanted this wrapped up as quickly and quietly as possible. Davis was simply happy he didn't have to serve a warrant to cut through red tape and get what he needed.

Security footage from the past seven days of the building where Williams died sat in his inbox waiting for him. Davis dragged the attached folders to his desktop and clicked to open the files, only to be interrupted by his captain, an unwelcome disturbance.

"Find anything yet?" Captain Jones murmured, standing over Davis. The position plucked his nerves. It was a trigger from his earlier years when his father would crowd over him, doling out insults about how he wasn't shit and would never be shit. Things never got physical, but his words were lethal enough, cruel and vicious.

"Nothing solid, but I'm about to go through the security footage from the night of the murder. Footage that we should have already had, but *I* had to request it."

Another gut punch signifying that Harper had dropped the ball. In the year that Davis had been with APD, Harper had proven to be good at his job. However, this one situation proved what Davis had always believed. Being emotionally attached was the best way to screw up an investigation.

"You alluding to something, Davis?" As always, their captain took the role of defending Harper. They had history; he and Davis had none.

"No, simply stating facts. We should have had this before the crime scene was wrapped up. I've lost valuable time locking down potential leads because of Harper's negligence."

"How about you stop pointing the finger and do your job? We're keeping this internal because of our relationship with Cass, but there's no guarantee that media outlets won't get their hands on this. We need to have something solid, considering the delicacy of the situation."

Something that took the heat off Cassidy Evans.

"I won't rush this, Captain. If that's what you expect—"

"I'm not asking you to. Only reminding you—"

"That *she's* one of you. Understood."

"*Us*. You're a part of this family now, Davis. Stop isolating yourself."

Davis chose not to respond, and neither said another word as Davis began clicking through the files the security company had sent over. They were organized into multiple folders, labeled by time segments, and broken up into three-hour increments. Knowing the potential time of death, Davis decided it was best to begin with the window of time closest to the actual crime. He bypassed the ones from earlier in the day.

The captain moved in closer to get a better view when the visual of the parking garage filled the screen. Davis clicked to fast-forward, advancing the footage and pausing when the camera picked up a familiar tracksuit, the one Williams wore the night he was murdered. Shortly after seeing Williams exit his vehicle, another familiar face caught Davis's attention as Williams entered the elevator bay. Cassidy Evans. She'd followed Williams at a safe distance, seemingly unnoticed by him.

Bingo.

"You see this?"

"What?"

"This . . ." Davis played the footage back and paused it once a clear visual of Cassidy was on the screen.

"Shit," Captain Jones mumbled. "That's all they sent? What about the interior cameras?"

"Don't exist."

Captain Jones's expression hardened. "What?"

"When I reached out to property management, they got me in touch with the owner. He informed me that many exclusive people lived in the building, and they valued their privacy. The only cameras on-site cover the exterior of the building and the parking garage. They don't even have 'em on the elevators."

"Fucking privilege," Captain Jones murmured.

"I guess, but this doesn't look good. She's not on record mentioning she was at the scene a few hours before the crime was committed . . . unless Harper left it out of his report."

The two shared a knowing look before Captain Jones discredited the accusation. "If he knew, it would've been in there." He motioned to the file, and Davis nodded.

"And hold on . . ."

Davis went back to the footage and allowed it to play. He took in the details of Williams disappearing into the elevator bay and then Cassidy shortly after. She reentered the garage and pulled out her phone while returning to her vehicle, making back-to-back calls. You could see her eventually engaging in a very animated conversation before returning to her car. At that point, with the distance from the camera and darkness hovering over the corner where she was parked, you couldn't see much else. He fast-forwarded again until three hours later when the car lights illuminated, and Cassidy slowly pulled from the space she was in and left the garage.

"A little over three hours, Captain. Evans was there for three hours, and that means she very well could have done this."

"Could have but didn't. She never got out of the vehicle again."

"Not that we know of, but look at this." Davis paused the video again and pointed to something on the screen. It was the dim glow of an exit sign. There was a stairwell in the corner near where Cassidy was parked. "Who's to say she didn't slip out the other side of the vehicle, go into the stairwell, and enter the building that way? There are no cameras inside. No one would have ever known."

"*I* know. There's *no way* she did this."

Davis scowled at the captain. "You do understand that if she did, she's not getting any special treatment or favors. At least not from me. I'm investigating this crime the same as I would any other."

"No one's asking you not to. Only that you don't rush to judgment.'"

"This isn't a rush to judgment. *This* . . ." He motioned to the screen, "is solid evidence that she needs to explain, and until she does, she's a prime suspect."

"Bring her in *discreetly*. And get that footage over to the experts. Maybe they can see something we can't," Captain Jones muttered and walked off without another word. Davis rewound the footage and watched closely several more times. Unfortunately, all he had was Cassidy being there. The angle of the cameras and poor quality of the equipment prevented any solid proof of whether Cassidy remained in the vehicle or if she'd managed to slip out the other side. Even if she hadn't, why the hell would she sit there for three hours?

You've got some explaining to do, Cassidy. Maybe you didn't murder your husband, but as of now, the evidence says you could have, and you also had motive.

✻

Detective Davis entered his house, swapping keys for the remote. The station was on SportsCenter because, on the rare occasions he watched TV, it was to catch up on his favorite teams. After listening to the latest injuries that could affect the upcoming seasons, he tossed the remote on the sofa and headed to his bedroom to shower and get comfortable.

His home was a rental in Sandy Springs that gave him proximity to the city without actually being in it. The two-bedroom ranch had been furnished with simple but cozy items he purchased online a few weeks before his move from New York. A king bedroom set made of dark wood and clean lines for his room, a two-piece leather sofa combination that came as a set that included a rug, coffee table, and one end table, and a glass-top dinette for the kitchen with brushed metal framing and ivory cushions. None of them matched or fit his personality, but they were affordable and promised to arrive on time.

He had very few personal items lying around. A handful of worn books and a few photos were about all. One of him as a child and his mother at the gym after an amateur fight; his father hadn't shown. One of him after he got promoted to detective. He'd celebrated with a handful of cops at the bar near the precinct, and someone had snapped a photo. He'd kept it all these years and found it when packing his things in New York. The walls of his rentals were still eggshell white, with no art or accents on the walls because he rarely had time, and shopping wasn't one of his favorite things. The place was comfortable enough.

There also hadn't been much he'd owned in the one-bedroom he'd left behind that was worthy of crossing state lines. For six months before his transfer, Davis had been living the life of a single man after a mutual breakup with a woman he'd dated for several years.

Stacy Mitchell, his ex, came from an affluent family. At the beginning of their relationship, she seemed okay with his career choice, but things shifted a few months in when Stacy began hinting that Davis should consider law. Her father and brothers were all lawyers and owned a very prestigious firm in Manhattan. A few months after they met, he finished his tour as a uniform and applied to become a detective. That had been the extent of where he chose to take his career at that time. Stacy, however, would always tell Davis he was halfway there as a cop and might as well consider taking things a step further with a law degree. He had no interest whatsoever in attending law school, nor did he want to spend his life representing high-society elites with their civil suits and blackmail cases.

Eventually, Stacy got the message, which led to a mutual separation. She packed his things and insisted they take a break. A few months later, an engagement announcement surfaced stating that Stacy was marrying a lawyer from Los Angeles who had recently relocated to New York to work for the DA's office. Davis cared about Stacy but didn't care enough to be what she wanted him to be.

After his shower, Davis dressed in lounge pants and a cotton tee that hugged his upper body. He traveled back through his home, bypassing the living room for a pit stop in the kitchen to decide what his dinner for the evening would be. After a quick scan of the contents of his refrigerator, he settled on grilling some chicken with a side of steamed vegetables since he'd remembered to transfer two breasts from the freezer to the fridge before leaving the house that morning. Someone was knocking at his door before he could fully commit to the decision.

After a little over a year in a new city, Davis still didn't have a group he considered friends, and only a handful of people knew where he lived. Most of them worked at the precinct and wouldn't dare drop by to share a beer or check in on him. He walked through the living room and peered out the glass panels, realizing it was the last person he expected to show up at his place without an invitation. They had an understanding, or so he thought. Exhaling a sigh, he turned the lock, opened the door, and stood dead center, not allowing the misconception that she was welcome.

"What are you doing here, Sam?"

"I missed you." She smiled in that sultry way that had gotten his attention the night they'd met and lifted both arms. In one hand, she held takeout from the place they'd met. Charlie's. No doubt, honey bourbon wings and fries, all flats. She knew Davis about as much as any woman could. In the other hand, she held a case of IPA beers. "And I brought dinner."

"You should have called first."

"I did. You didn't answer."

He knew that, and she should have accepted that he didn't want to be bothered. He would have called back when he felt like it. Sam shrugged and stepped forward, pushing past him. He let her. Samantha Douglass, or Sam, was a stylist Davis had met at a bar and grill close to his house a few days after moving to Atlanta. They'd shared wings, too much liquor, very little conversation, and ended up at his house. The sex was great, and the company was decent, so they hooked up a couple of times a month, but mostly when Sam reached out. Davis made it clear that he was new in town and that his focus would be on gaining his footing within the department. Sam said she understood, but here she was at his house uninvited like they did this all the time.

"Then you should have waited for me to call you back."

Sam grinned over her shoulder, taking him in slowly from head to toe. "I'm impatient, but I'm also worth it. You eat already?"

"No," he mumbled and joined her in the kitchen. He grabbed two plates, which he handed over before digging through a junk drawer to locate a bottle opener. He ripped open the cardboard casing protecting the beer, grabbed two and some napkins while she carried the loaded plates, and followed behind him. Once the two settled on the sofa, she kicked off her running shoes and settled next to Davis, crossing her legs while she balanced a plate of wings and fries in her lap. He sat forward with his food on the coffee table, dragging it closer for convenience.

"Oh God, these are so good. I could eat like this daily and never get tired of it."

"Says the health nut who runs five miles a day and overdoses on green juices." Davis tore into a wing but glanced back at Sam just in time to catch her smile.

He loved her smile . . .

His eyes lowered, taking in the fitted, lightweight hoodie she wore and matching yoga pants.

Amongst other things.

"I didn't say I *would*, just that I *could*." She lifted another wing and quickly cleaned the meat from the bone. "Besides, you're no better than me. You might not run five miles a day, but you're in the gym religiously, and boxing is hard work."

"I don't box," he murmured, lifting the beer toward his lips again, taking some down.

"Pounding a heavy bag until your muscles are screaming and your knuckles are raw is pretty much boxing, Nate. Just a more civilized version." She winked, and he chuckled, nodding in approval before tipping his beer back again.

"How are things? Business good?"

She smirked and leaned forward to grab one of the napkins he'd brought. After wiping her mouth, she answered. "Great, actually, but it's not like you care. I know you disapprove of small talk. You don't have to force it."

He tossed the clean bone onto the plate and smiled over his shoulder. "I don't *dislike* small talk. I simply prefer to skip it. My life is so intrusive sometimes because of the job, I find that in my personal time, I appreciate the luxury of not asking questions."

"I get it. I'm not complaining. That's one of the things I like about you. You're a straight shooter. You don't bullshit around, and I know what I get with you."

"Is that *all* you like?" He glanced over his shoulder again and noticed when her eyes lowered, taking in his body.

"Definitely not *all* I like, and definitely not the thing that tops my list, but it *is* on the list."

He chuckled and lifted his beer. Davis was partial to Sam. Sam would be a viable option if he considered being in a relationship again. Even after her impromptu visit intruding on his personal time, he still didn't mind much. She didn't push too hard for things he wouldn't give at this point in his life, and the sex was damn sure worth it.

"So . . ." She began, pausing to sip some of her beer to wash down the fries she'd just shoved into her mouth, "working on any interesting cases?"

Davis stilled briefly. His mind drifted to Cassidy but not to the possibility that she had killed her husband. No, his thoughts were of her eyes, her lips, and how she'd smelled like cinnamon and vanilla. He imagined it was what her home smelled like based on how it clung to her clothes the night he'd questioned her.

"No," Davis murmured in response to the question, then lifted another wing without looking back at Sam. He could hear the smile in her voice when she spoke again.

"I bet you are. Not that you would tell me. So secretive, Detective Davis. I think that's another thing I like about you. There's so much hidden in that head of yours that no one will ever know."

He scoffed, and she added, "And the fact that you're well over a ten in the looks and sexual appeal departments doesn't hurt either."

"A ten? What's the scale?" He turned, offering a cocky smile, and she matched it with a smile of her own.

"One to one hundred." She winked, and he barked out a laugh, throwing his head back.

"That's bullshit."

"Yeah, it is. You're a solid one hundred on a scale of one to ten."

"That's more like it."

"Arrogant ass." She tossed a fry at him, and he chuckled, lifting his beer. The two settled into watching a game with occasional trash talking banter between them while finishing their food. Sam cleaned up the mess, then rejoined Davis in the living room. Instead of settling in beside him, she stepped between his legs. She slowly removed her fitted hoodie and bra, dropping them both to the floor before she peeled out of her yoga pants, moving them over her hips and down her legs, stepping out of them once the spandex material was at her ankles.

Davis's eyes slowly crawled over her body, enjoying each curve and every exposed inch of smooth, brown skin until Sam leaned forward and placed her palms flat on his thighs to brace herself as she lowered to her knees. She reached forward, working her hands beyond the elastic band of his pants and briefs, and wrapped her fingers around him. Sam's eyes lifted to meet his, and a smile tugged at her lips.

"I was thinking since we're done eating, I could show you how much I missed you."

She didn't wait for a response, and Davis groaned under his breath when her head lowered to his lap, and he felt her tongue and lips as she slowly took him in. Sometimes, the best things were unexpected, and Davis decided that Sam was the best at being unexpected.

5.

Staying busy was hard. The first few hours after learning that Niles had been murdered, Cassidy was in shock. When she eventually made it home that night, she'd sat in the dark for hours, not moving, thinking, or feeling; just existing. A suffocating wave of sadness and pain followed that. Her husband was gone. Their life had been a lie, and she had been cheated of the opportunity to get answers from him. No matter the circumstances, Niles was gone. Her life would never be the same, and Cassidy had nothing left but intense sadness and far too many unanswered questions.

Then there was anger. She was so fucking angry. Niles had utterly betrayed her trust, and he knew how difficult it was for Cassidy to trust. Having a past like hers had deeply wounded Cassidy. She found it hard to believe people cared without hidden agendas or seeking personal gain. Ms. Clara had been there, and she truly loved Cassidy, but the act of taking her in as a child wasn't exactly selfless. Ms. Clara had always wanted a daughter, and Cassidy had been the perfect consolation prize.

Had Ms. Clara had a child of her own, Cassidy was convinced she wouldn't have loved her the way she did. And then there were the biggest frauds in her life. Jana and Donald. She was their biological child, and they'd still refused to love Cassidy the way she deserved to be loved. Scarred. That was Cassidy's default state of being, and Niles knew that. He knew her story and still chose to deceive her, breaking her further than she already was. The man who had promised to love her forever honestly hadn't planned to honor that commitment.

Cassidy did her best to keep her mind occupied with anything other than her murdered husband or the fact that he wasn't who she had known him to be, but it was damn near impossible while confined to the home they'd shared. Everything around her reminded Cassidy of Niles. The light scent of his cologne lingered in the closet. One side of their bathroom held his personal belongings—toothbrush, skin care items, and the moisturizer he used to keep his beard that she had been obsessed with soft to the touch. She used to love the woodsy, citrusy scent that lingered on her face and neck when she snuggled close to him at night.

Now, those memories, things, and scents angered her. As familiar as they felt, they were also a constant reminder that their life had been a lie. The reality she'd known with Niles Anderson had been fictional. She'd been married to a stranger. A stranger who she loved then and still now, no matter how much the thought of his betrayal hurt. There were so many things that didn't make sense about his life. Things that now, being viewed from a different perspective, all felt so surreal.

Niles's parents had passed during his first year of college. Neither of his parents had siblings, so there was no other family he was close to. Cassidy had never questioned him too much because she could relate to his family structure. She'd only had Ms. Clara as a solid fixture in her life until she passed away. It made sense that someone else's story could mirror her own. But unlike Niles, Cassidy did have friends, college alumni, and peers from her career that she added throughout the years.

With Niles, there was no one, so it completely threw her when he mentioned dinner with a couple he kept in touch with from his past. Sure, Cassidy had complained about wanting to meet someone—anyone—from his past, but she'd never expected it to happen. Jake and Niles had been friends in college, and Jake's wife, Zoey, had only met Niles a handful of times after they had married. Niles's job kept him busy, so the story made sense. Cassidy was so thrilled to share a piece of Niles's past that she overlooked many things back then. Neither Jake nor Niles disclosed any pertinent information about their past or their friendship. The conversation that evening had been safe and cautious, mostly about work, how Cassidy and Niles had met, and their future plans. Easy to overlook that it lacked depth.

"Cass, this is Jake and his wife, Zoey."

"Nice to meet you both."

"Same. I can't believe this guy is actually with the same woman for longer than a few months. And one as beautiful as you, Cassidy. You sure you want to marry this guy? I have a few other friends I can introduce you to that are much better options than Niles."

Cassidy snuggled in closer to her husband's side. They were having drinks at a rooftop bar during a trip to New York. Cassidy had been asking Niles for months about his past and friends, and he always pushed it off, saying that he was a loner because of his job. It was easier that way.

In reality, she hadn't been invited to share a piece of Niles's past. What if that had all been staged because she'd kept pushing? So, he created a way to appease her. After dinner that night, there was very little discussion about their evening. Niles distracted Cassidy with the most amazing sex ever. At the time, she hadn't minded one bit.

Occasionally, she'd ask about the couple, and all Niles would offer was that they were doing well and they should plan to have them visit soon. That never happened. They hadn't seen them again after that evening, but Jake and Zoey had sent a gift with a sweet card expressing their congratulations for their union. That would have been easy enough to arrange. Were Jake and Zoey truly people he knew, or had it all been a game? Actors maybe?

How could I not have known?

You loved him. You trusted him, and you wanted to believe he loved you too.

The question had been in rotation since Cassidy's life had been tossed in a bag and shaken to the point of total disarray. Things between her and Niles hadn't been great over the past few months. Niles had been traveling more than usual and becoming distant. The conversations where he excused himself to speak privately had more than doubled, and the way he had been there but not there became more of an issue.

Niles functioned like a man who had secrets, but never in a million years did Cassidy believe those secrets meant that he was living another life under another name. Cheating maybe, but not an apartment, bills—and an entire world that Cassidy wasn't a part of.

She'd confronted him with assumptions of cheating the night he was killed. They argued about everything she'd been noticing lately, and then Niles made promises, told lies.

There's only you, Cassidy. No one but you.

He repeated that affirmation repeatedly while he planted kisses on the curve of her jaw, neck, and shoulder. While his intense gaze remained fastened to her, he stroked her slow and deep, allowing his body to make that same promise.

There's only you, Cass. No one but you.

She believed him. Maybe because she wanted to. If she didn't, that would mean her world was crumbling, and Cassidy needed to feel safe, secure, and loved. Niles gave her that. So she believed him . . . until it became impossible to keep on believing.

After they made love, Cassidy showered to prepare for bed. She assumed Niles would join her, but he mentioned having somewhere to be. *Work.* A lead on a client that he had to explore right away.

And again, Cassidy believed him . . . until she heard a whispered conversation.

"I told you to stop fucking calling. She's getting suspicious. I'll be there. I'm working right now. Yes, I care, but there are some things I can't control. Don't call me again. I'll be there."

Cassidy's chest tightened as she stood still, trying to decide what to do next. There were so many things rushing through her mind. A small part of her wanted to believe that Niles wouldn't betray her, but a bigger part of her subconscious mind knew better.

That night, after Niles made promises not to be gone long, Cassidy smiled, kissed him softly, and told him she'd wait up. He returned a smile and left the house moments later. Cassidy followed.

Staring blankly over her backyard, Cassidy snapped out of her thoughts about Niles and glanced at the phone vibrating in her lap. The number wasn't saved, but it was local, so she answered.

"Hello."

"Ms. Evans . . ." The deep baritone was familiar, and she immediately knew who the caller was but waited until he confirmed. "This is Detective Davis."

"Yes?"

"I hope I didn't catch you at a bad time."

"No, you didn't. What can I do for you, Detective?"

"I was wondering if you might be available to come down to the station. I have a few questions for you and want your official statement on record."

Wondering?

How nonabrasive. Basically, it wasn't a request, more or less a demand. If I decline, someone will show up soon to decide for me.

"Absolutely. When?"

"Now, if that works for you."

She exhaled a sigh, gripping the phone tighter. "Sure, I can be there in under an hour."

"Perfect. I'll be waiting. I assume you know where to go."

The *assumption* lingered as a reminder of her connections.

"I do."

"Great. I'll see you soon."

"See you soon, Detective."

6.

Davis felt Cassidy the minute she entered the bullpen, and he discreetly watched her from his desk, listening as she interacted with his colleagues.

"Cass, hey. How you holding up? I've been meaning to check in on you."

No, you need to stay as far away from her and this case as humanly possible.

"As well as can be expected given the circumstances." Her tentative expression was noticeable as her eyes moved around the precinct. She briefly caught a familiar pair of deep brown orbs watching her.

"Yeah, I get that. What are you doing here?"

Davis's gaze shifted from Cassidy to Harper as he stood from his chair. She smiled softly at Harper and accepted the hug he offered.

"Davis called and asked me to come in."

"You being questioned?" Davis's eyes shifted to Harper, who grimaced and leaned in closer to Cassidy.

"Apparently so."

"You want me to sit in with you? Just so you know you have a familiar face in there?"

"I'm sorry, but that won't be possible." Davis stepped up beside Harper and slipped his hands into the pockets of his slacks.

"It's not your call, Davis," Harper gritted, narrowing his eyes.

"Unless you're sitting in as Ms. Evans's legal representation, it *is* my call."

Davis kept his eyes on Cassidy, taking in her reaction to the interaction between him and his colleague. She didn't seem moved one way or another.

"I'm not her lawyer, but I am a detective here with more tenure—"

"A tenured detective that was removed from the case." Davis stepped forward and extended a hand, motioning for Cassidy to follow him, ignoring the heated stare from Harper. "This way, Ms. Evans."

"Arrogant muthafucker," Harper hissed as the two of them moved past him. Davis only smirked, shaking his head. Once he and Cassidy entered one of the more comfortable interrogation rooms that subbed as a conference space, he stood by the door, waiting for her to sit.

"Can I get you anything before we get started?"

"No, I'm fine, thank you."

He tilted his head in acknowledgment before slowly closing the door and then taking a seat across from Cassidy. She was the first to speak.

"You and Greg don't get along, I take it."

"I wouldn't say that."

"It certainly appears that way. Your exchange wasn't exactly *friendly.*"

Davis offered the slightest hint of a smile. She was analyzing his relationship with his colleague to understand better who he was.

"Me denying him access to me questioning you isn't a reflection of how I feel about the guy personally. More so protecting

the integrity of my investigation. One that has already been
compromised because of unprincipled decisions made by Harper."

"So he's pissed because they took him off the case, and you
decided to rub it in a little?" She arched a brow, and he shrugged
noncommittally.

"Not sure. You'd have to ask him for confirmation on how
he feels. My decision was about the integrity of the investigation.
Shall we get started?"

Once she nodded her approval, he lifted the remote that
controlled the cameras and audio in the room. "I'm going to record
this."

"Understood."

Davis wanted Cassidy's attention purposefully focused on
being recorded. As a profiler, Cassidy had watched and reviewed
countless situations similar to the one where she found herself.
She'd witnessed numerous potential suspects answering questions
about crimes they were suspected of committing. She was to study
their behaviors to identify their truths *or lies* through their posture,
body language, delivery, and tone of their answers. Now, she was
potentially in a situation where someone was doing the same to her.

They quickly navigated through her personal information
before Davis began to dive a little deeper, possibly to rattle Cassidy.

"You arrived without a lawyer. Is there any specific reason
why you choose not to have one present?"

"I didn't think I needed one, Detective. This is just questioning,
correct?"

He slowly nodded. "How were things between you and Mr.
Williams?"

"Anderson," Cassidy corrected with a stern look. "My
husband's name is Niles Anderson. I do not know Jerrod Williams."

"Right. How were things between you and *Niles*? Any issues
in your marriage?"

"Yes, actually, there were."

"Such as?"

"I recently began to suspect that something was off. That my husband was keeping things from me."

"Such as?"

"I wasn't sure, but things were different between us. Niles was traveling more over the past few months. Spending more time on his phone—"

"Staying out late?" Davis interrupted.

Cassidy's expression shifted immediately, as if she understood the intent of Davis's question. The night Niles was murdered, he hadn't come home, and she'd previously told Davis that Niles wasn't the type to stay out late.

"No, actually. He didn't often stay out late."

"But he occasionally did?"

"Yes, on rare occasions."

"But his recent behaviors led you to believe he was keeping things from you? That he was hiding something?"

"Yes."

"And you weren't aware of the alternate identity or the apartment he kept?"

Cassidy tilted her head slightly to the side, her fingers curled softly into her palm, creating a fist before she could stop herself. Davis caught the reaction. "Is that a statement or a question, Detective?"

"A question."

"Then no, I wasn't aware of either."

"But you did feel as if he had secrets."

"Yes. Secrets, like another woman, not that he had a secret life," she stated firmly as her fingers further tightened.

"So you thought that Niles was cheating on you?"

"I did."

Davis stared at her intently for a long moment. "Had your sex life changed or shifted?"

Cassidy's brows pinched, and Davis followed with, "Just trying to put all the pieces together. You mentioned he was traveling more, spending more time on his phone. In most cases, when a spouse is cheating, their sex life shifts. More often than not, it decreases, but in some cases, the guilty party overdoes it, trying to cover any signs of their indiscretions. You know the whole, 'you can't possibly be cheating if things are good with us in the bedroom' angle."

The question was necessary, but Davis found himself asking for inappropriate reasons, which had him shifting in his chair.

"Things were different, yes. When we were together, it was great, same as it had always been, but I will admit to spending less time together *intimately.*"

Davis hated how her response created a slight bit of relief. This woman was married and possibly killed her husband, and he was annoyed by the fact that Cassidy perhaps had an active sex life. He decided it was best to switch gears.

"I'd like to show you something." He reached for the iPad on the table, unlocked the screen, and slid it across the table. The video was queued to the spot Cassidy's car pulled into the parking garage the night of the murder.

Davis noted how Cassidy made sure she had no detectable physical reaction. She merely glanced at the device, then locked her gaze on Davis, who rattled off, "I'd like you to watch the video."

Cassidy's finger gently touched the screen, focusing on the device until the video ended. The video was comprised of three clips showing Cassidy arriving, following Niles into the elevator bay, then making the call as she went to her car and leaving several hours later. All very incriminating.

When Davis had her attention again, he pointed to the device. "You were there that night."

"In the garage, yes. I followed him from our house."

"Because you thought he was *cheating*?"

"Yes."

"And what gave you that indication that he was going to be cheating that specific night?"

"I overheard a call just before he left where he told someone he would be there soon." The way she paused, Davis knew there was more, but she was holding back.

"Anything else?"

"No. He said he had a lead on someone he had been having trouble locating and had to go immediately, or he might lose them again."

"Was that normal behavior for him?"

Cassidy frowned thoughtfully. "Sometimes, yes. But mostly, Niles's work required travel."

"But not this specific case?"

"No."

"Do you know who he was trying to locate or who he was locating them for?"

"No. His job required discretion, which I'm sure you can understand."

"Right. He was a private investigator for exclusive clients. *Wealthy* clients, I'm assuming?"

"Yes."

"Do you think his job is why your husband assumed a false identity?"

"Do you?" Cassidy shot back, and Davis leaned back, allowing one hand to rest in his lap, the other on the table.

"Still trying to put all the pieces together, but I'm not sure as of now. So, you followed him that night expecting what?"

"I wasn't *expecting* anything."

"But you assumed that you would catch him with another woman?"

"Yes."

"Did you?"

"No, Detective. You can see from the video that I didn't follow him inside. I went back to my car."

"You did, but you were there for over three hours. Based on where you were parked, plus the lighting and angle of the camera, I can't be sure that you didn't slip out the other side to enter the building through the stairwell."

"I didn't."

He nodded. "Why didn't you mention that you were there the night your husband was murdered, *Cassidy*?"

He intentionally used her first name this time. She had insisted on them being familiar when he questioned her at her home. Using her name now was more or less a taunt.

"Because I hadn't yet understood what was happening and how my life was changing. I had no idea who my husband truly was, and I was still processing that information."

"You intentionally kept evidence concealed? Evidence that could help find your husband's killer."

"Yes. I suppose if that's how you'd like to look at it."

"You realize how this looks, don't you?"

"Of course I do, Detective. It *looks* like a woman still processing that her husband was a fraud. That our life together was a lie. It *looks* like a woman who felt betrayed and devastated after finding out that her happily ever after wasn't so *happy*." Her tone was clipped, the first display of any real emotion since the questioning began, and Davis was almost inclined to believe her.

Almost.

"Which means you had motive."

"As does anyone else connected to the life that Niles was living completely separate and unbeknownst to me. Maybe you should consider that, *Detective*."

Davis kept his eyes trained on Cassidy. She was once again guarded. The mask was back on. He wasn't surprised. This wasn't her first rodeo; it was simply her first one in her current position—as a suspect.

"Are you insinuating that I'm incapable of doing my job, Ms. Evans?"

"Absolutely not, Detective. Only that there's more than one possibility here. Your job is to find the killer. Mine is to prove it's not me. We're not exactly on the same team, are we?"

"It appears we're not."

Cassidy tucked a few loose strands of hair behind her ear, but her eyes remained on Davis.

"Are you arresting me?"

"Not at the moment. Everything we have is circumstantial, and you're willingly cooperating."

I also want you to be free to move around so that I can see if you are hiding anything.

"Do you have any more questions?"

"No. You're free to go, but I will need you to hand over your passport and stay close to home for now."

"I have seminars scheduled. They've been confirmed for months now. Should I cancel them?"

"If they're out of state, I would prefer you did. However, if you need to travel, I must insist you inform me of your whereabouts. But otherwise, use your own discretion."

"Right."

Cassidy stood and lifted her purse, sliding an arm through the strap and pulling it over her shoulder. "If that's all, I'll be on my way."

"Yes, that's all for now. Thank you for coming in. If I have any further questions, I'll be in touch."

"But while I'm here, you may as well ask the more important one."

"Which is?"

"If I murdered Niles."

Tension pulsed around them, and the room instantly felt ten times smaller.

"Did you?"

"No." Her eyes remained fastened to his, and her body language and demeanor supported the idea that she was telling the truth. Confident. Expressing certainty.

"Well, there you have it." Davis nodded with a ghost of a smile tugging at his lips, and watched Cassidy as she left the room. His thoughts drifted back to her answer, and he considered what it truly could have meant. Maybe she was telling the truth. Cassidy hadn't murdered Niles because, in her mind, Niles hadn't been the person shot that night. The victim had been his alias, *Jerrod Williams*.

Maybe I asked the right question but referenced the wrong name.

7.

"Tia, come in, please." Cassidy stepped aside, allowing space for her assistant to enter.

Tia Murphy was a college graduate who had been hopeful about breaking into the entertainment industry. She planned to work for as many celebrities, athletes, and musicians as she could attach herself to until she'd made enough connections to branch out on her own. Her first job was working for a local rapper, and after one party too many, Tia found herself in a compromising position where she had almost been assaulted. That incident was enough to pause her aspirations to become a singer and shift her goals. A few months later, she interviewed with Cassidy, who offered her a salary she couldn't refuse. They'd been working together for the past three years, with Tia starting a year after Cassidy married her husband.

"What's going on? You sounded urgent when you called." Tia's brows pinched slightly as she peered at Cassidy, dressed in jeans and an oversized sweater. Her feet were bare, and her bob was pulled back into a ponytail that sprouted from the nape of her neck. Tia was also in jeans but sported a crisp, white, boyfriend-style button-down that offered a casual yet chic look, which she paired with an expensive purse and matching ankle boots. As usual, the two women were like polar opposites, given Tia's runway-ready style, which greatly contrasted with Cassidy's comfy appearance.

"I need to tell you something, and I also need your help with a few things." Cassidy inhaled, releasing it slowly. "Come have a seat so we can talk."

Tia followed Cassidy deeper into the house but stopped in the living room and sat on the sofa. She placed her purse on the arm beside her while Cassidy continued toward the kitchen.

"I'm going to have wine. Would you like some?"

"Uh, sure, but only one glass. I have a date later and don't need to pregame."

Smiling as she grabbed the wine from one of the glass enclosures, Cassidy stepped back and placed the bottle on the counter, immediately securing two glasses and the electronic opener from a nearby cabinet.

"A date? That's new."

Or is it?

Cassidy racked her brain, trying to remember if Tia had mentioned meeting anyone recently. She faintly recalled Tia saying she was tired of being alone and that dating in Atlanta was exhausting.

"It's very new. Only been a little over a month." She smiled at Cassidy, accepted the glass of wine she handed over, then took a sip. "Oh, you brought out the good stuff. Should I be worried?" Tia smiled again, taking another sip.

"Maybe a little. So, tell me about this guy. I can't believe you've been dating someone for over a month and haven't mentioned it."

"We haven't talked much lately."

Cassidy cringed slightly, but Tia quickly added, "Mostly because we've finally gotten your schedule together after that overflow of inquiries and demands for you to speak. I can do everything else remotely and without much input on your end. It's why you pay me the big bucks, which, my passion for shopping truly thanks you." Tia winked. "But his name is Derrick, and he's super sweet. We met on a dating app—"

"Tia, you didn't?" Cassidy had warned her multiple times about the hazards of dating apps. She had plenty of horror stories where she'd analyzed disturbed people with even sicker intentions who used those apps as their personal playgrounds for finding victims.

"I did, but before you give me a lecture, just know that I thoroughly vetted him before we ever met, and when we did meet, it was in a group setting. Our first five dates were with other people. One was with his best friend and sister who just happened to be dating each other. I promise I was smart about it. I could literally hear you in my head . . ." She playfully rolled her eyes.

"Good, but I suppose I need to tell you why you're here."

Maybe it was strange that Niles had been murdered wasn't the first thing out of Cassidy's mouth, but in her mind, saying it out loud further confirmed that it was real. Discussing things with Davis hadn't really counted because he hadn't known Niles, but Tia had. She'd been to their house, had dinner with them, made reservations for anniversary dinners, and picked up gifts for birthdays and holidays at Cassidy's request.

"What's wrong? You look upset, pale even."

"It's Niles."

"Niles? Is he okay? Did something happen?"

"He, uhhh . . ." Cassidy gripped her glass so tightly she feared it would shatter. "He was shot a week ago."

"Shot! Oh my God. What happened? Is he okay? Shit, are *you* okay?" Tia's eyes began nervously roaming Cassidy's body, and Cassidy knew Tia was searching for any indication that she was harmed. She wasn't. Physically, she was fine, but emotionally, she was struggling.

"I'm fine, and Niles, he—"

Tia threw her empty hand over her mouth and began shaking her head. "No, no. Niles is . . ."

"Yes," Cassidy whispered. "He was murdered."

"Oh God." Tia gasped, shaking her head again. "How? Why? What happened?"

Cassidy turned and placed her wineglass on the end table beside her. "I need to ask you something, and please, don't be afraid to tell me the truth."

"I wouldn't lie to you, Cass. You know that."

Cassidy nodded. "I do, but this is about Niles."

"What about him?"

"He had an apartment in Buckhead under the name Jerrod Williams. He also had a New York license with that same name. Did you know *anything* about that?"

Cassidy wasn't sure why she asked, but a small part of her was feeling exposed and wondering just how exposed she had truly been.

"Hell no. And if I did, I would have told you."

Cassidy felt the anger and certainty in Tia's response and relaxed a little. It would have killed her to pick up any signs that Tia had known about her husband and kept it from her.

"Why would he . . ." Tia started, then narrowed her eyes. "Wait, was he cheating? Is *that* why he had an apartment under another name? No, he couldn't have been cheating. He loved you. I've seen you two together. Your marriage was perfect, Cass. So perfect."

Cassidy's chest tightened. Tia wasn't around daily because most of the work she did could be done remotely, but she had spent time with Niles and her a handful of dinners and occasional celebratory events. Even though she managed Cassidy's social media accounts, handled her website and schedule, and took care

INNOCENT INTENT   71

of requests for speaking engagements that had begun flooding in after Cassidy's book hit the NYT Bestsellers List, Tia still had enough insight to have an opinion on their marriage.

"No one's perfect, Tia. We certainly were not."

"So he was cheating?"

"I don't know for sure, but I assume he was. Even if he wasn't, he had another life I didn't know anything about. Are you sure you didn't know?"

"Cass, I swear I didn't." Once again, Cassidy watched her body language, searching for any signs that Tia was lying. She knew the young woman fairly well, and Cassidy was far more observant than most. She'd documented Tia's tells early on in their relationship, but she had never mentioned that to Tia. Because of who she was, she didn't want things to be weird between them or for Tia to feel like she was constantly analyzing her. Tia's tells were easily detected. Tia wouldn't maintain eye contact if she told a lie and unintentionally wrinkled her nose. Neither happened as they conversed.

"I believe you. I know you didn't spend much time around Niles—"

"I didn't spend *any* time around him. Well, at least not when you weren't around as well."

Tia was offended, and that hadn't been Cassidy's intention. Cassidy wanted to be clear that she trusted Tia. "I'm not accusing you of anything. I was only asking if anything about him didn't make sense to you. Anything you can think of that he'd said or done that might help me make sense of this."

Tia's brows furrowed, and Cassidy presumed she was thinking about her interactions with Niles. "No, nothing that I can think of. I know you said you weren't perfect, but to me, you were. You guys were what I wanted to be. Niles was the type of husband I could only hope to have one day, and you were the type of wife I aspired to be." She shook her head softly. "I can't believe this. That he's gone, and he had a secret life. How? He loved you, Cass. I know he did. I could literally feel it when I was around the two of you."

Cassidy hated how much that confirmation soothed her. If he truly loved her, why have an alternate life? She couldn't erase the thoughts that what she and Niles had was all a lie. "Again, nobody's perfect, Tia. This only proves it."

"Yeah," Tia said lowly before sipping her wine. "So what now? Are they investigating? Do they have any leads? God, this is insane, and what about you? Are you okay? This is a lot. You have to be struggling to make sense of things."

"You have no idea. It still doesn't feel real, and I do not know what's next. The only thing I know is that he was my husband. Even if under pretense, I have to figure things out. For now, I need to clear my schedule."

"Done. Don't you worry, I'll take care of it."

"You can't tell anyone what's going on. For now, I would prefer to keep things under wraps. I don't know for how long; maybe until they figure out who did this. Just tell anyone who asks that something came up. Some of the engagements are paid. Return the deposits they sent to get me on their schedules and—"

Tia placed her glass on the coffee table and scooted closer to Cassidy, placing her hand over the clasped ones resting in Cassidy's lap. "Hey, let me handle this. You have enough to worry about, and anything else you need, you just tell me, and it's done. What about funeral arrangements? How does that work?"

"I plan on doing something small. No service or anything. I'll get that taken care of. He doesn't have family or friends I know how to contact." Cassidy shook her head, annoyed that she hadn't pushed the issue to gain more insight into who her husband was previously. Now, she was paying the price—a very steep one that could cost Cassidy her freedom.

"Makes sense. Well, whatever you need, I'm here. You just call, okay?"

"Thanks, Tia. I appreciate you."

"Shit, Cass. I really can't believe this. I just can't."

"Neither can I, but I guess I will have to wrap my mind around this at some point."

Tia glanced at the watch on her wrist and then peeked at Cassidy. "Maybe I should cancel my plans for tonight. I could hang out for a while . . ."

"No, absolutely not. Like it or not, this is my life now. I have to figure this out, and you have a date waiting for you." Cassidy delivered a genuine smile. Her life was falling apart while Tia's was coming together. She wouldn't get in the way of someone else's happiness. "I do appreciate the offer, and I hope that I get to meet him soon. Maybe when things settle down."

"I promise you will." Tia stood and lifted her purse. Cassidy stood right after, and Tia caught her off guard when she pulled Cassidy into a hug. It was the first real physical contact she'd had with anyone in days, and her heart clenched with the reminder that she was once again alone.

"I love you, Cass. You're gonna be okay."

Tia hugged her tighter, and Cassidy allowed her to. When the two separated, Cassidy walked Tia to the door. She promised again to handle all of Cassidy's upcoming commitments for the rest of the month. Then she was gone.

And Cassidy was alone.

Again.

◄•———✺———•►

Cassidy pulled up CJIS—Criminal Justice Information System— grateful that she had decided it was worth keeping. She quickly keyed the name in question, knowing that if anything were there, it would be a closed case. She couldn't access open cases, but anything was worth a shot. Her first instinct was to call in some favors to gain access to the case file, but that would mean providing information on her husband's alias and herself. Instead, she decided to use paid databases to gather anything she could. It still amazed and disgusted Cassidy that anyone willing to pay could have access to just about anyone else's personal information. Doing so made her feel every bit of the criminal Davis believed her to be. She was a suspect, and, based on the way Davis handled the questioning the day prior, she was the only suspect. If not the only one, she was most certainly his main focus.

He thinks that I did this.

That I murdered my husband.

I need to change that.

After the third paid search for Jerrod Williams, all Cassidy learned was that his New York license was valid and that he had two known addresses attached to that name: the address where he was murdered and a small one-bedroom in Brooklyn.

There was no criminal record. However, two phone numbers and a personal credit report were attached to the same name. She was baffled as to how that was possible, considering there was no known job history or business ownership listed for Jerrod Williams.

Fake identification with a perfect credit score.

How fucking ironic.

Cassidy drummed her fingers on the sleek desk surface, running through what she knew of the man her husband was pretending to be. Apparently, Jerrod existed a year before Niles, but neither had existed before six years ago. The first known record for Jerrod Williams dated back eight years, whereas Niles Anderson's had only existed for a little over five. He and Cassidy had only been married for three years.

Yet another mystery. Niles Anderson hadn't existed until a few years before he and Cassidy met. She couldn't stomach the reality that the man she'd married barely existed before their union.

She mentally ran through the months after she'd first met Niles. He was handsome, smart, and charismatic but very closed off with his life. He later explained that it was because he had always been a loner. With no family in his life or anyone he could truly rely on, Niles found it easier to employ solitude. Losing his parents had made it hard to trust lasting bonds or that people would stay around. Cassidy related to that side of him and felt it brought them closer. Gave them something unique that very few others could understand.

Fear of trusting and then being left alone.

What if that had been a lie too? It seemed so real, but thinking back with what she now knew of the man, Cassidy hadn't truly known him. What if he had researched and used what he knew of Cassidy's life to get close to her? To gain her trust and make her believe she could feel safe with him.

She closed her eyes, embracing a memory. Cassidy could see his handsome face and feel the warmth of his breath as it whispered across her lips when he promised he'd always be there. That she could trust him to be her one constant.

"We're all we have, Cass. That's why we have to make this work. No one will ever understand me the way you do or you the way I do. This is forever, Cass. Forever."

Another round of nausea raced through her system. Cassidy's bio was online. Bits and pieces about who she was had been easily accessible. She had also spoken publicly in interviews about her life, her trust issues, and how those flaws had helped throughout her career. She channeled those flaws to become better at her job, more efficient. Cassidy analyzed what was most overlooked repeatedly, searching for anything that felt off or uncertain. It was what she had done early in life, trying to understand why her parents couldn't love her the way other parents loved their children. She picked apart her earlier years piece by piece, analyzing every detail, and still nothing. Even if she never got the answers she was searching for when it came to Jana and Donald, she'd found answers in the cases she worked on, which had become her passion. Her vice of choice.

She had even done that with Niles and believed in him, believed he loved her. She was now beating herself up for missing so many essential things.

Love disrupts your thought process. Clouds logic with feelings and makes truths become abstract, and lies possess more clarity.

This was something she had told victims time and time again when they asked the same question that had been on repeat in Cassidy's mind since discovering her own life held secrets.

Niles wasn't who he claimed to be.

And that statement had proven to be true. Love did disrupt your thoughts and make you believe the lies, but not Cassidy. She should have known better.

But I didn't.

The nausea was gone, and her belly clenched and blazed with another feeling. A stronger emotion. *Anger.* The same anger she'd felt when following Niles that evening.

He was a gotdamn liar.

A fraud.

Cassidy slammed the lid of her laptop closed and shut her eyes, trying to control the rage boiling in her core. Rage that had her about to do something incredibly stupid. Her freedom was already on the line, so what did it matter?

Pushing away from her desk, Cassidy hurried to the custom, secured file cabinet she kept in the office. She'd wanted something modern with a soft appeal that matched the elegant style of her decor—a metal desk with a smoked glass surface and matching hand-stitched leather desk chairs with hints of black, white, and gray accents. If nothing else, it was aesthetically pleasing.

The file cabinet kept all of Cassidy's pertinent information—contracts, degrees, past case files, and recent manuscripts. She keyed in the passcode, the lock clicked, and the drawer gave way, gently moving back. She pulled it open further and began digging through the contents. Her breath caught slightly when her finger brushed across the thick file folder that had haunted her for years. Her stomach contracted as she bypassed it and removed the tiny metal box behind the files. She placed the box on top of the file cabinet and flipped the lid open.

Thank God.

Cassidy exhaled a sigh of relief at being a hoarder of everything involving her career. Fingering the dated identification card briefly, she slid it into the pocket of her jeans and hurried to her room. After shoving her feet into a pair of shoes and grabbing a coat, keys, and purse, Cassidy headed to the door. She would deal with whatever consequences, if and when they surfaced. But for now, she needed answers and would do whatever was necessary to get them.

❦

Walking into The Atrium, Cassidy felt her pulse thumping more rapidly with each step. She was risking so much with the potential to gain nothing, but instinct said she didn't have a choice. With her life spiraling out of control, she needed to take control. This was the only way she knew how.

As soon as she reached the on-site rental office, Cassidy inhaled deeply before wrapping her fingers around the brushed nickel handle to pull on the paneled glass door.

"Welcome to The Atrium. How can I help you?"

She's young. Good.

"Uh, yes." Cassidy plastered on a confident smile and clutched the identification she held, prepared to flash it to whoever she needed to in order to certify the lie she was about to tell. "I'm Cassidy Evans. I'm working with APD. There was a shooting here—"

"The sexy guy on the third floor?"

Cassidy nodded, tensing at this young lady referencing her husband—Jerrod Williams—as sexy. "Yes, Jerrod Williams. There's an open investigation, and I need to go up to the apartment once more to finalize a few things."

"I thought they finished all that."

"They did, but we have a few more questions that can be answered with one last walk-through. To my understanding, they want this wrapped up as quickly as possible. A shooting in a place as prestigious as this has to be a disruption."

Cassidy didn't know for sure, but in most cases, a dead body in a fancy high-rise being an active crime scene wasn't what residents would call a "favorable" environment.

"Right. So you're like with the police department? Do you have a badge?"

"Not a badge, but I have identification. I'm a forensic profiler, not a cop. I analyze crime scenes and suspects to help the cops solve their cases."

Cassidy glanced at her hand, sliding the identification around until the date was covered, but her photo and name were visible. She held it up, fast-talking her way through the next moment, shifting the woman's focus from the ID and praying she wouldn't ask to take possession of it.

"You're more than welcome to go in with me to make sure—"

"No, thank you. I'll have maintenance go up there with you. I'm not trying to be anywhere near that mess." The young woman shivered, tensing her face. "Hold on. Let me call them."

She picked up the phone, and Cassidy listened while she explained to whoever was on the other end that a cop was there and needed to get into Unit 302. After a few uh-huhs and rights, she ended the call and addressed Cassidy.

"Elevator's that way. Lewis will meet you up there. You know where you're going, right?"

Cassidy nodded. "Yes, thank you."

As soon as she stepped off the elevator and turned the corner, Cassidy laid eyes on an older gentleman dressed in uniform, a short-sleeved, light blue Polo shirt and matching pants that were a shade or two darker. He didn't smile or greet Cassidy; he only used a universal key to unlock the door. A green light flashed on the keypad, overriding the control, before he yanked down on the handle and pushed open the door.

"How long you gonna be?"

"Not long. I'll make this as quick as possible. I'm sure you're busy," Cassidy offered, opting to keep things cordial.

"Very," he grunted. "We're short-staffed today, and I've got a list a mile long. This isn't helping."

"Got it. I promise I'll hurry."

Cassidy gave him a soft nod before she stepped into the apartment. She removed a pair of latex gloves from her purse she'd brought from home. She would have to risk tracking in debris from her shoes because she didn't have booties. Not that she cared at this point.

The air inside the place smelled stiff and closed in. It had been a few days since the shooting, and no air was currently circulating. Cassidy glanced around the living room, taking in her surroundings. There were a few signs that CSU had searched the place, but the apartment was still orderly, for the most part, appearing only slightly lived in.

Cassidy traveled to the bedroom. There, things were less organized. The bed had been tousled. The sheets and comforter were moved away from the bed, and the pillows were tossed around but not in the way of someone sleeping there. CSU had been searching for evidence. DNA. Cassidy swallowed thickly, wondering what they'd found and who it might have belonged to—*if* there was anything there.

She slowly walked around the bed and peered at the bloodstained carpet, staring blankly at memories of Niles's— *Jerrod's*—body playing in her mind. When she felt overwhelmed, Cassidy closed her eyes, blinking away the image to center her focus.

"Why am I here?" she whispered.

She knew CSU would have collected anything relevant, but she had to come. Cassidy needed to see if there was anything they'd missed. *Anything.*

She lifted the strap to her purse and repositioned the small bag to hang across her body and out of the way before starting with the dresser. Slowly, she pulled open each drawer, pushing around clothing. Anger crawled up her spine as she thought about how the contents were the same as the ones on his side of the closet at the house she and Niles had shared—socks, briefs, tees, all bearing similar labels.

Nothing.

Her next stop was the nightstand, where she found stacks of bills, bank statements, and credit card statements.

Jerrod Williams.

One in particular caught her eye: a renewal notice for a safe deposit box. The bank wasn't one she and Niles were associated with. Opening the statement, she realized there was also a checking account at the same bank in Jerrod Williams's name. The balance on the most recent statement was $682,987.32. That had been two months ago.

Where did you get that type of money?

Cassidy took a photo of the statements, then neatly tucked them back into the drawer before searching the bathroom and the closet. By all accounts, Jerrod's life mirrored Niles's life with Cassidy through clothing and personal items such as jewelry and cologne. Yet, another confusing layer to this mess that was now her life. Why have a secret identity if he was basically the same person?

But it isn't the same, is it?

This life that Jerrod Williams lived didn't include me.

Despite the similarities, Jerrod's life had erased Cassidy's existence.

"Lady, you about done in there?" The terse, irritated voice from outside the apartment startled Cassidy but made her refocus.

"Yes, coming now."

She hurried out of the bedroom, through the living room, past the maintenance guy, mumbled thank you, and then hurried toward the elevator. She now had one more piece of a puzzle she had no clue how to solve. Despite her reckless behavior, Cassidy had no other choice if she wanted to prove her innocence. So, her next stop was Capital Bank.

8.

"Davis . . ."

At the sound of his name, Davis paused and backtracked, peering into the corner office.

"Yeah, Captain."

"Where are we with the Williams case?"

"Nothing new. Got a few leads. I'm waiting on a warrant to access a safe deposit box Williams has to see if that gives me anything."

"That's it? It's almost been a week. We need to get an arrest on the books. Our UCR stats haven't been that great over the past few months."

After twenty-plus years of referencing UCR, Uniform Crime Reporting, Captain rarely acknowledged NIBRS, National Incident-Based Reporting System. However, he didn't have to because, much like himself, his colleagues were programmed to use specific metrics.

"There's not much to go on at this point. I'm going to dig a little deeper into Williams to see if . . ."

"None of that is relevant to the case, Davis. We need an arrest, and going on some witch hunt isn't going to get us there any faster."

"I'd be more than happy to bring Evans in, but considering we don't have a weapon, DNA, or solid evidence that ties her to the crime scene, nor would anyone around here appreciate me hauling her ass back in here with an official charge, digging into Williams is the best lead I have right now."

Davis had gone over the fine details of Cassidy Evans's life. Nothing was out of place or suspicious. Sure, her husband was living an alternate life and cheating, albeit still unconfirmed, but that wasn't nearly enough to get a conviction. The DA would hand him his ass if he presented a case against Evans seconds before they laughed him right out of their office.

"Well, if Cass is clean, you need to figure out who had a motive to kill the guy. If he's living a double life, then he had to have pissed off somebody. You don't have anything?"

"Not yet, but as I said, I'm looking a little deeper into Williams's life and trying to understand why neither name goes back any further than eight years. Both are clean. No criminal history, not so much as a traffic ticket. You don't recreate yourself if you're a standup kind of guy. There's something there. I just need to figure out what the hell it is."

Captain leaned back in his chair, brushing a palm down his face. "Yeah, you do, and you need to light a fire under your ass. Maybe I should put someone else with you to speed this thing up. Make sure the case is moving in the proper direction."

Captain's heated glare fastened to Davis's with a warning. Get something solid, or Davis would be assigned a partner on his case regardless of whether he liked it.

"I don't need someone else getting in my way. Let me do what I do, Captain. Rushing creates mistakes, and I'm sure you'd much rather not travel down that road again."

Captain offered a stiff nod. "See what you can find about Williams, but if nothing comes up, you need to figure out something else. We need a solid arrest on the books."

"And if that arrest is Cassidy Evans?"

Davis knew everyone here wanted her to be clean on the murder of her husband. Hell, he even wanted to pin the shooting on someone else. The woman deserved vindication, considering her husband had played her, but a small part of Davis believed Cassidy had already played judge and jury.

Nothing like a woman scorned.

"Is there anything pointing to her?"

"Not at the moment, but my gut is telling me something isn't right. I can't say for certain she did this, but things aren't piecing together properly with the woman."

"I expect you to handle this case like you would any other, but if you put this on Cass, you had damn well better have iron-clad evidence, or you'll find yourself on the wrong side of a complicated situation."

"Is that a threat, Captain?"

"No. Just offering a reminder that if this investigation leads you that way, make sure what you have is solid before you go tossing out charges, especially if you're charging Cassidy Evans."

"I know better than to compromise myself or this precinct, Captain. If you don't trust that, then put someone else on the case. Until then, I will handle this how I see fit."

Davis delivered a warning of his own, which he felt the captain didn't appreciate. When it came to the job, Davis never allowed his personal feelings to cloud how he handled a case. Apparently, their captain needed to adopt the same policy. "I've got work to do, so if that's all . . ."

Captain offered a sigh paired with a tight nod. "That's all, but keep me updated."

"Yeah."

Davis walked back to his desk and plopped down in his chair, staring blankly at his computer screen while he drummed his fingers atop the case file for the Williams murder. So many things didn't add up, but none of those loose ends got him any closer to finding out who had murdered Williams.

He flipped open the file and began shifting through what he had so far. A bunch of nothing. Witness statements, eighteen to be exact, with no solid details about the guy. After doing a little door-to-door on the third floor where Williams's apartment was located, all of his neighbors gave various stories with the same details. Nice guy, kept to himself, seen with several different women. They could not provide any reliable information other than the women were attractive.

Cassidy was attractive. Beautiful even. Had she been one of those women? Was she lying about knowledge of the apartment or her husband's alternate life? Davis shifted his attention once again, annoyed to be thinking about Cassidy as more than a suspect.

Refocusing, he circled back to the details he could rely on. Williams's apartment was clean. No DNA or prints other than his own. He was careful about covering his tracks. He was the type of man who didn't want to leave anything behind that could connect him to anyone with valuable information about who he was and what he was up to. Not even the rental office could say anything about Williams other than that he'd paid for the apartment a year in advance with a cashier's check.

Thinking of the bank, Davis leaned forward to lift the phone to check on his only hindrance. He'd reached a dead end with finding anything crucial on Anderson or Williams to aid his case, which was frustrating as hell. One man and two identities, neither of which had ties to anyone or anything other than . . .

Cassidy Evans.

"District Attorney's office. How can I help you?"

"This is Detective Davis. Badge number 6112. I'm calling to check on a warrant I requested."

"When was the request placed?"

Davis ground his back teeth. It had only been a few hours since he'd signed off on the affidavit. He was new and couldn't call in favors, so he typically had to wait his turn. "This morning."

"Well, Detective, we're a little backed up. DA Greene has been in back-to-back meetings since this morning. It's not likely she's gotten around to it."

"Yeah, see, I'm at a bit of a standstill here. I really could use a little help getting that on her desk."

"Detective Davis, was it?"

"Yeah, and before you shoot me down, just know I would forever be in your debt with anything you could do to help."

"I'm sure. Why don't you head on over, and I'll see what I can do."

"Yeah, sure, I can do that. On my way now."

"Fine, but no promises. Like I said—"

"You're behind. Got it. Again, I appreciate you even trying."

Davis ended the call, grabbed his cell phone and keys, and headed out of the office, only to be stopped by one of his colleagues.

"You in a hurry, Davis?"

"Yeah, I am. Excuse me."

"Look, I get it. You're new, a loner, and not looking to make friends with any of us." Irritation flooded Davis's expression when Detective Braxton Reese refused to get out of his way. Davis would have to reiterate the point the other detectives didn't seem to understand. They needed to let him be.

"Then, if you get it, why the hell are you still in my way?"

"Because you might not need friends, but allies come in handy." Reese lifted the phone and quickly made a call.

"Hey, Chelle. It's Detective Reese. Good, and you?" Reese issued a lazy grin. "Of course you are, and I'll see what I can do. Listen, one of our guys called about a warrant. Yeah, Davis. He's on his way over. Why don't you do me a favor and make sure it's ready for him?" Reese smiled wider but kept his eyes on Davis. "I know, but if you do this for me, you know I'll return the favor. Perfect. He's heading your way now."

Davis ground his teeth behind Reese getting involved. "I didn't need your help with that."

"Maybe not, but you got it. Only it's gonna cost you. One beer, tonight at Charlie's."

"No, thanks."

"Come on, Davis. I'm not trying to overstep . . ."

"That's exactly what you're doing."

Reese grinned smugly, shrugging lazily. "Okay, maybe I am, but can you blame me, or any of us, for that matter? We're a family around here, and you insist on keeping yourself exclusive. Might not mean much to you now, but I promise having at least one of us on your side will prove beneficial. It damn sure won't be Harper, so I'm your best choice."

"And why the fuck do you care?"

Reese grinned again. "I don't actually, but I've been where you are, so I get it. One beer. After that, do whatever you want around here. Tonight, eight o'clock, Charlie's."

After speaking his piece, Reese walked back to his desk. Davis left the precinct with a warrant in his hand twenty minutes later.

Davis parked his car in front of the bank and was about to get out when something, or rather someone, caught his eye. Before he decided to get out to see what she was up to, a call came through on his cell. He answered but kept his eyes on Cassidy as she entered the bank and walked to the customer service desk.

"Detective Davis."

"Good afternoon, Detective. This is Angel Diaz."

"Ms. Diaz, yes. You have something for me?"

"I do. It took a little digging, but it seems that the names and Socials you provided are valid but shouldn't be in circulation."

Davis noticed Cassidy's expression turn to frustration as she leaned closer to the woman at the customer service desk, who was nodding quickly before she rounded it and hurried away.

"I don't follow," he muttered, focusing on his call once more.

"Both Socials match the respective names. However, the numbers are from deceased infants. Williams was born on August 2, 1989, and passed away from SIDS on November 13, 1989. Same with Niles Anderson, born June 8, 1987. He died of SIDS on October 4, 1987."

"Shit. The sick bastard took the identity of dead kids," he murmured more to himself than to Diaz.

"Seems that way."

"You sure?"

"Completely. Both deaths were recorded with the hospital, and obituaries are in the papers, but neither the funeral home nor the parents reported the deaths to the SSI offices."

"No one checked."

"Apparently not. It happens. The death of a child is hard enough, so I can see how reporting the loss of your child to the SSI office isn't really a priority. The parents were likely grieving, trying to make sense of things, and not all funeral homes are efficient. They also forget all about the families they service after the checks clear. If no parents or loved ones apply for survivors benefits, then it makes sense that the deaths were never reported, leaving the numbers and identities active and available for—"

"For any heartless asshole that wants to take it over."

"Exactly."

"Can I get you to email that over to the office for me?"

"Sure thing. I have the address you provided. It will be on the way as soon as I hang up."

"Thanks."

A few minutes after Davis ended the call, he noticed Cassidy leaving the bank. She wore a look of frustration and came out empty-handed. He quickly navigated to the camera app on his phone and captured a few shots of the highly irritated suspect walking to her vehicle and then sliding behind the steering wheel. A few moments of Cassidy slamming her fist down on that same steering wheel passed before she started the car and backed out of the space, driving aggressively out of the bank's parking lot.

"What the hell were you in there looking for, and why didn't they hand it over to you?" Davis mumbled to himself before he lifted the warrant, opened his glove box, and removed a pair of latex gloves and a clear evidence bag from the box he kept on hand. He climbed out of his vehicle, folded the gloves and bag into the breast pocket of his jacket, and navigated to the door. Once inside, he walked to the same customer service desk where Cassidy had been, plastered on a smile, and greeted the young woman sitting below him.

"Welcome to Capital Bank. How can I help you today, sir?"

This was a rare occasion where Davis actually had on a sports coat, so he pushed it out of the way and pointed to his shield affixed to his pants. "The woman who just left, Cassidy Evans. What was she here for?"

The bank associate's eyes darted around as if she wasn't sure how to respond. Davis moved closer, leaning over her desk.

"I'm a detective. You can tell me." He tapped his badge with two fingers, and she slumped her shoulders, conspicuously looking around again before responding.

"She asked about a safe deposit box."

So she knows. Interesting.

"Under the name Jerrod Williams?"

The woman's brows pinched as she nodded. "Yes. She said she was married to the guy, and when I asked for identification, the one she gave me didn't match his name. When I looked up the account, she wasn't listed as the wife. I couldn't give her access without something official or his permission."

"Official, like a warrant?" Davis flashed a charming smile, and she returned a flirtatious one, nodding.

"Yes, a warrant would work.

"Good thing I have one of those then." He extended the papers, and the woman hesitantly accepted and stood moments later.

"If you'll give me just a minute, I must show this to our bank manager. I'm sure you understand why."

"Absolutely. Take your time."

Davis didn't really want the woman to take her time, but he decided playing nice was the quickest way to get what he wanted. He watched as she crossed the bank and paused at one of the offices before she knocked and stuck her head in the open door. Through the paneled glass, he could see her hand over the warrant, and an older, balding white man flipped through the pages and then glanced his way. Davis lifted his head in acknowledgment before the guy handed the paperwork back to the woman, who immediately rejoined him.

"This way, Detective."

After being handed off to one of the attendants behind the counter, Davis was escorted into the vault that held the safe deposit boxes. He handed over the key they found at Williams's apartment. She moved to the wall of boxes and removed the one that belonged to Williams, handing it over to Davis.

Once she was gone, Davis pulled on the gloves and carefully lifted the lid, frowning at the contents. He found three passports with matching identification cards with Williams's photos on them.

"Who the hell is this guy?"

After carefully lifting the items from the box and placing them in one of the clear evidence bags, Davis examined the last thing in the box, a flash drive—one he couldn't wait to get on screen because his gut was telling him that he finally had the lead he was hoping for.

9.

"Were there any complaints?"

"No. Truthfully, everyone was very understanding but also very eager to reschedule. I told them I would be in touch soon to have a new date on the books."

"As soon as I know something, we can work on alternative dates."

Cassidy had no clue if and when her life would be settled again. It seemed as if she received one blow after another.

Dead husband.

False identity.

No access to any parts of his life.

Being the main murder suspect.

"Shit, Cass. How are you? I probably should have begun there instead of diving right into business."

"No . . ." Cassidy softly shook her head, staring into the sky as the colors shifted once again. The orange, hazy glow was being swallowed by the darkness of night. "Regardless of what's going on with my personal life, the world doesn't stop."

"True, but that doesn't mean I can't be considerate of what you're going through. I can't begin to imagine how you're handling this."

Cassidy released a sharp laugh. "I'm *not* handling this. I suppose that's the best explanation. My life for the past three years has been a complete lie. I'm not sleeping because the idea of doing so has my anxiety spiking. Lie or not, someone shot my husband. Who's to say I'm not at risk? I have no idea who killed him or why, and the cops think I'm the murderer. They don't give a shit whether I'm safe or a target. I'm so damn exhausted and don't have any idea what to do with any of those feelings. So, there you have it. I'm *not* handling any of this. I'm just . . ." After a brief pause, Cassidy exhaled the last word. "Here."

"Oh, Cass. I'm coming over. You really shouldn't be alone . . ."

"No, please don't. You being here won't change any of what's happening."

The line went quiet, and Cassidy realized her tone might have been a little harsher than she intended. "What I mean is, this is my new reality, Tia. I can't expect anyone to make sense of this for me. As much as I appreciate you wanting to help, there's nothing you can do."

"I understand. I just want to help. You have been so amazing to me, and I feel like I need to return the favor. To do something— *anything*."

"You're doing enough. You're handling the business side of things, so I don't have to. I can focus on my personal life, or what's left of it."

"That's my job, Cass. You pay me to handle the business stuff."

"But it still matters, so I don't want to demean your efforts. I have to go, Tia. If I need anything, I'll reach out, but for now, just continue handling things on your end."

"I will, and please don't hesitate to call for anything at all, Cass."

"I won't."

After Cassidy ended the call, she lifted her wineglass and swallowed a hefty gulp while staring at the paperwork in her lap. She was notified two days ago that Niles's body would be released from the coroner's office. That meant she would be responsible for handling the arrangements. A plethora of mixed emotions surfaced. She was burying both her husband and a stranger. She was mourning the loss of the man she loved and angry that her life would forever be attached to a man she never knew.

Cassidy went back and forth, trying to decide which of the identities she should count on. Niles was sweet, caring, and consistent, while this Jerrod was a complex mystery. Maybe neither of them was real. The unanswered questions were what bothered her the most. Who had she fallen in love with, and why had he purposely chosen to attach himself to a life he never intended to honor? The only certainty she could rely on was that her world with Niles was over, and she was burying all the happiness she'd dreamed of with him.

10.

"Well, damn, you really showed."

Davis shrugged, filling the spot at the bar next to Reese. "It's hard to respect a man who doesn't keep his word."

Reese nodded before signaling the bartender and finishing the last of his beer while waiting for the guy to make his way to them.

"You get that warrant you needed?"

"Yeah, she had it waiting on me when I got there. Thanks for that."

"You're welcome. See, it's not so bad being a part of the team."

"Never said I had a problem with being a team player."

"You didn't have to. The way you shut all of us out is explanation enough. Mind if I ask what that's about? The whole loner thing?"

Davis glanced at Reese before focusing on the bartender when he approached.

"What can I get you?"

"I'll take a beer." Davis pointed to the import Reese had in front of him.

"You can bring me another one with his. Put it on my tab, Lou."

Davis wanted to decline the offer but felt accepting a few beers was the least he could do. He didn't have any real issues with the guys he worked with. He simply didn't care enough about building bonds to put any effort into getting to know them.

Once the bartender was gone, Reese turned to Davis to pick up the conversation again. "So, the working solo thing?"

"It's not a *thing*. I just prefer to work alone."

"You didn't have a partner in New York?"

Davis knew that was the opening for Reese to dig a little into his background, and he decided to let him.

"No, not one designated partner. I worked with the guys when cases called for it, but I like my space and privacy."

"Maybe I should consider giving that a try. Parker talks too damn much and always about his wife busting his balls. I swear we stop at least ten times a day so he can smoke those gotdamn cigarettes too. Working alone doesn't sound all that bad the more I think about it."

Davis chuckled, nodding thanks to the bartender who dropped off their beers. "Parker seems like a decent guy."

"He is . . ." Reese shrugged. "But he does talk too much. I feel like I know way too much about this wife, and I've never laid eyes on the lady."

Reese grinned. "You see my struggle?"

"Yeah, I do." Davis smiled behind his beer after lifting it to his lips.

"So New York to Atlanta. Why'd you transfer?"

Because working alongside a district attorney who was engaged to my ex-fiancée didn't exactly make for a peaceful work environment.

"Personal reasons," Davis muttered, not wanting to get into it.

"Come on, Davis. You can give me more than that. Unlike some of the other guys, I don't entertain *teenage-girl gossiping.* Your personal shit's safe with me."

Davis laughed at the reference to the back-and-forth he and Harper had engaged in shortly after he took over the Williams case. "I guess you heard that."

Reese smirked and shrugged again. "We all did. It was funny as shit because Harper really fucking hates that they took Evans's case from him and put you on it. He was very vocal about the power exchange, and now the guys keep giving him shit about running his mouth. You're not his favorite person at the moment."

"I don't give a damn how Harper feels."

"Which is why you have more allies than you think. Harper's a decent-enough guy and a damn good detective most days, but sometimes, he forgets that we're all on the same team. The guys appreciate that you don't give a damn about what Harper thinks. Don't discount their stance on things. Like I said before, you might not want friends, but it won't hurt to have allies, and you've got them *if* you want them."

Davis lifted his beer, taking down some before he nodded. "'Preciate it."

He decided that since Reese was being genuine, he'd open up some about why he transferred to their precinct.

"My ex thought that me being a detective wasn't good enough. She kept urging me to get a law degree. When I refused, she ended up engaged to a lawyer, a district attorney, to be exact. Seems she was more interested in being with the title, regardless of the package it came in."

Reese nodded to Davis before he clarified. "The reason I transferred was because her fiancé ended up becoming the DA for my precinct. Annoyed the shit out of me every time I had to work with him. I didn't give a damn that he was marrying my ex, but I guess it made him feel special, which meant he always gave me shit trying to flex his position. I needed a change, so I transferred here. A new city where I'm not attached to anyone or anything and plenty of cases to solve."

"Was it a coincidence that he was assigned to your precinct?"

Davis scoffed. "Doubtful. If I had to guess, her father pulled some strings at her request. He's very connected in New York. She wanted me to be reminded of what I passed up, like I gave a shit."

"That's a fucking blow to the ego. You regret not getting your law degree?"

"Fuck no. I like being on this side of things. Being on the other side blurs the lines. Lawyers bend and twist the rules to get the results they want. We deal in facts. We let the evidence guide us. They manipulate the truth, which doesn't always mean the good guys win or the bad guys pay for their sins."

"We deal in the facts to solve our cases, but the evidence sometimes tells a far different story than the one that truly happened. We don't always find the truth either."

"Agreed, but once we hand it over, we can confidently walk away knowing we did our part. That's what makes this side the lesser of two evils. We use the evidence to tell the story; they use it to tell the story they want to be told."

"A *good* detective, that is. Not all of us play by the same rules," Reese added. Davis agreed. Some functioned by the letter of the law, and others saw nothing wrong with cutting corners or misrepresenting the facts.

"I'll drink to that." Davis lifted his beer and tipped it toward Reese. Reese returned the gesture, finishing the one he was working on while Davis drained half of his.

"You want another one of those?"

"Might as well make this worth my while since it's on your dime."

Reese chuckled amusedly. "Damn, and here I was thinking I was good company when it's really the free beers keeping your ass on that stool."

Davis grinned and shrugged. "We'll consider it an even split for now. But I'm starting to think that Parker might have rubbed off on you with the talking too much thing."

Reese threw his head back and laughed. "Motherfucker, I knew that shit would be contagious, and you didn't have to call me on it."

"Hey, you wanted me here. You'll have to live with what you get."

Reese held up two fingers to signal for another round. Once he got acknowledgment from the bartender, he nodded, lifting his beer.

"I guess I do, don't I?"

A few hours later, Davis felt a little buzz as he parked in his driveway. Wasn't the wisest decision driving home after six beers and two glasses of cognac, but he had always been able to handle his liquor. Even with the buzz, he was still in complete control of all his faculties.

Davis opened the glove box and removed the flash drive. Once he'd dropped the contents of Williams's safety deposit box by the precinct to be properly bagged and tagged, he'd requested a copy of the flash drive. Davis was hopeful there would be something on it he could use. They'd dusted for fingerprints, and the only ones present belonged to Williams, which had Davis eager to find out what he was hiding. By the time CSU finished and made his copy, Davis had a little less than half an hour to get to Charlie's to meet Reese. Finally home, he was motivated to see what he had. He stepped out of his car, hit the locks to secure his vehicle, and navigated inside the house, moving through the motions of his regular routine.

Car keys were tossed on the coffee table, and the remote was in hand shortly after, allowing Davis to flick on the TV more out of habit than with the intent of watching. He had a flash drive to check out, which meant the TV would end up being background noise.

A quick trip to his room to grab his laptop brought Davis back to the kitchen, where he removed a bottle of water from the refrigerator and then folded his long frame into one of the small wooden chairs of his kitchen dinette to power up the device.

While he waited, he downed the bottle of water, then keyed his password before lifting from the chair to get another bottle, tossing the empty one in the trash. When he was seated again, he plugged in the flash drive and clicked on the file as soon as it illuminated on his screen.

Davis quickly sobered up when he realized what he was looking at: a case file. A very old one. He wasn't familiar with this particular one because it'd happened almost eighteen years prior when he was just a uniformed officer in New York. The case was worked here in his new city, but he immediately recognized something as he shifted through the photos of the case file. Post-it Notes were attached to the pages with handwritten notes and questions.

"Why the hell do you have one of Cassidy's case files on a flash drive tucked away in the safety deposit box?"

Davis continued clicking through the files, analyzing the notes. It appeared that Cassidy was second-guessing certain aspects of the case, evidence, and witness statements—one in particular she had placed a Post-it Note on with the words "reasonable doubt" in all caps, underlined. The statement was from the victim's ten-year-old daughter.

What's that about?

Curious for answers, Davis navigated to a search engine and typed in the defendant's name, Johnathan Arnold. The first article that appeared was from the day of his sentencing.

> *Johnathan Arnold, 36, was convicted and sentenced to thirty years in prison for the rape and murder of Alison March. March was a college student.*

Davis scanned through the details of the murder listed in the article. March reportedly had a flat tire late one night while driving home alone from an off-campus party. Arnold offered to help but stated he didn't have the tools to change the tire. As a compromise, he offered a ride to the nearest gas station, where she could safely wait for a cop to assist. All according to Arnold. He planned on leaving her there; however, she flirted with him. When he suggested they get a room, she willingly agreed.

Arnold had been *accused* of raping twelve other women, which March hadn't been aware of at the time. Arnold was known for using a police badge he purchased online and would often tell his victims he was an off-duty cop.

Arnold was convicted of raping, then murdering, March at a local hotel, where she was later discovered. Based on the drugs found in her system, it was believed that Arnold drugged March to get her to the hotel.

DNA from Arnold was identified throughout the hotel, and Arnold's semen was found in March. The room where March's body had been discovered was rented by Arnold. His testimony was that she'd willingly joined him and that he'd left March alive before going home to his family. Arnold agreed to being a cheating bastard but not a rapist or murderer. Based on the time of the murder and witness statements that Arnold's car was seen leaving the hotel hours before, prosecutors had a tough time building the case against him. His only alibi during the time of the murder came from his wife and daughter. However, neither could say with certainty when he'd arrived home that evening. They could only agree that he was there at some point, which meant both mother and daughter were unreliable witnesses.

After further scrolling, Davis also took note of two significant things. The case was Cassidy's first right after she finished her training with the department, and it was also the case that skyrocketed her career. Cassidy's testimony after speaking with Arnold had been a huge deciding factor in convicting the guy. Her testimony as an expert witness discredited the statements from Arnold's wife and daughter, which meant no alibi. The conviction gained Cassidy and Lance Trent, the lead detective, a lot of media attention.

Davis leaned back, massaging his chin, trying to understand what he was looking at. Why did Cassidy have the file with notes questioning the details of the case? More than anything, why was her focus on the testimony of Arnold's wife and daughter? There was something there. Davis simply had to piece it all together.

❦

The following day, Davis found himself at an office building across town. He had been up most of the night doing a deep dive into the case involving Arnold as well as Cassidy's career. That case was important enough to create motive for Cassidy to kill her husband. Davis decided he needed to go back to where it all began, but also that he needed to speak to those who weren't directly involved. They had just as much to lose as Cassidy. After being associated with Arnold's case, several people's careers were elevated positively. Those same cops and detectives worked hundreds of cases after Arnold was sentenced. If there were indiscretion with anyone involved in the Arnold case, the department would have a mess on their hands. Numerous other cases worked by those individuals could potentially be called into question.

Arnold's case was somehow connected to Williams, or he wouldn't have had evidence of it locked away in a safe deposit box. Several scenarios came to mind, none of which looked good for Cassidy. Was it possible Williams discovered something that incriminated Cassidy related to the case? Something that could ruin Cassidy's very honorable and decorated career? Cassidy could have been blackmailed by her husband, which provided motive. The guy was a fraud, so blackmailing his wife wouldn't be far beyond his purview.

"Detective, what can I do for you?" Sidney Tyler greeted Davis with a curious look as she invited him into her office.

"Ms. Tyler, thanks for seeing me on such short notice. I wanted to ask you a few questions about an old college alum of yours."

"Okay . . ." She frowned slightly, and Davis could sense that she was already analyzing him. She was a psychologist, after all. Being cautious and perceptive were to be expected. "Who would that be?"

"Cassidy Evans." Davis was now doing the analyzing. He watched Tyler's reaction, noticing the slight flare of her nostrils and squinting of her eyes before he continued. "I understand the two of you graduated together and both trained with the department to become criminologists. However, you ended up in private practice, while Cassidy—"

"Ended up as the god of all gods when it comes to understanding the criminal mind and behaviors."

There is animosity between the two.

"Cassidy's career has been stellar, yes."

"She could have been any of us, Detective. We all make choices that lead us down different paths."

Interesting.

"Care to elaborate?"

"Why are you here? I haven't seen or communicated with Cassidy in years. If she's receiving another award or honor where you want those of us who *knew her when* to chime in on what an amazing person she is, you might want to pick another alum. I'm sure plenty would be willing to sing her praises for a chance at being associated with her."

"And you wouldn't?"

She leaned against her desk, locking thin arms firmly across her chest. "No, Detective, I would not. *Again*, we haven't spoken in years."

He nodded. "How about you tell me what you meant by different choices that led down different paths? I assume that means the two of you didn't see eye to eye when it came to your chosen paths?"

Tyler laughed, rolling her eyes. "I chose to earn things with hard work and respect. Cassidy, not so much."

"Sounds like you're saying she didn't *earn* her career."

"I'm saying had I chosen to give more attention to the detective assigned to train us in the field as Cassidy had done, then you might be prying into *my* background instead of hers. Choices, Detective."

Cassidy was sleeping with the detective in charge of her field training?

That brought another round of questions. "What would that have to do with Cassidy's career?"

"Her first case was the Arnold case. Cassidy's expert testimony discrediting the guy's alibi is what essentially won the case. The wife and daughter were adamant about Arnold being home that evening. It was even rumored that Cassidy promised the kid that she believed her. No record of that promise exists, however. That case didn't fast-track *only* Cassidy's career. Chief Trent had a very stellar career as well. You do the math."

"Are you saying she lied?"

"I'm saying that the guy was guilty. Everyone knew it, but the prosecution struggled with providing evidence that could prove he killed the woman. He was there. Admitted to having sex with her. He said it was a mutual exchange. That couldn't be disputed. The smoking gun was putting him there at the time she was murdered. Cassidy gave the jurors what they needed, which was an open window for Arnold to have been there when March was killed. I get it. You guys shift things all the time, especially in cases like Arnold's. He was a sick bastard who deserved exactly what he got. However, is justice really served if the details were manipulated to get the conviction?"

No.

But that's sometimes necessary.

Davis understood the game. He simply didn't enjoy it when the rules were broken. Now, he understood why Cassidy was obsessing over the case. Guilty conscience or possibly a severe case of imposter syndrome. Her entire career was based on manipulating the facts to serve an intended purpose. In her case, it was a conviction she felt wasn't earned. For some, that was hard to let go.

"I see. Well, I think I have what I need. Thank you for your time, Ms. Tyler."

As Davis tipped his head to leave, Tyler stopped him. "I have a question for you, Detective."

Davis again granted Tyler his full attention, standing in the doorway of her office with his hands submerged in his pockets while he waited. She neared him, stopping about a foot from his rigid frame. "You being here obviously isn't about celebrating Cassidy's career. If I had to guess, and I'm pretty good at reading people, you're here because you have doubts about Cassidy, her career, or possibly both."

Davis didn't respond, and Tyler smiled smugly. "Your silence is loud, Detective. What I would like to know is, why me? Of all the people you could have contacted, why did you choose me?"

"Easy. There was a photo online of the day Arnold was convicted. A group of you stood in the room while Cassidy was honored. The look in your eyes is the same as it is now . . . begrudging. I decided to cut through the bullshit and get straight to the people who were less than impressed by their colleague's success. I'm good at my job, Ms. Tyler, as are you. Have a great day."

He left her office with a new motivation contradicting what he wanted to believe about Cassidy Evans. Not only was she hiding something, but she was also potentially just as much a fraud as the man she was married to.

11.

The mood was strange. Although the sun was shining, the sky was clear, and the air was clean and crisp as a gentle breeze drifted around Cassidy, her spirit felt dark. Standing graveside, alone, to bury the man she both loved and now hated, was the cause of that darkness. No matter how hard Cassidy tried to block the way her heart ached, to channel anger instead of disappointment, she failed miserably. Tears welled in her eyes behind the dark shades she wore. However, she managed to prevent them from escaping. With her nerves frayed and anxieties running haywire, Cassidy mindlessly brushed a palm across her waist. She had bypassed the typical funeral attire and was instead dressed in jeans and a cream, cable-knit sweater.

There is no point in following protocol.

This isn't my husband.

This is a stranger.

Cassidy didn't owe this man the respect of going through formalities. Out of respect for the lives attached to the names he'd stolen, Cassidy elected to bury her husband with the name John Doe. He didn't deserve to be identified or remembered by the names he violated. Jerrod Williams hadn't earned her love or loyalty. Niles had possibly, but this wasn't Niles. She refused to allow herself to feel a connection.

But my heart still aches for the love that no longer exists.
Had it ever really existed?

"You lied to me."

One tear fell, then another before Cassidy swiped a knuckle across her cheek.

"Why? Why pretend to love me, only to rip out my heart with no care or consideration of the consequences?"

Her body trembled with sadness that slowly shifted to anger.

"I trusted you," she whispered over and over again before she was yelling. "I. Trusted. You."

Cassidy's head swiped left and right, her fists clenched at a painful degree at her sides. She didn't know what she was looking for until her eyes landed on the beautiful arrangement of flowers. Several vases were positioned in the grass surrounding one large design of white roses and calla lilies that sat on an easel. The funeral home had provided them. Of course, they provided superior service. She had paid an exorbitant amount to bury a man she didn't even know.

Why wouldn't they?

Moments later, she reached for the flowers, lifted the first arrangement, and hurled it into the grave. It crashed against the casket while she turned and lifted another. One by one, she unloaded the arrangements onto the casket, her body trembling with rage, chest heaving. Once she dragged the easel and shoved it behind the rest, she yelled one last time.

"I trusted you!"

Cassidy collapsed to her knees, sobbing uncontrollably. The anger shifted back into sadness and heartache yet again. She never considered herself weak or emotional. She had always been the type of woman who schooled her emotions—kept them locked away because others couldn't be trusted with handling them. She trusted Niles, and he'd betrayed her. The thought caused Cassidy to sob harder. The emotions she'd been holding back since his murder finally reached the surface. She was so lost in the moment that she hadn't realized she was no longer alone until an arm circled her waist, and she was being lifted from the ground and dragged into a solid, warm frame.

Her body stilled, tensed with unease, until she looked up and found concerned brown eyes staring down at her. *Detective Davis.* His face was void of emotion, but his eyes gave her comfort, so when he cuffed the back of her head and tucked her face into his chest, she allowed him to. She needed *something—someone*—at the moment, and he was there. She allowed herself to be vulnerable. As time passed, so did the moment, and she eventually managed to pull away.

"What are you doing here?"

"We need to talk."

Cassidy scowled at Davis, who seemed composed and detached. His eyes no longer seemed caring but more accusatory.

"How did you know I was here?"

He smiled arrogantly, and Cassidy hated how handsome the man was while doing so. Davis was undeniably easy on the eyes, but none of that mattered, considering he thought she was a murderer.

"I'm a detective, Ms. Evans. It's my job to *know* things."

"It's also rude to disrupt my personal and very private moment."

Something flashed behind his eyes for a second before they seemed to soften. "You're right. Are you okay?"

Cassidy's gaze lowered briefly to the casket. "Clearly, no, but I'm sure your job isn't to be concerned with my personal feelings, Detective. What is it you want to discuss?"

Davis nodded stiffly, and Cassidy hated how his eyes locked on hers, fully taking her in. She also loathed that he'd been there to witness her unraveling and had also been a source of comfort. The man who was trying to convict her of a crime she didn't commit shouldn't have been a shoulder to lean on.

"Might be best if we take this somewhere else."

"Such as?"

"Precinct, if that's okay with you. Considering . . ." His eyes lowered to the grave. "We can do this another time if you'd prefer."

"No better time than the present, right? The sooner you ask me whatever you have on your mind, the sooner you can find out who put him there." Cassidy's hand motioned to the grave, but Davis kept his eyes on her. The two maintained a visual standoff before he nodded, conceding first.

"If you're sure you're up to it."

"I'm fine, Detective. Not that you'd care. I have my car. I'll meet you there."

She turned to walk off, but he called after her. "Cassidy, I care. This situation can't be easy to deal with, and you're allowed to feel however you need to feel to make sense of things."

She paused and glanced at him over her shoulder. "Thanks for your approval to grieve my fraud of a husband's death, Detective. But again, I'm fine."

Her walls were up once more. She'd trusted one man who betrayed her. Cassidy had no plans on allowing another the opportunity to do so. Especially not one who was convinced she was a killer.

Sitting in the interrogation room, Cassidy was reminded of how much her life had changed. She wasn't foreign in this space. However, in years prior, she had been asking questions, not on the other side of things.

Davis entered a few moments later with two bottles of water, one of which he placed in front of Cassidy before filling the seat across from her.

"Thank you."

"You're welcome."

After he uncapped his and had taken down a healthy amount, his intense gaze was on Cassidy. She rolled her shoulders back, preparing for his questions, and Davis didn't disappoint.

"You were alone today."

"I'm sure you understand why."

My husband was a loner without family, friends, or other connections.

"I understand your husband didn't have anyone in his life, but certainly you do, right?"

"I'm not in the position to invite people into my life right now, Detective. What would I tell them? My husband Niles was shot in an apartment that he'd kept, which I wasn't aware of. Oh, and let's not forget, he wasn't actually my *husband*. He was a man with two identities, neither of which truly belonged to him. I wasn't jumping at the opportunity to share that story with my intimate circle or stomach the questions that would surely follow. Alone felt like the best option."

Cassidy stared at Davis unflinchingly. She was angry again. Angry about her reality. Angry that Davis had her here to dig deeper, trying to prove she was responsible for taking a life. He wasn't going to play nice or dance around the obvious. He had a job to do, which meant finding a killer. She could only hold firmly to her innocence.

"Ask me whatever you want. Let's get this over with."

Once again, the two were in a visual standoff, and Davis was the first to concede. Cassidy kept her eyes on him while he began.

"I saw you at Capital Bank yesterday."

"And?"

"Would you like to tell me why you were there?"

Cassidy smirked. "Would you like to tell me why *you* were there?"

They were both experts at their jobs—two very strong personalities, and neither willing to give much.

"Williams had a safe deposit box. One that held information about you. I'm assuming that was why you were there. To clean up behind yourself."

Cassidy faltered briefly. Yes, she was there for the safe deposit box but had naturally assumed it would hold information about Niles or Jerrod. Not once had it crossed her mind there would be something incriminating about her.

"What did you find?"

"Passports, identification that matched them. There were additional names besides the two you were familiar with, but more importantly, a flash drive with case file photos. One of *your* case files."

Cassidy frowned before asking. "Why would he have one of my case files?"

"I was hoping you had the answer to that question."

"I haven't got a clue. We rarely discussed my cases. Which one did he have photos of?"

"Your first one."

Cassidy's chest constricted like someone had wound a rubber band around her, hindering her ability to breathe.

"You okay, Ms. Evans?"

When the fog cleared, she placed a hand on the table. Her fist was clenched tightly, and Davis's eyes were on her.

"Yes, I'm fine."

"You sure? It seems that you got lost there for a minute."

"I assure you I'm fine. I have no idea why Niles would have a copy of that case file."

"Cut the shit, Cassidy. Was your husband blackmailing you?"

Her defenses heightened, and her expression hardened. "Why would he be blackmailing me?"

"If I had to guess, I'd say because he discovered you lied on that case. Your testimony sealed the conviction, and all these years later, you're second-guessing your actions."

Her eyes flared with anger. "I didn't lie."

"Maybe not, but if you had, that would mean your entire career and the careers of those involved with that case would be questioned. Hundreds of cases that *you* were attached to that they handled would be brought into question. I'm sure you can imagine what a mess that would create. If your husband found out that you lied . . ."

"I *didn't* lie." Cassidy slammed her hand down on the table, glaring at Davis. The outburst had him smiling smugly, and she realized her mistake. He wanted a reaction, and she'd given him just that.

"Then what happened, Cassidy? Tell me why that case mattered so much to you. To *him*. Why would he have a copy on a flash drive in a safe deposit box with your notes and questions about specific aspects of the case? It only makes sense that he was blackmailing you, and if he wasn't, then he planned to. Maybe you found out and decided you couldn't allow that to happen, which means motive."

Cassidy had her composure again. "I didn't kill my husband, Detective."

"Possibly not, but did you kill Jerrod Williams?" Davis countered.

Cassidy chuckled bitterly, pushed her chair back, and extended to her full height. She traveled to the door and opened it.

"We're not done here, Evans. Where are you going?"

"We're going to see Dixon. You believe I killed Niles, Jerrod, or whoever the hell you want him to be, but I didn't. I need you to focus the energy you're wasting on me toward finding out who the *real* killer is. You'll only do that if you no longer believe that person is me."

Davis stared at her introspectively for a long moment before he pushed his chair back and stood. "Dixon retired last year. Grant administers polygraphs now. You still want to do this?"

He thinks I'm counting on a favor from Dixon.

"I don't care who does that test. Only that it's done properly."

He nodded, crossing the small conference room until he was right in her personal space. "We can do this, but you understand it's not admissible in court."

Cassidy nodded as well. "I have no plans on needing it in court, and if it comes to it, I'll deal with defending myself in front of a judge at a later date. Right now, the only person's trust I need is yours, Detective." Her eyes bore into his for a long moment before she left the room, not bothering to check that Davis would follow.

12.

"What the hell was that?" Harper growled once Davis was back at his desk.

With a cool demeanor, Davis took his time handing his attention over to Harper, who had undoubtedly witnessed him bringing Cassidy in for additional questioning. It also hadn't escaped him that Harper potentially knew about the lie detector test. The precinct was small. People talked, and unlike Davis, Harper had more friends than foes there.

"Do you hear me talking to you, Davis? I asked you a question."

"I heard you perfectly clearly, but APD, not Gregory Harper, issued my badge the last time I checked. Now, if you would like to tone that shit down and try this again like a sensible person and not an entitled asshole, then I might consider answering or, at the very least, extending you the respect of not punching you in your face for addressing me like I'm not a grown-ass man."

Harper's cheeks flushed red with anger. "This tough-guy act is not earning you any brownie points around here, Davis. You box—so what? I'm just as handy with my fists."

Is this guy serious?

"Not likely."

Realizing he wasn't getting the intended result, Harper decided to try a more civilized approach. "Why did you bring Cassidy in and have her do a lie detector test?"

"I had questions pertaining to *my* case. The test was *her* decision, *not* mine."

"I'm sure it was since you seem hell-bent on making her your only suspect when she's innocent."

"Is she?" Davis initially believed Cassidy to be guilty but had since shifted his opinion of her. The way she navigated through the questions asked while attached to the polygraph with certainty and ease had been the reason. She was either telling the truth or an incredibly good liar. His gut leaned toward Cassidy telling the truth. Davis rarely went against his gut feelings because they never steered him wrong.

"You had her in the box; you didn't ask?"

I would have been a fool not to.

Davis smirked, leaning back in his chair, chest expanded and legs wide. A show of dominance. His elbows were bent with his hands clasped behind his head. "I did, actually."

"And?"

Davis's smile expanded. "I choose to keep that between myself and Ms. Evans for now. You know, just in case things change one way or another."

"You don't have to be a dick, Davis. Everything is not about a show of power."

"I disagree . . ."

"Harper, let's go. We have the lead we've been waiting on."

Davis's eyes moved past Harper to where his partner waited a few feet away, watching their exchange with a hard expression locked in place.

"Looks like you have somewhere to be."

"Fuck you," Harper ground out. "You're gonna need me, Davis, and when you do—"

"I won't," Davis retorted. He would do whatever to ensure needing Harper would *never* be an option. In the event it was, he'd still find an alternative, at least until Harper was willing to hand over the respect he so arrogantly demanded. With one last heated stare, Harper turned to leave. Davis felt eyes on him and looked up in time to find Reese glancing his way, sporting a smug expression. Reese smiled, shaking his head before he lowered it and went back to banging on his keyboard with very little finesse.

Davis shrugged nonchalantly, realizing that Reese wasn't the only one with eyes on him. He caught the captain's disapproving stare seconds before he turned, entered his office, and closed the door.

I guess he isn't a fan of my actions today, either.

At this point, Davis was more concerned with finding another suspect because if he didn't, he would have no other choice than to circle back to Cassidy. The more time he spent around her, the more he found himself wanting to believe that she genuinely hadn't been the one who killed her husband. Instead of allowing his thoughts to go there, Davis leaned over his desk and began shuffling through the bank statements he had for Jerrod Williams. He'd learned early on in his career to follow the money. It would always lead to something or someone who had answers.

By eight that evening, Davis had enough investigating for the day. After spending hours traveling in circles, only to come up empty, there was no point in further torturing himself. He also had a few more questions that needed answers, which was why he found himself pulling up unannounced to the last place he should be. Had he been honest with himself, he would have settled into the fact that he could have initiated a call, but that would have cheated him of the opportunity to look into Cassidy's eyes to gauge her answers. Finding truth to her responses wasn't the only reason he had a strong desire to gain access to those maple-brown orbs. Even if he wouldn't allow himself to cross those lines, he couldn't seem to deny himself the pleasure of her company.

"Uh, Detective Davis, what are you doing here?"

"Hope I'm not interrupting . . ." He suddenly had the urge to look past Cassidy when thoughts of her not being alone found their way into his subconscious. She hadn't seemed like the type to cheat, but her husband was dead, and that *husband* had betrayed her. Maybe there was someone new.

Nah, too soon.

Why the hell do I care?

"No, I just finished putting dinner away and cleaning the kitchen." Her brows pinched as she stared at him.

"Yeah . . ." He lifted a hand and massaged his chin, briefly looking down uncomfortably before he gave her his eyes again. "I had a few more questions."

Cassidy squared her shoulders, narrowing her stare. "I thought we covered everything earlier."

Davis smiled smugly when he noticed the annoyance that quickly altered her mood. He was immensely enjoying the many layers of Cassidy Evans. "We did, at the time, but I came across something and wanted to run it by you."

She relaxed slightly. "Oh, well, would you like to come in?"

Yes.

No.

Fuck.

"If you're sure I'm not interrupting anything."

"Nope. Nothing that can't wait." She moved back, offering space to welcome him into her home. Davis accepted and stepped inside. The smell of vanilla and cinnamon subtly tickled his senses and created a sense of familiarity.

His eyes moved around as if trying to decide which way to go when Cassidy decided for him by pointing to his left. "Living room."

Davis offered a nod and followed Cassidy into the living room. "Please." She motioned to the sofa, and he settled on one side while Cassidy stood a few feet away. "Can I get you anything? Water, wine, coffee."

"*Coffee*?" Davis questioned with a smug grin, which had Cassidy's brows pinched.

"What's wrong with coffee?"

He chuckled, shaking his head. "Nothing. I'm fine, I won't be long. I have to feed myself at some point this evening."

"Detective, is there some hidden meaning to offering someone coffee I'm unaware of?" He realized she hadn't understood the reference and decided not to elaborate.

He smiled. "Absolutely not, and you can call me Nate. Name's Nathaniel."

"I'm aware, but unless you've decided to accept my invitation to call me Cassidy finally, I'll stick to Davis or Detective."

"Fair enough, *Cassidy*, it is then."

"I have extras if you're okay with pasta?"

Cassidy watched his face shift and added, "You mentioned feeding yourself. I haven't quite mastered the art of cooking for one." She huffed. "I suppose it takes time."

"*Or* never happens. I haven't quite figured that out either. Tons of leftovers throughout the years, but I guess that works too."

Cassidy nodded on her way to the kitchen. She felt Davis tracking her movements. "So you're not married then."

"No, came close but never made it to the finish line. No wife or kids. Just me."

She hated how the admission sparked a twinge of happiness regarding his single status but pushed the thought to the back of her mind.

"Sounds ominous."

"Story for another day," he muttered.

She wouldn't push. "Right. This is an official, *unofficial* visit. Probably shouldn't be prying into your personal life," she stated quietly, retrieving a covered glass dish that she had placed in the refrigerator not too long ago. It held the remainder of the Cajun pasta she'd prepared for dinner.

"Official, *unofficial*. Care to elaborate?"

She felt Davis near before she lifted her eyes to find that he'd joined her in the kitchen and made himself comfortable leaning against the counter, arms folded across his chest, legs spread shoulder width apart. The muscles in his arms and chest were at war with the thin material of his dress shirt. She tried not to notice, but it was unavoidable.

"On what?" She frowned, piling pasta onto a plate she retrieved from the cabinet beside her.

"Official, unofficial."

She glanced over her shoulder, arching a brow at Davis, who still had his eyes on her. "You're here to ask questions that I would guess are official. But you're also about to have dinner, so I'll classify that as official, unofficial, *Nate*."

She loved how saying his name shifted the energy between them. His lazy smile as his eyes casually moved from the plate in her hand back to her face was appreciated as much as the view he offered.

"You have a point, and this technically isn't us having dinner if I'm the only one eating."

She nodded softly. "Well, that won't change. I've had my fill. Have a seat."

Cassidy motioned to the massive kitchen table. Davis made his way there as well, pulling out a chair and settling in.

"I take it you're not a fan of coffee, so that leaves wine, soda, and water."

"What about a beer? I'll take one of those if you've got it."

She nodded slightly. "I do. Samuel Adams. I hope that's okay."

"I'm not picky."

Cassidy retrieved a beer from the refrigerator, removed the cap, and placed the long-necked bottle in front of Davis. Moments later, the microwave went off, and she moved the steaming hot plate of pasta and silverware in front of him. The proximity granted her a whiff of his cologne. The spicy, clean scent settled warmly in the pit of her stomach. She quickly moved away and selected a seat at the opposite end of the table, leaving four seats between them.

What am I doing?

This man thinks you're a murderer.

I shouldn't be attracted to him.

I just lost my husband.

A man who lied to me and betrayed my trust.

"Hey, you okay over there?"

Cassidy snapped out of her thoughts as Davis stared her way with both arms resting on the table beside his plate. He appeared concerned.

"Just thinking; sorry."

"Yeah, this is a little weird."

"Weird?"

"The whole me being here and you offering me dinner. You have to admit it's a bit ..."

"We're not friends, Nate, so, no, this isn't a typical occurrence, but that doesn't mean we have to be weird or consider this more than it is. You were hungry; I had food." She shrugged, knowing it was more than either of them would admit, but that more couldn't happen. What would people think of her? Of him? She would be willing to bet he wouldn't compromise his case like Lance had by sleeping with someone so intimately involved in such an important case. Only now, she wasn't exactly *involved*. *She* was the case—the suspect.

"Good way to look at it." She watched as Davis lifted the first forkful of pasta to his mouth. Cassidy waited with bated breath for his thoughts.

"Damn, this is good." He flashed her a satisfied smile moments before enjoying a second forkful. "Or maybe I'm just famished."

She laughed, shaking her head, enjoying the moment shared between them too much and needing to get things back on track. "You said you had questions."

"Right." He lifted the napkin next to his plate and brushed it over his mouth in such a manly way that had Cassidy smiling again. "I found several considerably sized money transfers from your account to one that belonged to Jerrod."

"That's impossible. I didn't know about his account, nor would I have transferred money to him. Had he done it, I would have noticed. How large are we talking?"

"There were six. Each for twenty grand."

Cassidy's eyes went wide as she began shaking her head. "There's no way I would have given him that kind of money, and before you go there, no, he wasn't blackmailing me."

"I no longer believe that was the case. You answered honestly when I asked earlier during your session with Grant. I do believe he intended to at some point, though."

"I can't say I disagree knowing what I do now," she stated firmly. Davis only nodded.

"The transfers were all within six months. One a month. I'm surprised the bank didn't contact you."

Cassidy appeared perplexed. "So am I. Doesn't make sense. And with that amount of money being moved, I would have noticed it missing."

"Do you have an account that you don't use as often? Maybe for business or something?"

Cassidy's mind began to wander . . . and then it hit her. "I do, but not one he should have known about, and definitely not one he would have access to. Excuse me for a moment, Detective."

She realized she'd slipped back into formalities by not referring to him as Nate. Maybe it was the situation, but she couldn't get sidetracked by irrelevant things. She left Davis in the kitchen and traveled to her office, where she located a stack of mail. She shifted through the unopened envelopes collecting three bank statements and returned to the kitchen with them gripped in her hand. Her heart raced as she stood above the table, ripping them open one by one. Each time, her anger heightened.

Sure enough, each of the three had one transaction, a wire transfer she wasn't familiar with for $20,000.

"How . . ." she whispered.

"I take it you found proof."

Cassidy stared at the statements in her hands, nodding mindlessly before walking over to Davis and dropping them on the table beside his plate. He lifted the stack and scanned them while she sank into the seat beside him.

"And you didn't know about this?"

She shook her head. When her eyes found his with questions lingering, she added, "I don't know how he did this. He didn't know about this account. It's one I don't touch. I haven't in years."

"But you have over half a million dollars in here, Cassidy. Even after the money that was transferred." Her eyes landed hard on Davis.

"I would have *never* given him this much money without good reasoning and not from this account—*ever*."

The account held the proceeds from the sale of Clara's house. It also held the balance of the insurance money Clara had left behind, minus the amount Cassidy used to pay for college. She'd held onto that money for years, afraid that depleting the funds would mean losing the only connection she had left to the one person who'd ever truly loved her. Knowing that Niles had not only stolen money from her but also from *that* account was an entirely new level of betrayal. He couldn't have known because she never told him, but the disappointment wasn't any less palpable.

"I don't know how he could have done this."

"You were married to the guy, Cassidy. It wouldn't have been that complicated for him to find out things you didn't think he was privy to."

"No." She shook her head. "I never told him about this account. He never should have had access to it."

"But he did because, if not, the alternative is—"

"I *didn't* make those transfers, Detective."

"Nate." She noted his annoyance from the lack of use of his name but couldn't find the energy to care. "And if he didn't, then someone did. Who else would have knowledge or access to that account?"

"No one."

"An assistant, possibly? Accountant? Estate guardianship?"

Tia.

But no, not possible.

"No, I have an assistant, but she wasn't aware of the account. I never discussed it with her or anyone, and she was never alone in my home. The account was personal to me. I just . . ." She shook her head. "I never shared knowledge of that money with them or anyone."

"Personal, how?"

She hoped Davis would overlook that minor detail, but he hadn't. She wasn't prepared to share any more of her life, not at the moment.

"Does it matter? I didn't share the information with anyone. No one should have known about the account."

"I understand you think they wouldn't, but this proves someone did."

"Right."

Cassidy moved through all the possibilities. She had the paperwork locked away in her office. Niles never used the space, but that didn't mean he hadn't discovered the statements at some point and went looking for access. It also shouldn't have been possible to access the account without her granting approval. She'd have to find out how that was, but it wouldn't happen tonight.

"Maybe I should go—"

"No, please, finish your food. Your eating will not change the fact that there's yet another way that Niles betrayed me."

Cassidy forced a smile, and Davis nodded sympathetically. While he ate, she sat wondering how she had missed so many things. With that new information, she embraced yet another reality. She couldn't trust herself any more than she could trust anyone else.

13.

Jab, cross, hook.

   Jab, cross, hook.

   Davis's arms burned from the exertion of consistent punches as he completed his second hour at the gym. Weights, jump rope, speed bag, and now, heavy bag. His mind was still reeling, although his body had finally begun to settle.

   Spending the evening with Cassidy hadn't been the smartest idea. The more time the two spent together, the more complicated and tangled his thoughts seemed to be. The lines were clear. Detective. Suspect. There was no world where the two of them should be more than what they were. Detective investigating a murder. Suspect maintaining their innocence.

   That was part of the issue. Davis believed that Cassidy was innocent. He couldn't dispel the whispers in the back of his mind that his belief was partially founded in his attraction to her. Those maple brown eyes, tempting lips, and subtle curves . . . It had been awhile since he was intrigued with a woman beyond the physical pleasure she could provide. Knowing *who* was currently holding his attention was what had him up at four a.m. heading to the gym by five after a long run hadn't cleared his mind of thoughts of Cassidy.

   Jab. Jab. Cross.

Jab. Jab. Cross.

"Fuck," he growled through his frustration, dropping his head forward between his shoulders while his hands pressed into his hips until the burn from his muscles had him releasing them to hang loosely at his sides.

It was Saturday morning, one of the few rare days when he had nothing pending. There was investigating that needed to be done with Cassidy's case, but nothing pressing that couldn't wait until the start of the week. The goal was to relax and enjoy a minute to himself. However, considering his current location, that hadn't worked out as planned.

Davis decided to give it a rest and made his way to the locker room to shower and dress. Like most days, the place was empty. A few bodies scattered about, none of whom gave much thought to anyone around them, or so he assumed . . . until he stepped out into the blazing sunlight. A woman's voice caught his attention as he moved from the curb.

"That workout seemed pretty intense." Davis glanced over his shoulder and followed the teasing smile as the woman moved into his view. She was pretty, of average height, with soft brown eyes and a body he found himself comparing to Cassidy's. The yoga pants and fitted shirt showed off the woman's slim physique of toned limbs, barely-there hips, and perky breasts.

Cassidy's curves are a little more defined.

Davis preferred a natural body type, soft to the touch and something to hold onto while . . .

Let that shit go. It isn't happening.

"Didn't know anyone was paying attention."

She smiled brightly, moving closer, tossing a nylon duffel over her shoulder.

"Hard to ignore with a body like yours." Her eyes crawled from Davis's face further south, unabashedly lingering below his waist before she met his eyes again. "I'm Lena, and you are?"

"Nathaniel. Nice to meet you, Lena." He smirked, already knowing the direction she was attempting to take their exchange.

"So, boxer?"

"Detective."

Her eyes flashed with curiosity and then narrowed. "Seriously? You don't look like any detective I've ever seen. Well, aside from those on TV, and even then . . ." Her eyes swept him again. "They don't look like *you*."

"You share company with a lot of detectives, Lena?" His tone was teasing, which had her smile expanding.

"Not exactly. I'm no angel, but I'm also not that level of bad."

"And what kind of bad would that be?"

"The kind that requires badges and handcuffs, unless . . ." she stepped closer, "my partner prefers role playing."

Davis chuckled and nodded. "Good to know."

"You busy, Detective? I was about to grab some breakfast." She motioned to the café next to the gym. Davis's eyes glanced in that direction before they were on Lena again.

"I could eat."

"Great, my treat. Let me just throw this into my car, and we can walk over."

"Not necessary. They pay me well enough. I can handle footing the bill for breakfast." He winked, and she grinned, moving to her vehicle while he made his way to his own. After discarding their gym bags, the two crossed the parking lot and entered the café, finding a table in the corner.

Once they ordered, Lena dove right in with her flirtation. "So, Detective, you're single, I assume."

Davis chuckled. "Yes, the job makes it difficult to date." That wasn't full disclosure, considering he hadn't been interested in dating recently, but he didn't need her running with the idea of anything solid between them. At the moment, he needed a distraction from the woman who had been overcrowding his thoughts.

"Difficult, maybe, but not impossible, I bet."

He lifted his coffee and smiled. "No, not impossible. Just takes some strategic planning and a little manipulation."

"Manipulation, hmmm? I like the sound of that." Her smile was devious, but she moved on, and Davis was grateful. "So, is your job like what they show on TV? Hunting down the bad guys, guns drawn, looking sexy while you threaten to lock them up and throw away the key?"

"Yes and no. Most of what I've seen loosely reflects my day to day. It is a little embellished at times. I must admit I admire TV detectives a little more than I should."

She leaned forward, propping her chin atop loosely hanging fingers. The movement was subtle yet intentional. It offered a peek down her top if he elected to take it. "Oh yeah. Why's that?"

"They mostly have the luxury of closing cases in their allotted forty-two-minute window. Mine tend to drag on for weeks. Sometimes months."

"Hmmm. I can see how that would give you admiration for your fictional counterparts."

Davis chuckled, watching as she sipped green juice and picked at her egg white and spinach omelet. "But I'm sure they can't possibly look as good as you while solving those cases." She winked, and he allowed his smile to expand behind his coffee cup.

The two spent the next half hour engaging in easy conversation while finishing their meal. Davis wouldn't deny that he enjoyed Lena's company or the view, so when she asked to exchange numbers, he agreed. However, when she leaned in and planted an unexpected kiss on his mouth, brushing her body against his, Davis realized he wouldn't be reaching out. There was nothing to give him motivation. No sparks, no desire to take things a step further, knowing full well that he could have if he wanted. She presented an invitation to get to know her better with subtle cues and the unexpected kiss.

"Did you have plans later?" Lena was hopeful. *Too* hopeful. He could see the eagerness in her eyes.

"Actually, I do."

"Well, if your plans change, don't hesitate to call me. I'll keep my schedule open, just in case." She flashed a seductive smile before turning to walk away, with a slight wiggle of her fingers and an extra focus on her steps, which had her slim hips swaying to give Davis a reason to consider calling.

He wouldn't because someone else had his attention. Someone he had no business wanting.

⋯⋯⋯❖⋯⋯⋯

"Detective . . ." Cassidy held the door blocking the entrance as she delivered a cautious stare to Davis. He had once again shown up at her house unannounced. After the gym and breakfast with Lena, he exerted his best efforts to remain busy throughout the day, doing small things around the house which managed to keep him occupied for a few hours before he settled into mindlessly watching a game while he did a little more digging into Cassidy's past. Mostly the case of Johnathan Arnold, which then led him to Lance Trent. The detective-turned-chief-of-police that Cassidy allegedly had a personal relationship with.

Once he could no longer pacify his need to see the woman who had completely consumed his thoughts, Davis called in an order, swung by Charlie's to pick it up, and drove across town to Cassidy's house. Not the most professional or smartest move for his career, but he was off duty, and no one could regulate how he spent his personal time.

"Figured I owed you dinner since I barged in last night and ate yours." He held up both hands, one holding the bag from Charlie's, the other a six-pack of beer. He chuckled at how unsettlingly similar his current move was to Sam's from not too long ago. Davis also couldn't deny their intentions likely hadn't varied all that much.

"I offered. It's not like you intruded."

"True, but I figured I still owed you." He shrugged nonchalantly, hopeful that she wouldn't turn him away.

She didn't.

"Come in."

Much like the night before, Davis entered Cassidy's home, immediately relaxing at the sweet scent assaulting him, but this time, he navigated to the kitchen instead of the living room. She followed, propping up next to him and watching as he lined up plastic containers on the counter. Cassidy leaned in close, inhaling deeply and offering a smile.

"Smells good."

"Because it *is* good. The best in the city. You've never had Charlie's?" He glanced to his left, arching a brow, and Cassidy gently shook her head.

"No, never."

"You're in for a treat then. Best wings you could ever imagine."

Cassidy left his side and moved to the cabinets, removing two plates and placing them on the counter. She collected forks and serving spoons, which she placed on the island before turning to the sink to wash her hands. She and Davis switched places after he removed the lids from the food. While he cleaned up, the savory blend of aromas filled the kitchen, and his stomach growled with anticipation. Cassidy swiped one of the wings and allowed her teeth to sink in, quickly humming her approval.

"Oh wow, this *is* good. It's buttery rich but sweet." She caught a slip of sauce that drizzled down her chin with a swipe of a finger before her tongue met the tip.

Davis turned just in time to catch the motion and groaned internally. "Honey Bourbon," he murmured pointing to the container she swiped the wing from. He followed up by pointing out the rest. "Carolina Barbecue and Sweet Heat."

Cassidy nodded, dropping the empty bone on one of the plates as she lifted a few wings from each container. "This is a lot of food."

"I can eat. Wanted to make sure there was enough." He motioned to the beers. "You want one?"

"Might as well. I'm guessing you paired them for a reason."

"Smart woman." He grabbed two while she lifted both plates once they were full of wings and carried them to the table. Davis took the beers and found his way to the same chair he had been in the night before. He was pleased when Cassidy sat to his right instead of at the end of the table when she returned with a handful of paper towels.

"So, is this just dinner, or are you back on official, *unofficial* business?"

Davis worked his way through a wing, cleaning his fingers and mouth with a paper towel before he answered.

"Just dinner, but I am curious about something since you asked."

Frowning a bit, Cassidy paused briefly. "What's that?"

"You say you didn't know about your husband's other life . . ."

"I didn't . . ." She turned defensive, only for Davis to assert his confidence in her answers.

"I believe you, but I'm curious about how he managed to exist in your life with two false identities."

"I should have known," she stated bluntly, and Davis shook his head, lifting another wing.

"Maybe, but you didn't. I guess I'm wondering how that is. I did a little digging myself, and both names he used were from deceased infants. Both died of SIDS . . ."

Cassidy cringed. "Wow."

"My thoughts exactly. It's not so hard to do if you know what you're looking for. The deaths were never reported to Social Security, and because they were infants, there was no record of their lives aside from their names and birth. Clean profile. People do it all the time. You can also buy credentials and identification from the black web. If you know enough, you can bypass paying someone and find what you need yourself. Apparently, he knew, which led me to the next thing. Who *was* this guy?"

"Definitely not the man I thought he was," she responded bitterly.

Davis nodded with understanding. He couldn't imagine spending years building a life with someone who'd pretended to be someone they weren't. His mind drifted to his ex. She wanted him to be someone else, but he never pretended for her sake. She had to accept him as he was.

"Niles was clever or, at least, *careful.* No prints or DNA in any of the official systems. It's like he doesn't exist."

"Well, technically, he doesn't. Not anymore."

As their eyes merged, he understood where her thoughts had gone.

Someone killed the guy.

"I'm sure you're also wondering how someone like me could be fooled into marrying a fraud."

Davis glanced in her direction. "The thought has crossed my mind."

"Probably not as much as it has mine." She smiled wryly before continuing. "He wasn't perfect, you know. No one is, but the man I knew, Niles, was *perfect* for me. His past, or at least the one he shared with me, made sense. He didn't have anyone, and neither did I. The lack of connection made it hard to trust. When the people in your life leave you, no matter the reason, you build up walls. You believe that it's easier not to let others in. Once you reach a certain point when you can fend for yourself, you don't have to let others in. He understood how that felt. He made me believe he was the same. I trusted my husband, Nate. Maybe because I was tired of being alone, or maybe I truly did love him and believe he loved me. Not that it matters because everything about us was a lie. I know that now. I'm only trying to clarify how someone like *me* fell for someone like *him*."

Davis stared into her eyes. He felt the hurt and betrayal. A part of him wanted to fix it somehow. Instead, he cleared his throat and offered what he could. "It wasn't a lie."

Cassidy glowered hard, and he continued. "What you felt for him wasn't a lie. He might not have been who he claimed to be. Might have even lied about things he told you, but regardless, *your* feelings, they weren't a lie. You're allowed to own them. If you want to, that is."

"Thank you." She smiled softly, lifting the beer she had been nursing.

"So you said you were tired of being alone. That's why you fell for the guy. You don't have a family? Parents? Siblings?"

He knew certain details of her background. It was necessary because of how their lives aligned, but he figured he'd ask and let her give whatever pieces of her life she wanted to share from her perspective, not from the articles and files where he'd learned the information.

"My parents left me when I was a kid. Back then, I was crushed. I didn't understand why they didn't want me. Still, don't most days. But now, I have a better understanding of who they were. Not everyone is meant to be in parental roles. They were certainly not parent material. They did care enough, however, to leave me with someone who was, and in a sense, that makes me grateful. My life wasn't all that terrible."

"Yeah? Who was that?"

"A neighbor." Cassidy laughed, shaking her head. "I guess that wasn't the best either, but it worked. She had worked in social services all her life. Babysat me occasionally, and when they left me with her, she applied to adopt me. Once she did, I was raised as her daughter. She never had kids. When she passed, that was the end— no more family for me. I was a kid when my parents left. I never knew anything about their past. Didn't care enough to look when I was old enough. I had one parent for a while, Ms. Clara. Which is why I don't understand how Niles knew about the account."

Davis was confused at the shift in conversation, but she explained.

"That account was one I kept private. When Ms. Clara passed, she left me money through her life insurance policy and her house. It wasn't worth much, but she wanted me to have both. I used some for college and kept the rest. Eventually, I sold the house. The upkeep became too much, and my life was hectic. I deposited the money from the sale into the same account. It was private. I never told Niles. I never touched the money, so I never looked at the statements. There was no need to."

"He had access to you. To your life, Cass. It wouldn't have been hard to discover if he truly wanted to, and considering the things he's done, I believe that may have been a part of the plan. We have to consider the obvious, at least."

He married you for money.

She exhaled and lifted her beer again. "You're right."

"Hey, people like your husband . . ." Davis paused, not liking referring to the guy as her husband. "People like Williams, they are intentional. They use others with little to no thought for the destruction they leave in their wake. You can't carry the weight of his actions one way or another. Vulnerability isn't weakness. Opening yourself to others isn't the end of the world. Sometimes, it's necessary."

"Doesn't make it hurt any less, Detective. But at least I can appreciate that he won't do this to anyone else because he *can't*."

They shared a look, and Cassidy's expression had Davis's mind wondering again. *Who is this woman, and is she capable of such a heinous crime?*

14.

"**M**s. Evans, I apologize for the wait. What can I do for you?"

"I was wondering if you could tell me about these." Cassidy reached into her purse and removed the statements that showed the wire transfers.

The bank associate shuffled through the paperwork, then lifted her eyes to Cassidy. "What about these?"

Cassidy pointed to them. "There's a wire transfer each month for twenty thousand dollars. How is this possible?"

The woman's face flushed with concern. "I assume you're asking because you didn't approve the transfers."

"No, I did *not*. I've had this account for over twenty years. I purposely set things up as an interest-bearing savings account because I had no intention of using the money I keep here. I would not have approved these transfers. I *didn't* approve these transfers."

"Would there be anyone—"

"No. No one else has access to this account," Cassidy stated with finality, which had the associate placing the statements on her desk and waking her computer screen.

"Let me take a look because wires of that amount would require approval, considering the type of account this is. I'll see what I can find."

Time passed by agonizingly slowly while Cassidy listened to the clicking of a mouse and rhythmic pecking of the keyboard. Eventually, the associate peeked at Cassidy with an anxious look.

"I see where the first transfer happened. It was on April nineteenth of this year. And I also see it noted in the account that the transfer was flagged as suspicious activity, and we immediately reached out to ensure the request was valid."

"Reached out how?"

"A call was initiated where we reached *you*, Ms. Evans."

"You absolutely did *not*. I *never* talked to anyone about transfers from this account."

"It's right here that one of our associates initiated a call, noted that they spoke to you, and that you mentioned several transfers would be coming through. One a month. To avoid them getting hung up, you demanded that it be noted in the account that you approved all future transfers to Mr. Williams's account."

"That's impossible. I never spoke to anyone about this. *Never*. I also wouldn't have ever approved transfers from that account." She pointed to the statements but kept her eyes on the associate. "What number do you have? What number did they call?"

The associate clicked her mouse several more times and rattled off an area code followed by seven digits: Cassidy's number. "The call was initiated immediately after the request came through on April nineteenth at three p.m."

Cassidy shook her head slightly. "How is this possible?"

"I'm not sure. We take such matters as this seriously. The integrity of our customers' accounts *is* our top priority. Would you like to speak with the bank manager or our fraud department?"

"I'm sure there's not much more your bank manager can do than you've already done. Do you mind giving me the number to your fraud department? I'll reach out to them to see if they can help."

"Sure, no problem. I'm sorry this happened. I'm sure it's frustrating, but if we can resolve the matter, we will certainly put forth our best efforts."

"I'm sure you will. Thank you," Cassidy muttered after accepting the number and the statements she'd handed the associate. She left the bank with no more information than she'd arrived with, which was frustrating.

Once Cassidy was in her car, she pulled up her schedule and traveled back six months to the date of the first transfer. She realized at that moment there was no way possible the bank could have contacted *her*.

On the day in question, she had a speaking engagement at Duke. The session was from two in the afternoon until five that evening. Tia had been with her up front as a focal point for Cassidy, who struggled with speaking to mass audiences. Cassidy also always kept her phone positioned on the podium with notes as a way to stay on topic. Had the bank called, she would have known. Unless their records were wrong or the associate was lying, they had to have dialed someone else to approve those transfers, but the question was . . . who?

Frustrated that as each day passed since Niles had been murdered, her life was unraveling more and more with no reprieve or recourse, Cassidy tossed her phone into the passenger seat and begrudgingly made the drive home.

◆━━━❈━━━◆

"So, how are things? I've been meaning to reach out."

She'd gotten another random visit from a detective. However, she couldn't curb the disappointment that today's visit wasn't from Davis but instead, from her old colleague and friend, Gregory Harper. Cassidy sat across from Harper, brushing her fingers over a fray in her jeans.

"Things are as well as to be expected, considering." She'd made the same statement to Harper the day Davis had brought her in for questions weeks ago. She was unwilling to open up and share with Harper as much as she had with Davis. The truth was disarming. Whereas Harper was a friend, Cassidy imagined Davis as having the potential to be more.

What is wrong with me? The man is trying to convict me of murder.

"Understood. Anything new with the case? Any new evidence to prove you didn't do this?"

She frowned. "I would expect you to know that."

He chuckled bitterly, confirming the pending animosity between the two men. "Davis isn't the sharing type. It's his case, and he makes sure we all know it's *his*."

"Oh . . ." Cassidy offered, not surprised. Davis was open with her, but she hadn't missed how he seemed a bit closed off from his colleagues.

So why is he open with me?

Maybe he . . .

No.

The man is just doing his job.

"You can't be offended, Harper. If I recall, you've never been big on sharing either."

"Maybe not, but I'm also not a dick to the people I work with. The guy could learn a few things about knowing his place."

"His *place*?" Cassidy didn't understand why she was offended, but she was. Harper kept going, oblivious to her concern with his choice of wording.

"Yeah, his place. He's new. Only been here a year. He refuses to make nice with any of the other detectives and acts like he doesn't need anyone."

"Maybe he doesn't," she defended, puzzled at her need to stand up for Davis in the first place.

"Come on, Cass, that's not how things work. You, more than anyone, know that everyone needs somebody in our line of work. You can't survive on an island."

"True." She nodded. "But you said he's new. Maybe he'll find his rhythm with everyone."

"Doubtful. Like I said, the guy's a fucking dick most days. Speaking of," he narrowed his eyes at her, "how's it going with the case and all? He treating you right? Being respectful, because if he's not . . ."

"He's been great." When Harper's expression shifted to one of speculation, Cassidy added. "With the case, I mean. He's doing his job."

"Is he? As far as I can tell, there's still no arrest and no major leads."

"Didn't you just say he's being a dick and not letting anyone in on the case? How would you know the intimate details?" She smiled smugly, and Harper groaned his disapproval.

"Captain's getting anxious. Even if he doesn't talk, everyone else does. You've been the only suspect, and he's wasting his time pointing the finger at you. There's no way you killed your husband. We all know that, Cass. There's no way."

She nodded softly. "Good to know because I didn't. I think Nathaniel knows that as well, but as you noted, there are no other leads, so—"

"Nathaniel? You two on a first-name basis, Cass? I'm sure the guy's charming, but getting too comfortable with him might not be the best thing . . . considering the past."

She didn't hide the offense his insinuation presented. "The past?"

"People talk, Cass. It's no secret about you and Trent. At least, not to those of us on the inside."

"I'm not sure what that has to do with my current situation or why you brought it up."

"Davis is a detective. You're a suspect in a case he's working. The lines can easily become blurred, and you don't need a repeat of past events. Not with your career and all."

"I see. Well, let me just be clear. Detective Davis and I both understand our positions. However, as I've stated, I didn't kill my husband, so suspect or not, I haven't done anything wrong. There is also no proof of any blurred lines. Not that it matters. And as for Detective Davis, you mentioned twice how much of a dick the guy is, so why would you be concerned that we would end up in a position to blur the lines? I'm not a fan of *arrogance* or *assholes*, Harper." She made sure their eyes locked when she emphasized those two specific words.

"I didn't mean anything by it."

"I'm sure you didn't, so no offense taken."

He nodded. "Maybe I should go."

"Yeah, that might be a good idea. Wouldn't want there to be any reason for anyone to question the authenticity of the department with you being here and all. Even as a *supportive* friend, they might assume the lines are blurred."

He nodded again as he stood and followed Cassidy to the door, fidgeting once he was on the porch. "Cass, I really am sorry if I offended you."

"Don't be because you didn't. I know who I am, Harper, and I don't have room for others' opinions or judgments about my life. In case you've forgotten, I have more important things to focus on."

A second detective pulled into Cassidy's driveway as if the universe decided to complicate matters further. The one she was initially hoping to see today. Harper didn't bother hiding his animosity once his eyes returned to Cassidy.

"I guess duty calls. You take care, Cass. I'd warn you to be careful, but don't think you'd listen anyway."

She watched from the porch as Harper traveled down the driveway to his vehicle, which Davis had parked beside. The two engaged in a heated exchange, with Harper leaning a little too close to get into Davis's face. Harper's tightly wound stature and red cheeks showed he wasn't happy, while Davis maintained a smug grin the entire time. His posture only changed after he watched Harper navigate out of the driveway and then made his way to Cassidy, delivering a curious stare.

"Since he's no longer on your case, I assume that was a friendly visit."

"You assume right, but what was that about?" She pointed to where their exchange had taken place.

"Office politics," Davis smirked and stepped into Cassidy's home without waiting for an invitation. She followed the path he traveled, watching as Davis stood, waiting for her to shut and lock the door.

"Was that anything I need to be concerned with?" She narrowed her eyes on Davis, who still sported a smug grin.

"Why would you think that?"

"Because he called you a dick, and from what I've seen, the two of you are not fond of each other. I don't like being in the middle of a dick-swinging contest."

Davis's face lit up with amusement. "I wasn't aware that you were sleeping with Harper."

Cassidy's eyes went wide. "What! No. Why the hell would you say that?"

"Because the only way I would entertain a dick-swinging contest with you in the middle is if it involved something more intimate than me investigating the murder of your husband, Cassidy. I'm very good at my job and have nothing to prove in that department. No need for swinging body parts."

"And you would have something to prove in relation to being intimate with a woman?" She arched a brow, and Davis stepped closer. Dangerously close. His presence, the scent of his cologne, the intensity of his stare, and the unspoken promise that lingered in the air made her feel slightly overwhelmed.

"No, not there, either. I'm actually quite skilled in that department too. No complaints to speak of."

She gasped softly. "Which is irrelevant because I'm not sleeping with either one of you and don't plan to."

Cassidy didn't appreciate the smugness of his smile before he chuckled lightly as if taunting her with some unspoken promise.

Not yet.

"Why are you here?" She locked her arms over her chest, attempting to hide the visibility of her nipples, which were no doubt visible beneath the thin cotton of her shirt. The way his eyes followed the motion was proof enough.

"We touched on you not knowing much about your husband's past. I was curious how much you *knew*. You were married for three years. Have you ever met anyone he was connected to outside of the people in your life?"

"No. He told me his parents passed when he was in college. He didn't have siblings and wasn't close to any other family. He was alone like *me*. That isolation is one of the ways we bonded. I guess that was stupid on my part."

"Not necessarily. You trusted him. No situation is black and white. What about friends? You never met any of his old classmates, colleagues, acquaintances?"

"No. Wait, yes, once. A couple, Jake and Zoey. We once traveled to New York on vacation, and they met us for dinner."

"And how were they? Did they discuss details from his past? Is there anything we could look into?"

Cassidy shook her head. "After this happened, I started going over all the details of my life with Niles in my head, attempting to make sense of how I couldn't have known. I doubled back to them. Thinking about it now, I realized their conversation that evening was generic. They didn't tell funny stories about Niles's past or give insight into who he was. Everything flowed easily and felt comfortable, but the discussions were more or less about our recent lives, jobs, things like that."

Davis nodded. "And that was the only time you met them?"

"Yes. I insisted they be invited to the wedding, but they never came. Makes sense now why they didn't. We did get a gift. A really nice one, actually, but it was mailed." She closed her eyes, briefly shaking her head. "It all seems so insane now."

"I know it's a stretch, but by any chance, would you know the address the gift was sent from?"

Cassidy felt hopeful. "Oddly enough, I do. I sent them a thank-you note. Only a handful of people, mostly friends of mine, sent gifts since we did a private destination ceremony. I have a file with all the addresses."

"You mind getting that for me?"

Cassidy left Davis standing in the living room, navigated to her office, and returned with her laptop. She carried it to the sofa, propped the device on her knees, and lifted the lid. Davis followed, sitting next to Cassidy, waiting while she searched for the address.

After locating and opening the file, she turned the laptop so that Davis could see the address on the screen.

"PO Box," he muttered.

"Right, and it's been years," she expressed, stifling the disappointment.

"But many people upstate keep PO Boxes to avoid having their mail stolen or because of constant moving. It's possible she still has that address." He glanced at the screen once more. "I will do some digging and see what I can find. You mind sending me that?"

"No, not at all."

"You have my number?"

"I do. I still have the card you gave me."

They stared at each other for a long moment before Davis extended to his full height again. "I'm going to get going. Got a few things I need to look into."

"With my case?"

He nodded but didn't elaborate. "Seems I've lost my main suspect. If I want to keep my job, I might need to be rounding up another."

She smiled softly. "Yeah, I heard your captain isn't too pleased with your lack of direction."

"Harper tell you that?" He angled his head to the side, leaning over Cassidy.

"Among other things."

"Such as . . ."

"Warned me about blurring lines with you."

"Harper should mind his gotdamn business," Davis murmured, and Cassidy smiled.

"You two really don't get along, do you?"

"More on his end than mine. He have an answer for why that is?"

"Something about you being a dick who didn't need anyone. And maybe thinking you're God's gift to the world might have also been mentioned."

He belted a laugh, and she loved the sound of it, along with the freeness of his spirit, because she felt he didn't often share that side of himself with many people. "I'd say he's a little biased, but he probably has a point."

"On the dick thing or the God's gift part?"

"Both, actually. I'm not lacking confidence, and I haven't been the most courteous."

"Why is that?"

"I'm a bit of a loner."

"I feel like I'm at a disadvantage here. You know more about me than I know about you."

"Considering the nature of our relationship, that's understandable, don't you think?"

"I do, but that still doesn't help me level the playing field regarding who *you* are."

Davis flashed her a charming smile. One that Cassidy was growing accustomed to enjoying a little too much. "Then maybe we should remedy that in the near future, but for now, I'm going to head out. Don't forget to send me the address."

"I won't." She watched Davis leave, hating the pinch of disappointment for wanting him to stay.

15.

A few days later, Davis stepped off the elevator at Police Palace, hoping to gain some clarity on another piece of Cassidy's past that had been bothering him the more he got to know her. His thoughts had been running rampant at her suppressing some deeply embedded guilt, but he no longer believed that guilt was connected to her husband's murder. He instead thought it had to do with a case from her past haunting Cassidy over the years. Davis needed to know why and what her husband had discovered that made him feel he could use that case as leverage.

With very little to go on concerning Williams's murder and the only lead being a PO Box in New York, Davis found himself digging into the past of the woman he was intrigued with.

"Good morning. How can I help you?" The woman manning the desk just outside Chief Trent's office smiled brightly as she admired Davis. He decided to use her obvious attraction to his advantage. He settled on the element of surprise since he hadn't requested an appointment to see Trent. Instead, he acted on a whim, showing up to dig into the background of a man who likely wouldn't appreciate landing on Davis's radar.

"That smile just made my day."

She shifted in her seat, leaning an elbow on the desk as she lowered her chin atop a closed fist. "Are you flirting with me, Mr. . . .?"

The question hung in the air. She wanted his name, and Davis complied.

"Detective Davis."

"Well, Detective Davis, are you flirting with me?"

His smile was luminous. "Just offering a compliment, and if you consider that flirting, then I suppose I am."

"I'll take it. Now, I know you're not here just to compliment my smile. What can I do for you?"

"I was wondering if I could have a minute with Chief Trent. Is he available?"

"Do you have an appointment?"

"No, actually, I don't. Maybe you could help me out?"

"Ah, so it wasn't about my smile."

Davis chuckled. "Come on, now. You can't possibly believe that I would lie about your beautiful smile."

"Men have lied about much less to get what they want, but . . ." She paused, taking him in. "A compliment from a man as good-looking as you is worth accepting, no matter the reason. Chief has about ten minutes before his next meeting. He may not appreciate the intrusion, but if you're willing to deal with his aversion to your pop-up, go on in by all means."

"I think I can manage. Thank you."

Davis headed to the door, knocking twice before he stepped inside. He was greeted by a pair of narrowed eyes that narrowed further once they took him in.

"Can I help you?"

"Hopefully, yes."

"And you are?" Chief Trent leaned back and expanded his chest, asserting his dominance and irritation. Davis tapped the badge affixed to his hip and slipped his hands into the pockets of his slacks.

"Detective Davis. I was wondering if I could ask you a few questions."

"About?"

"Cassidy Evans. More specifically, the case that the two of you worked years back."

He and Cassidy had only ever worked one case together. The one that landed him in this office. Davis watched Trent closely to see what his reaction would be.

"Which case is that? I've worked hundreds throughout my career."

Davis smirked. "But only one with Evans. I'm sure you're more than familiar with which case I'm referencing."

He offered a tight nod. "Arnold."

"Yes, Johnathan Arnold."

"Why are you curious about that case, Detective?"

"Several reasons, actually." Davis moved closer to Trent's desk but remained standing, asserting his dominance. He felt the need to level things between them since Trent wanted the appearance of having an upper hand. "For starters, what was the nature of your relationship with Evans when the two of you were assigned to the case?"

Trent's lips flattened, and his jaw tensed. "I'm not sure what that has to do with the case. Care to elaborate?"

"I will. How about you humor me for now and answer the question?"

"Humor you?" Trent's deep tenor rattled with his disapproval. "Detective, as I'm sure you're aware, I am *your* superior. You showing up here unannounced, asking me questions about a case from fifteen years ago while demanding I 'humor' your line of inappropriate questioning seems to be a gross misuse of city time.

How about you get to the point before I find myself doing some digging of my own."

David smiled smugly. "Fair enough. I'll get to the point. Were you sleeping with Cassidy when the two of you worked the Arnold case?"

"Who the hell are you to accuse me of sleeping with a subordinate, Detective?"

"Who I am isn't quite as important as the details of the case that I'm asking about—"

"And why the fuck are you asking about that case?"

"Because it's closely linked to one I'm currently working on."

The irritation from Trent was apparent. Trent's defensive nature and anger confirmed what Sidney Tyler had told Davis. Trent and Cassidy had an intimate relationship all those years ago.

It was possible to believe Cassidy's guilt behind the case was related to being manipulated in a specific direction with the case under Trent's persuasion. She was young, fresh out of college, and had just earned her training through the department. Her mentor crossed lines, and she ended up in his bed. Not that Cassidy didn't bear any blame for potentially manipulating facts with the case, but Trent was her superior. He knew better than getting involved with a subordinate, then not speaking up to recuse himself or Cassidy from working the same case. One where Cassidy's testimony had been the deciding factor for a conviction on a case where Trent was the lead detective.

"Do all the investigating you want, but keep my personal shit out of it. Regardless of my relationship with Cassidy, she and I both did good police work. Arnold was a piece-of-shit psycho who raped and murdered multiple women. He was guilty and is right where he belongs—rotting in prison for the rest of his life. Now, if you don't mind. I have a meeting that I'm scheduled for."

"No, don't mind at all. I have what I need."

"Good, now get the fuck out of my office."

Davis smirked and nodded. "Have a good day, Chief."

By the time Davis reached the door, Trent was speaking again. "And, Detective . . ."

Davis turned to face him, and Trent wasted no time issuing his threat. "Don't you ever in your life come in my office like this again, accusing me of shit that you have no business sticking your nose in. I can guarantee that you don't want to deal with the consequences when I start digging into *your* background. I'm *not* a problem you want, Davis."

Without responding, Davis left his office. His jacket was clean, and he didn't buckle under fruitless threats. He had no intention of unraveling the case concerning Arnold. His only goal was to understand Cassidy better. Some things were better left as they were. As much as he may not have approved of the methods, the outcome was favorable. A dangerous man was in prison and no longer had access to harm innocent people.

Now, there was the small detail of knowing that Cassidy had potentially lied about or withheld evidence on a case. Davis had to decide what to do with that information since Trent had confirmed that he and Cassidy had a past, one that would have been frowned on by the department. Was that a reflection of Cassidy's character? Should he be concerned with what other things she would be okay lying about or withholding to get a favored result? Only time would tell, but for now, there was cause for him to err on the side of caution. Yet another reason he should be staying away from Cassidy. Deep down, he knew that he wouldn't, and now the lingering question was, what did that say about him?

❖

Back at the station, Davis decided to give an update. He was about to explore his one lead, learn more about Williams, and gain more insight into who wanted him dead.

"Captain . . ." When Davis knocked, Captain Jones lifted his head and waved Davis into his office.

"You here to tell me why the hell you were down at Police Palace pissing off Chief Trent?"

That was fast.

"I had questions."

"About a case that doesn't have squat to do with the one you're working. I get that you're new, but you have to know better than pissing off the guys that make the final call on whether or not you keep your job."

Davis shrugged nonchalantly from just inside the captain's doorway. "Being liked isn't a quality of me doing my job. If Chief Trent prefers his detectives to half-ass with cases, then maybe his job should be in question."

"Cute, Davis. If you want to go on a suicide mission, that's on you, but leave the rest of us out of it. Stay the hell away from Trent and that case. It has nothing to do with what you're working on."

"Technically, it does."

Captain's face went hard. "How so?"

"Williams had a flash drive with information about the Arnold case on it. It was in the safe deposit box."

"How the hell did he get that, and why am I just now finding out?"

"Cassidy. She has a copy of the case file at her house. There were handwritten notes and questions regarding the case, things she was concerned about years later. If she somehow mishandled the case, then Williams was likely considering blackmailing her."

"You saying that's her motive?"

"Could be. Many careers were fast-tracked, thanks to the outcome of that case. APD put an end to a national manhunt for a serial rapist. The case got a lot of press. If word got out that Cassidy was second-guessing . . ."

"You ask her about it?" Davis noticed something in his eyes.

"I did."

"And?"

"I don't think she killed the guy because of it."

I don't think she killed him at all.

"Then leave it alone. You go digging into that case, and you'll make a lot of enemies."

"Like Chief? Did you know he had an intimate relationship with Cassidy while they were on the case? You were only a sergeant back then, but—"

"Of course, I knew. I know everything that goes on under my roof. Past and present."

"And you didn't have a problem with it?"

"What I have a problem with is why you're so concerned about the two of them. Should I consider this a problem?"

Davis smirked. "Not at all, Captain. Just doing my job as thoroughly as possible. Had a lead, followed it, and nothing panned out."

"Then what *do* you have? I'm beginning to wonder if I made a wrong move handing this case over to you. No new evidence. No current suspects other than Cassidy. Not a damn thing getting us any closer to the finish line."

"I have a lead—someone who can potentially give more insight on Williams. The guy is an utter mystery. If I can figure out who he is, then I can figure out who he pissed off enough to kill him."

"Sounds to me like the only one with a motive is his *wife*."

Davis tensed at the thought of his captain potentially wanting him to press forward, with Cassidy being the only suspect.

"Regardless of what we think, nothing solid points to Cassidy. Everything we have is circumstantial. There's no real evidence we can take to the DA without them laughing us out of their office."

"Then find something. At this point, I don't care if it's pointing to Cassidy or someone else. We need to get this case closed. If she did this—"

"*If*, Captain."

"*If* she did this, we'll have to handle things as we would for any other case. I might not like it, but the job comes first."

Davis nodded, feeling annoyed. "I'll be out of town for a day or so. Heading to New York to investigate the lead I have."

"Do what you must, but if you're putting this on the department's dime, I suggest you come back with something solid."

Instead of entertaining the threat, Davis left his captain's office and decided to find a better use for his time. He was equally frustrated that there wasn't much else he could go on. No leads that amounted to anything, nor had he discovered anything that brought him closer to clearing Cassidy's name. At present, she was still the only suspect, and that bothered him more than anything.

❦

A few hours later, Davis was exhausted from combing through details connected to the Williams case, only to come up short. He decided to call it a day and start fresh in the morning. With the planned trip to New York to prayerfully chase down the one lead he did have, his mind traveled back to the person who'd provided it.

Cassidy.

As he stepped into the humid night air, Davis removed his phone from his pocket to call the woman who had his mind wrapped up for most of the day. Before he could get her on the line, Harper stepped out of his car, slamming the door behind him.

Davis's eyes darted from Harper to his partner Gary Richards, who paused his steps as if trying to decide whether he should stay and be the voice of reason between the two. The friction between Davis and Harper wasn't foreign to any of them.

"You coming inside?" Richards asked as he eyed the two detectives.

"In a minute. I need to have a word with Davis." Harper glared at his target, not bothering to acknowledge his partner visually. Richards issued one last weary look before releasing an annoyed sigh but walking away from whatever was about to happen. The two could engage in a complete brawl right there in the parking lot for all he cared.

"You want to tell me what the fuck that whole scene was about, Davis?" Harper pushed forward, stepping into Davis's personal space. Davis didn't move. He only lowered his chin and angled his head slightly to the right, looking down on Harper. The smug grin that appeared seconds after only intensified matters between the two.

"You know your partner much better than I do, so maybe you can tell me what that was about?" Davis noticed the pulsing vein at Harper's temple and smiled more arrogantly.

"You know gotdamn well that's not what I'm talking about."

"Then what *are* you talking about?"

"You and Cass. You make a habit of spending time with suspects at their *homes?*"

"Not that it's any of your business, but when necessary, yes."

"You two cozy now? She more than just your suspect? Because if that's the case—"

"If that's the case, it's not your concern, so fuck off."

Harper's eyes narrowed further, expressing his anger. "Fuck off? Right. Seems to me like that's more your forte. You're wasting a lot of time on this case and possibly for the wrong reasons. You might want to think about your clearance rate versus using the job as a way to add a few notches to your belt."

"I thought you and Cassidy were friends."

"We are."

"Then act like it. Show some gotdamn respect. You talk about all your friends that way?"

"In what way?"

"Unjustly condemning them for their personal choices? If you do, seems like I've made the right decision keeping things professional where you're concerned."

"Professional? You don't know the meaning of professional, or you wouldn't have taken your ass down to Police Palace questioning Chief Trent. You like pissing people off, don't you? Might want to be more selective about *who* you piss off. Just a word of advice."

"I appreciate the concern, but I'm fully capable of handling my life and my career. You stick to your cases, and I'll stick to mine."

"My clearance rate is not in question. It's well over 80 percent. Can you say the same?"

"I can. In fact, your clearance rate might be 80 percent, but how many cold cases do you have?"

The acknowledgment and anger flooded Harper's expression in a matter of seconds.

Davis stepped closer, locking his arms over his chest. "You seem to be struggling to come up with a number. I'll help you out. Last I checked, it was twenty-two. I have *none*."

With his final word, Davis turned toward his car, leaving Harper fuming behind him. "I've been on the job a lot longer, you arrogant son of a bitch. You think you're that much better—"

"No. Never said I was better. Just making sure you understand I'm good at what I do. I don't need you or anyone else worrying about how I handle myself on the job. Especially when that attention can be better utilized handling your own shit."

After making his point, Davis settled into his car, immediately starting the engine. As he pulled out of the parking space, Harper remained affixed to where Davis left him, glaring at the vehicle through a haze of anger. Another day, another fucking pointless argument.

16.

"You okay?"

Cassidy slowly peeled her eyes away from the passenger window and gave her attention to Davis. The two of them were sitting outside the UPS Store, where Zoey Wright would hopefully show up soon. The plan was for Davis to ambush the woman with an unsanctioned interrogation to see if she knew anything that would help in their search to find out who Jerrod Williams was, if she was willing to share.

"I'm great; why?" She scrunched her nose slightly and shifted her position in the seat of the compact car they'd rented after landing at LaGuardia Airport a few hours earlier.

"That's why." He motioned in her direction, and Cassidy looked down before her eyes lifted again and landed on Davis when he followed with, "You've been fidgeting for the past ten minutes. You don't have to—"

"No, I do have to be here. This is important."

"To you personally or for the case?"

"Both." Cassidy huffed a sigh of irritation. "I know you're taking a risk, allowing me to tag along. You're still on the fence about whether I killed my husband, so I understand what's happening here. I'm anxious because if she shows, I'll be face-to-face with another one of his lies. I'm not worried you'll find some hidden evidence that will further convince you that I'm guilty of killing Niles."

Davis stared at Cassidy pensively. She matched his stare, trying to decide what he might be thinking.

"You have the right to be anxious. The man lied to you. Zoey helped him do it. I'm only asking if you're okay because I get it. This can't be easy. Truthfully, it has to be an entire pain in the ass. He lied to you for years. Left you in a complicated space, and now you're doing your best to make sense of it all. I don't know that I would be holding up as well as you are."

She flashed a smile. "Maybe I'm managing because I already got my retribution."

Davis scoffed. "If I believed that were true, you wouldn't be here. I would have already tossed your ass in county, and you'd be awaiting trial."

Cassidy's brows pinched as she processed the affirmation hidden in the words. "Does that mean you believe I wasn't the one who killed him?"

"For now, yes."

"Thank you," she stated quietly, and Davis was quick to follow that thought.

"Don't thank me just yet. My opinion could change pending what happens in there."

"Right."

Moments later, a woman came strolling down the block. She tugged at her coat, shaking away a chill caused by the crisp fall air. Davis and Cassidy both watched her intently, then Davis's eyes lowered to his phone. Once they'd arrived, he'd spoken to the clerk after flashing his badge and asking questions about the owner of the PO Box. Cautiously, the clerk answered but refused to hand over the woman's home address. He did agree to a compromise, which Davis suggested. Call Zoey and ask if she would come down to the store to pick up a package with the insistence that it had to be picked up that day.

When Davis's phone vibrated with a call, he answered while Cassidy held her breath, listening.

"You sure that's her? Okay, heading in now. Stall until I get there."

Once he ended the call, Cassidy glanced at the store and then Davis. "That's her?"

"Yeah, let's go because I know there's not a chance in hell you'll wait for me out here, *but* let me do the talking."

She nodded, reaching for the handle to release the door before he added, "I mean it, Cassidy. Let me handle this."

"Okay."

He offered a firm visual warning before they both got out of the car and headed into the store. He opened the door, allowing Cassidy in first. The minute they were inside, Cassidy opened her mouth, doing the opposite of what Davis had asked.

"It really is you. I mean, your hair is longer and has highlights, but it's definitely *you*."

"Christ, I thought we agreed to let me do the talking." Davis stepped around Cassidy, approaching the woman. Her expression was laced with apprehension as her eyes bounced between the two strangers who now had her cornered.

"Do I know you?"

"No."

"Yes." When Cassidy's voice followed Davis's, he issued another warning look. She held her hands up in surrender and made a mental note to keep her mouth shut.

"Ms. Wright, I presume."

"Yes. Who are you?"

"Detective Davis with Atlanta PD. I'd like to ask you a few questions if that's okay."

She glared at him. "Do I have to?"

Davis glanced at Cassidy to make sure she didn't intervene and quietly shook his head. "No, you don't, but I would appreciate it if you did. You're not in any trouble, and the questions are about someone you know, not necessarily about you."

"Atlanta PD. That means you don't have jurisdiction here, right?"

Davis smirked and shrugged. "Depends on the situation. But for now, let's just consider this officially *unofficial*." His eyes subtly shifted to Cassidy before he continued. "I'd like to ask you about Niles Anderson."

"Niles Anderson. I don't know that name."

"Are you sure?"

"Yes, why? Should I? Did he say he knows me?"

Cassidy spoke up. "Not exactly. Niles is dead now, so you'll have to take our word for it, but you knew him or at least one of his aliases. Possibly not that one, but you had dinner with us years ago. You and your husband."

Her expression revealed an overwhelming sense of irritation. "I'm not married, so that can't be true."

"Well, maybe not, but you pretended to be. To a guy named Jake."

Recognition flashed on her face. She remembered.

"You're the wife. That doctor he was engaged to."

"Yes, that was me."

"I remember now. He paid me five grand to pretend we knew him."

"You and Jake?"

"Yes."

"And you didn't?"

"No. Never seen the guy before. He showed up at an acting class that Jake and I took evenings at a community college. Asked if we wanted to make some extra cash." She shrugged. "I needed the money."

"And you didn't think about the consequences of lying to someone? Lying to *me*?" Cassidy screeched.

"What I was thinking about was that my rent was due. Seemed harmless. It was only dinner."

"It *wasn't* harmless," Cassidy hissed, lunging forward. Davis managed to insert himself between the two women before Cassidy made matters worse.

"Was at the time. We didn't do anything wrong. There's no law against pretending to be someone you're not. Right, Detective? We didn't commit a crime."

Davis shook his head. "No, you didn't. However, you did help a criminal convince someone of a false identity where he committed a crime. More or less an accessory."

It was a stretch but worth the threat if that got what he needed from her.

"Not my problem. He paid, and I played the part. I didn't commit a crime."

Cassidy scoffed. "Right, and rent got paid."

"You're damn right it did. And if you have a problem with that, take it up with him." Zoey argued back defensively.

"Kind of hard to do. Did you miss the part where I said he's no longer alive?" Cassidy muttered angrily.

She walked away, pushed through the glass door, and stormed back to the car. She leaned against the sedan, dropping her head back between her shoulder blades, inhaling deeply before she closed her eyes and repeated the process a few more times.

Not long after, Davis walked out of the shop and chirped the key fob to unlock the vehicle. Cassidy landed hard in the passenger seat while he filled the space behind the steering wheel.

"Not great with following orders, are you?" His narrowed stare landed on Cassidy, who didn't meet his eyes and instead, chose to stare out the passenger window.

"You'll have to excuse me for reacting poorly to a woman who willingly participated in conning me because her rent was due."

Davis groaned as he started the car. "I never said I didn't understand why you neglected to follow my orders. Only noting that you didn't."

Cassidy's eyes shot across the car, and his were waiting. "So, now what?"

"Now, we go back to the hotel and eat something. Maybe even get a few drinks in you. After another dead end, I figured you deserve to unwind a little."

"Right, because that was utterly pointless. And we're still no closer to knowing who my husband was or who killed him. Doesn't that bother you?"

"Yeah, it does, but seeing your reaction in there also further confirmed something for me."

"Which is?"

"She's the actor; you are not."

Her brows pinched more. "Was I supposed to be?"

"No, and I was hoping you weren't. Your reaction there was genuine and not that of a woman who has been plotting to kill her husband. More of a woman who was devastated to get confirmation that he had been conning her from the very beginning. If you had killed him, the anger would no longer be there. I believe that had you already played judge and jury and satisfied your need for retribution, your reaction there would have been a little less explosive."

Cassidy smiled softly. "Explosive, huh?"

"Pretty much, but again, justified."

"Good to know."

"Now, what about dinner and those drinks?"

She shrugged. "Not like I have anything else to occupy my time now."

"Looks like it's a date then." Davis winked at Cassidy, and she had to fight hard not to allow that one simple gesture make her to travel down a very dangerous road . . . one that led to *Davis* being her distraction and escape instead of those drinks he offered.

⚜

"Does your boss know that I'm here?"

Davis smiled behind a glass as he leaned back in his chair. "Would it matter?"

"Not really. Just curious to know how much of a rebel you truly are."

Davis had presented the idea of traveling to New York. He told Cassidy that calling and trying to get the information they sought would be more difficult. Zoey would be less likely to cooperate via phone communication. Not that she had been willing in person. Cassidy insisted on going, and when Davis gave in, she covered her own expenses. The two had remained on the phone coordinating flights and hotel reservations. Although they sat side by side on the plane, their overnight stay would be in separate rooms.

"No."

"Why didn't you tell him I was accompanying you?"

"Wasn't his business."

She smiled widely. "Clearly, it is. I can't imagine he'd be happy about you flying me out of state to help investigate a lead for a case where I'm a suspect."

Davis smiled, and Cassidy both loved and disliked how disarming his smile had become to her senses. "Then problem solved. I didn't fly you here, and you didn't help me investigate anything. Quite the opposite, actually, seeing as how I had to do more damage control than investigating."

She was midswallow of a hefty gulp of wine and sputtered a laugh that left her dangerously close to spraying their table with the expensive Merlot. "Don't hold back now, Detective."

He chuckled lightly, and the heavenly vibration settled into her bones. Or it could have possibly been the wine.

"I pride myself in being honest."

"That you are. Which I appreciate, considering . . ."

That my husband lied to me for years.

"Can I ask you a question?" His expression turned serious, and she nodded.

"Fire away."

Davis downed more of his drink before lowering the glass onto the table next to his empty plate, keeping his finger wrapped around the fine crystal.

"Why did you bury him?"

"Why not?"

A hard line formed between Davis's brows. "I can think of plenty of reasons why not. The most important being that he conned you for years when you trusted him with your heart."

A tight lump seized Cassidy's throat, which she struggled to swallow, along with the very raw truth, before lifting a shoulder in a lazy shrug. "I can't say why, really, other than I needed closure. Burying Niles allowed me the peace of mind to accept that I wasn't okay and the space to move forward with my life so that I could eventually be. It's important to embrace the past, and not having answers makes it that much worse, but at least I can have closure somewhat, you know."

"I get it."

"Do you?" Her eyes intently bored into his while she waited, seeing the truth before he spoke it.

"Yes, I do."

"And what was it that you needed closure for, Nathaniel?"

His name on her tongue felt like sin, but sin of the best kind, so she embraced it, but the moment was interrupted by another woman's voice shattering the lingering possibilities.

"Nathaniel, I thought that was you."

17.

Davis lifted his eyes to the woman he hadn't seen in a little over a year while thinking how insanely small the universe had to be for this very moment to exist.

"Stacy," he greeted dryly before his eyes shifted to the right, where her husband stood protectively, peering at him. His body language almost made Davis offer reassurance that he didn't have to fear competition for his wife. She was the last person he wanted in his life.

"I didn't know you were in town."

"Why would you? We don't talk, Stacy." Davis noticed how she cringed at the truth, but she quickly recovered, plastering on her fake smile. One he didn't miss in the least.

"You're right; we don't. I suppose I meant I'm surprised to see you *here*. Didn't think you'd find your way back to the city after you left so abruptly."

Davis could feel Cassidy staring, and his mind quickly shifted to what she might have been thinking, watching the exchange between him and his ex. There was no doubt he'd have to explain later, but now he needed to get rid of his ex-fiancée and her insecure husband.

"Well, here I am."

"Indeed you are." Her eyes moved to Cassidy. "And who's this?"

Warmth covered Davis's hand, and when his eyes lowered, he found Cassidy's delicate fingers layered over his before she answered, "A close friend. And who are you?"

"Nathaniel's *ex*-fiancée, and I didn't get your name."

"Because I didn't offer it to you."

Davis chuckled at the snarky way Cassidy responded. He'd have to thank her for that later, if only for the way her reaction grated Stacy's nerves.

"No, you didn't, did you?" That fake smile was back.

"So, Davis, seems you're not making any friends down there in Atlanta."

His eyes shot up to Tony Samuels, who smiled smugly. "You been asking about me?"

"No, don't have a reason to, also don't care enough to invest the time in how you're making out down there."

"Then how would you know if I was making friends?"

"A couple of inquiries about you have been circulating. Seems your new team is curious about how you got along here. One just came through this morning from your chief. Mentioned you were an arrogant and nosy son of a bitch. The arrogant part I agreed with. I did tell him you never were the nosy type that I remembered. Maybe something about him got under your skin and had you putting your nose where it didn't belong. You were always good at your job. Wouldn't ever deny that."

"I'm sure you could if given enough time."

"You're probably right. Well, we should get going. You two enjoy the rest of your evening."

With a dip of his chin, he placed his hand on Stacy's back and navigated her through the restaurant. Davis wasn't surprised to see them in the same place. Although their dining choice for the evening was attached to their hotel, many locals enjoyed the food and frequented the place.

"Well, that was interesting." Cassidy attempted humor, but Davis wasn't in the mood. Not that he cared much about seeing Stacy, but he most certainly had an issue with his new colleagues reaching out to find information about his past in New York. Davis's mood had shifted completely, and he was no longer interested in sharing a meal or company with anyone, even if it were Cassidy.

"I'm going to get the bill so we can head up. It's getting late, and we have an early flight tomorrow."

"Late?" She reared her head back in surprise. "It's barely nine. I wouldn't exactly call that late. Would you like to talk about the happy couple that just left? This abrupt ending to our evening seems to be attributed to the two of them."

"Doesn't have anything to do with them. Like I said—"

"Early flight. Got it."

Davis flagged down the server and requested the bill, which he covered with cash before he and Cassidy made their way to the elevators and up to their floor. Their rooms were across from one another, so there was no way to avoid the tension-charged ride and silence that followed. Davis didn't bother trying. Once they were at their doors, Cassidy hesitated. He noticed she kept peeking over her shoulder while he dug out a room key. She stopped him as soon as he held it to the magnetic lock, and the light flashed green.

"I don't know what happened down there, but it really seems to be bothering you. It might help to talk about it."

Davis glanced over his shoulder to find Cassidy with her back pressed against her room door. He turned and mirrored her position but crossed his legs at the ankle and slipped his hands into his pockets. He was still in his attire from earlier that day: slacks and a collared shirt, sleeves rolled up to the elbows.

Cassidy had elected to change out of her jeans, tee, and blazer into another pair of jeans and an oversized sweater, which hung off her shoulder. Davis couldn't help but enjoy the visual of her soft brown skin, which taunted him. To the average person, they looked like any other people—but were anything but. He was a detective, and she was a suspect accused of killing her husband. He was investigating the case; she was navigating how to prove her innocence, and yet, at this very moment, their thoughts weren't on any of those things. At least, Davis's weren't. He assumed her mind had also drifted based on the concern in her eyes as they fastened with his. This woman cared about his well-being. The one he'd just engaged downstairs only cared about imploding his happiness.

I'd have to be happy for her to do that.

"Well?" Cassidy pressed, pulling her lip between her teeth, worrying it a bit before she released it. "Want to talk about your ex?"

"Not particularly, but I will on one condition."

Cassidy's face tensed a little as her eyes narrowed slightly, her lids a bit hooded from the wine she'd enjoyed with dinner.

"You tell me about yours first."

"My ex?"

Davis nodded.

"You already know everything I know. I'm not sure what else I can tell you about Niles . . ."

Davis shook his head gently as he closed the space between them, placing his palms flat against the door above Cassidy's head, lowering his so he could see her eyes. "Not Niles. Lance Trent."

Her lids fluttered, and her lips parted slightly before she found the words that struggled to surface. "What makes you think he's my ex?"

Davis smiled lazily. "The way you just openly expressed your surprise at me asking about him is a surefire confirmation. Now, do we have a deal or not?"

"I . . . sure . . . We can talk about him, but I don't understand why you think he's relevant."

"Let's go inside and talk." Davis remained hovering over Cassidy while she turned to face the door. His body brushed hers as she held the key card up and waited for access to enter. She stepped inside, and when Davis didn't follow, he explained. "Leave the door open. I'll be right there. I need a minute." She nodded and didn't question him further. He joined her moments later, and once inside, they both moved to the tiny table in the corner near the bed.

Davis filled one chair, legs set wide, arms lazy in his lap until he lifted one and allowed it to rest on the table. Cassidy sat with her spine straight after she kicked off her flats and tucked one leg beneath her. He took note of how nervous she was.

"I supposed you want to know how that happened since it's immensely frowned upon."

"I'd rather know if your relationship with him is why you've been questioning things with the Arnold case all these years later."

"Yes." She huffed as her shoulders deflated. "It feels good actually to say that out loud. I've been wanting to for a while. I just . . ." She shook her head and lowered her eyes. "Who could I hand my concerns over to? So many lives would be affected. The department, the families that received justice because of my testimony. It would be such a mess."

"They would, but the truth is the truth, Cass. Sometimes, the truth is ugly."

"What Arnold did was uglier. Those women . . ." She paused and swallowed. "He was guilty. There was never a doubt in my mind, and had I not handled things the way I did, he would have gone free—*again*."

"What exactly did you do?" Davis's body was stiff with anxiety while he waited. He didn't want to believe Cassidy to be dishonorable, and even if she lied, that didn't make her one. Only someone who chose to serve a greater justice than the facts presented would have allowed. He would never judge. How the hell could he? No one was perfect—least of all him.

Here he was, sitting across from a beautiful woman, wanting the opportunity to have more of her than he should be allowed to have. He *desperately* wanted that opportunity.

"His wife and daughter were his alibi. They both remembered him being home that night. Arnold and his wife argued. It got bad. Their stories contradicted, but there was no way to prove the timeline for him being home that night."

"Did you believe them?"

"The wife, no. She'd lied for him before. They had him, but she provided an alibi, and he got away with killing another woman. She knew who he truly was back then. I could see it in her eyes when I watched the tape of when I talked to her. She believed him guilty back then and with Allison's case. There was no missing the truth. I felt her lies, and she knew I had."

"Then what's the problem? It doesn't seem like you did anything wrong."

"I didn't," she quietly defended.

"What am I missing, Cass?" Davis frowned at Cassidy, and she looked away when she said the next thing.

"His daughter. I believed her. She wasn't lying, and she remembered him being there. The wife wasn't credible. Everyone knew her history of lying for Arnold, but his daughter, she would have raised reasonable doubt. I kept my true thoughts out of my notes that I believed the daughter's testimony when she said her father was home during the time of the murder. One slip, a small margin of doubt, and he would be free again. I shouldn't have caved, but . . ."

"Trent convinced you to?"

"Yeah," she said softly.

"He used you, Cass. He was your superior. Your training officer and someone you should have been able to trust. He took advantage of the fact that he was sleeping with you to manipulate the case."

"But I agreed."

"You did, and there's accountability for your role, but *he* should have never asked."

"Right, but there's not much I can do about it now. It just . . ."

"Haunts you?"

Cassidy's eyes expressed so much remorse. "I lied to her. His daughter. She asked me if I believed her, and I said yes. I made her a promise to make sure everyone knew that she was telling the truth, which I broke. She was a kid protecting her family. No matter how dysfunctional they were, they were hers. I can't blame the child for wanting to protect her father . . ."

"Who was a rapist and a murderer."

"You don't think I know who and what he was? That I haven't gone over my decision a million and one times trying to justify my actions?"

"I'm sure you have. With the case file and all the notes and questions, I *know* you have."

"Which makes me a horrible person."

He shook his head. "Not a horrible person. Someone with a conscience who considered the greater good, and that's okay."

She nodded. "So now what? You know what I did."

"Doesn't matter. Sometimes, you have to allow things to be what they are. Arnold deserved what he got."

"You're not going to tell anyone? You have the case file that was in his safe deposit box. It's evidence."

"It was, but no one has to know why. Did you kill him because of that file?"

"No."

"Then I don't see how tearing down the department and the reputations of all its key players behind a case that served justice is necessary."

She nodded and released a breath that had Davis relaxing as well . . . until the next thing came out of her mouth.

"My turn to ask a question . . ."

18.

"So, fiancée, huh? You know all my secrets. It's only fair that I get to know yours."

Cassidy watched Davis intently. His handsome face shifted through several emotions before his eyes fastened on hers.

"That feels like a very long time ago."

"Was it?"

He smirked. "Not exactly. She ended things shortly before I packed up and moved to Atlanta."

"So, less than two years. That's recent enough to still feel things."

"The only thing I feel is contentment that she married him and not me."

"But you were engaged."

"Unofficially. No ring, just a promise that it would happen. Thinking back, I realize that was one of our issues."

"Women love the presentation. It's not official without a show," she joked. "What were the other issues? The ones that mattered the most."

"She wanted a lawyer, and I was content being a cop."

"She cheated?"

"No. Just kept urging me to get my law degree. I wasn't interested, so we took a break, and she surfaced a few months later engaged to the new DA for my precinct."

"Ahh, I can see how that would be awkward."

"For me, no. At least, not at first. But the guy had a bit of a hard-on for complicating my life. Seems he didn't appreciate the idea of being the consolation prize. Had I gotten my law degree like she wanted, like her father wanted, then I would have been the one with her at dinner tonight. Not him."

"Which means you wouldn't have been there with me." She smiled softly.

"I'm okay with how things turned out." His look communicated so much more. Emotions she felt but shouldn't have.

"Do you still have feelings for her?"

Davis scoffed. "I have plenty of feelings for her . . ."

"Oh . . ." Cassidy rushed out on a husky breath right before he added, "But none that are favorable."

"*Oh.*" That time, her tone was a little lighter.

After long moments of silence, Davis stood and glanced around the room. "So, I guess we're done here. I should go. Early flight."

Cassidy stood seconds after and cautiously moved to him. "Or, you could stay for a while. That is, if—"

Before she could finish the sentence, his arm hooked around her waist. She collided with his body, and his mouth crashed against hers. The kiss was perfect. Nothing was gentle about the way he pushed his tongue into her mouth, exploring. Cassidy's mind was reeling with so many different reasons why this was a bad idea, but she couldn't settle on one bad enough to make her stop what was happening.

Stepping back, Cassidy removed her jeans by forcing them slowly over her hips and down her legs. Davis's eyes warmed her skin, so she settled into the assumption that the visual she had provided worked in her favor. A cocky smile surfaced on his face as he unbuttoned his pants, allowing them to hang loosely while he worked on the buttons of his shirt, revealing rippled abs. There was the faintest line of hair that disappeared into his pants and briefs. Cassidy's breath grew slightly labored from anticipating what was to come.

Are we really doing this?

Before Cassidy was allowed to second-guess, Davis responded, allowing his lips to crash into hers once again. One hand moved to her hip while the other slid under her sweater until the pad of his thumb roughly moved over her nipple. It tightened from the warmth and pressure of his contact.

"Fuck," he murmured, allowing his mouth to travel to her jaw and neck. "You sure about this?"

"Very."

So very sure.

"Good."

Cassidy's sweater was ripped up and over her head, then tossed to the floor. She pushed the thin fabric of his shirt from his shoulders as he walked her toward the bed.

"You're beautiful."

She blushed when Davis took in every inch of her exposed skin, and another rush of warmth blazed through Cassidy's veins. As she sat on the edge of the bed, her fingers found his zipper, which she dragged down slowly, admiring the thick impression of his dick beneath the cotton fabric of his briefs. Her eyes lifted briefly before her hands went forward, but he quickly grabbed her wrist and leaned in to place a kiss just below her palm.

"Starting with me in your mouth might not work in our favor."

Davis slipped a hand into his pocket and revealed a condom, which he tossed on the bed.

"Should I be concerned that you have that?"

He smiled smugly as Cassidy leaned back on her elbow. "I had them with me here but not on me. It's why I asked you to give me a minute."

"So, you had expectations?" She arched a brow.

"No, but I'm a man spending time with a very beautiful woman I'm attracted to. I also have it on good authority that she is attracted to me. I was hopeful and learned never to leave anything to chance."

Davis kneeled between her thighs, dragging his hands from Cassidy's ankles up her legs before pressing his palms firmly against the inside of her thighs. They spread at his silent command.

"Now would be the time to object if you disagree with anything I just confessed, Cass."

He didn't give her a chance to argue and, instead, leaned in and placed a kiss just below her navel. His mouth continued to move down her body, leaving a trail of warmth on her skin until his tongue swiped the entire length of her pussy.

Cassidy exhaled a shaky breath. "You can't expect me to object to any of this after that."

Her statement drew a wide grin out of Davis before his face was out of sight again. "No, I can't, which was my intention. Not playing fair gets us both what we want tonight."

He added a little more pressure, further spreading her thighs. The tip of his tongue made slow, torturous circles while he introduced one finger and then two. They dragged in and out of Cassidy, causing her body to clench and release, climbing slowly toward her peak. While Davis's mouth pulled pleasure from her body, he watched with a trained focus, examining her reaction. She felt his eyes on her even during the brief moments when hers were closed. Each time Cassidy braved a glance at his position between her thighs, his intense eyes were waiting, heightening her experience.

One last very intentional swipe of his tongue, slowly dragging from bottom to top, set Cassidy's climax in orbit. The sensual drag back and forth of his fingers, which were eventually replaced by his tongue, prolonged the downward spiral that had Cassidy feeling as if she were completely falling apart. By the time her body relaxed, Davis was between her legs again. When his thighs brushed hers, she realized his pants were no longer there.

The slow pull of desire quickly shifted to frantic need as the hard muscles of his body settled against her softness. The minute his dick nudged forward, Cassidy swung her head left, sighing in relief when she noticed the ripped condom wrapper near her head.

Oh, thank God. I don't think I have the restraint to stop this moment.

Cassidy spread her thighs wider the more he pressed forward. There was no guilt, remorse, or contemplation. Only an instant desire for more, and Davis delivered. He shielded her from his weight with one hand, and the other grabbed her jaw, holding her steady while his mouth consumed hers.

"I . . . oh . . ."

He was buried deep after one meaningful thrust. Her body tensed, and her pussy embraced him. The deep, throaty moan that barely escaped his mouth had Cassidy tilting her hips, wanting him deeper. Davis lifted onto his arms, hovering slightly above her, and adjusted his position, driving in harder.

Wish granted.

Cassidy was lost. She clung to him, needing something to keep her grounded. When she felt the warmth of his hand moving up her side and then the tug and pull of her nipple, she inhaled a sharp breath. The sensation traveled south, sending a strong, pulsing throb all the way to her clit.

"Focus, Cass. I need to see it."

If?

See me.

Unraveling.

His hand trailed higher and settled at the base of her throat with a gentle, leveling pressure that had her eyes fastened to his. The slow smile and arrogance in his stare was a mind trip. Punishing thrusts, back-to-back, pressing her deeper into the mattress had the ecstasy settling in. Davis's tongue slipping into her mouth triggered the implosion. She crashed hard. Shattering.

He tipped into bliss right behind her, pushing the last waves of Cassidy's release to the surface. His plunges slowed to an impossibly torturous pace once more, his dick dragging in and out while he kissed Cassidy through her climax and his own. She handed it all over to him, even if it was just for that moment.

19.

It had only been a few hours since Davis and Cassidy had landed, and both were exhausted from the quick turnaround. Back-to-back flights were never easy; the two had been to New York and back in less than thirty-six hours. Davis was physically spent and would much rather be heading home to crawl into his bed, or better yet, Cassidy's, but that wasn't an option. He needed to get to the precinct and figure out how to make something of his case.

Not only had he crossed lines by sleeping with Cassidy, but he'd also enjoyed every minute of their time together and was hopeful about crossing those same lines again. Hence, the hesitation he currently felt as they pulled into her driveway after he demanded to provide a ride home instead of Cassidy taking a ride share from the airport.

"So, I guess I'll wait to hear from you." Cassidy blushed and quickly added, "about the case. You know, if anything new comes up."

Davis chuckled lightly, reaching across the vehicle and clasping his hand over hers. He laced their fingers, bringing her wrist toward him, placing a chaste kiss against her skin. He watched Cassidy exhale slightly before she gently tugged her wrist away.

"Maybe we should leave New York in New York."

Davis's expression hardened. As much as he wanted to play it cool, everything about the woman sitting next to him had already seeped into his soul and created a need that only she could satisfy. "Is that seriously what you want?"

Her eyes darted around briefly before landing on his. "No, but you can't be confused about how this looks."

"I'm not. It's complicated."

"*Complicated?*" She scoffed sarcastically.

"Yes, complicated, but not impossible. We'll figure this out."

"My deceased husband conned me into a fraud of a marriage, stole money, and intended to blackmail me with a case that could end my career. Regardless of my intentions to make sure no other women suffered being assaulted and murdered, my decision was still unethical in the eyes of the law. After I discovered all of the above, I then shot my husband to get retribution for the way he lied to me and mishandled my trust. Definitely a little more than complicated, Nate."

Davis's muscles locked tight. "You didn't kill your husband, Cassidy."

Her shoulders sank, and some of the tension also escaped Davis's body as well. "No, I didn't, and you may believe the truth, but there's no way the rest of the world will. At least, not until we know who actually shot and killed Niles."

"Then I work harder to figure that out." He was part of the problem. There was no way he shouldn't already have a suspect or at least a valid trail leading to them.

Cassidy nodded. "And until then . . ."

"You want to put this on hold."

"I think that's best. This isn't smart. Nowhere near practical . . ."

"It wasn't practical in New York, but you still allowed me in your bed."

"I have no regrets, Detective."

"Detective?"

"Nate ..." she said softly.

"What you're saying and not saying sounds like regret, Cass."

She quietly shook her head. "No regrets. I'm only being practical."

"I hear you loud and clear," he muttered before popping the trunk and getting out of the vehicle. He rounded the back, lifting Cassidy's travel bag. When she got out and tried to intercept it, he turned slightly, moving the luggage out of her reach.

"I got it."

"You don't have to walk me to the door."

"I didn't have to sleep with you either, but I did. The least I can do now is be a gentleman." He could sense that Cassidy wanted to object further, but she allowed him to carry her things to the porch and put them inside once she unlocked the door, and the two of them stepped into the foyer.

"Well, thanks for allowing me to tag along ..."

She shifted awkwardly, and Nate smirked, stepping into her personal space. Without much notice, he had one hand gripping the back of her neck, pulling Cassidy into a kiss that left them both breathless. When he stepped back and saw her flushed cheeks and dilated pupils, Davis felt he'd accomplished his goal. Give Cassidy a reminder why pressing pause might be practical, but it wouldn't be easy.

"Looks like neither of us is big on following orders."

Nate chuckled, nodding. "Appears that way." His eyes moved around her house. "I guess I'd better be going. I've got a suspect to track down."

"Yeah." She smiled softly.

"I'll call you." He paused. "About the case."

After another nod from Cassidy, Davis walked out the front door, closing it behind him. He only made it a few steps before his phone vibrated in his pocket, notifying him of an incoming call. Once he had it in hand, he frowned at the screen, immediately recognizing the number. Davis answered dryly, not in the mood to hear any of his captain's shit, assuming word might have gotten back to him by now that he hadn't been alone in New York.

"Yeah, Captain."

"Davis, where the hell are you? I've called you three times and left you several messages." The annoyance in his captain's voice was hard to ignore. There had been messages, but Davis elected not to check them, knowing that he would be on his way to the precinct after he got Cassidy home. Whatever had crawled up his captain's ass could wait until then.

"I was on the plane. Just got back . . ."

"Wanna tell me why you dropped the ball on the most important part of Evans's case?"

"What are you talking about?" With a tight expression, he lowered his head, peering at the running shoes on his feet. Dressed casually in jeans and a long-sleeved tee for comfort on the plane, Davis wasn't in his usual attire of slacks and a dress shirt.

"Running a list of firearms that might match the one used to kill Williams. How the hell did you miss that?"

"I didn't; just hadn't gotten around to it."

Fuck.

Davis silently cursed himself for doing precisely what he was being accused of—missing a vital part of the investigation. He had been sidetracked with so many other things that led to dead ends he hadn't considered tracking down the gun. Nothing pointed him in any real direction of finding it, and there was no ballistics linking the bullets to anything in the system.

"Well, you should have. We have the gun, Davis. It was dropped off anonymously at a local firehouse, and guess who it's registered to?"

Don't say it . . .

"Cassidy Evans."

Fuck.

"It's time that you get your ass in gear, Davis. Wherever you are, drop what you're doing and bring her in, unless you need someone else to do it for you."

"I'm perfectly capable of bringing her in." Davis's tone was clipped.

"I used to think so, but now, I'm not so sure if you can be partial where she's concerned."

Davis laughed cockily. "I see someone's been pillow talking with you, Captain."

"Bad analogy, Davis, and not one that I appreciate. I'm not sleeping with Harper, so pillow talking isn't possible. But he did mention you've been spending a lot of personal time with Evans. If I need to pull you off the case . . ."

"No, that won't be necessary. I can do my job."

"Good, then prove it. Get her ass in here now. A partial print was found on the weapon. If it's hers, then you know what's next."

I'll have to arrest her, and she'll be charged.

"I hear you loud and clear, Captain. I'll bring her in."

"Don't be all day either."

The line went quiet, and Davis realized the captain had ended the call. He slipped his phone into his pocket and used that same hand to massage his temple. The mounting frustration created the beginnings of a tension headache.

How the hell did I miss that?

Am I too caught up in the woman that I'm overlooking the reality of things?

Is that what she wanted, for me to be emotionally connected and blur the lines, making missteps with the case? She was trained at manipulating people's thoughts and feelings.

Davis turned on his heels, feeling very annoyed as he climbed the stairs and banged on Cassidy's door. When she didn't answer immediately, his fist made contact again until she stood before him with a frown.

"Did you forget something?"

"Yeah, a lot of shit, like the fact that I need to start investigating this case with a clear head."

"Nate, what's going on?"

Nate.

Is she playing with me?

Personalizing us so that I would get sidetracked.

"Do you own a gun?"

"What?"

Cassidy's face flashed with something Davis couldn't decipher, which only fueled his anger and made him ask the question again more aggressively this time. "Simple question, Evans. A simple yes or no answer. Do. You. Own. A. Gun?"

"Yes, I own a gun."

"Where is it?"

"Why? What's going on?"

"You're not the one asking questions right now, Evans. I am. Where's the gun? Show it to me."

"It's in the bedroom. My closet."

"Let's go." His fingers wrapped around her arm, and he began moving. Not once had he been to Cassidy's bedroom, so he wasn't sure why he was taking the lead other than the frustration of needing to get there faster. She snatched away from his hold and frowned up at him.

"I assume you're accusing me of something based on how you're acting right now. Given the circumstances, I'll humor you, but keep your damn hands to yourself."

He laughed cockily. "Now, you want me to keep my hands to myself?"

The words felt bitter on his tongue, but at the moment, he was being driven by the blow to his ego now that his captain was on his ass and believed he wasn't adequately doing his job. Then there was the slight feeling in the back of his mind that Cassidy had possibly been playing him this entire time.

"Wow. This way, *Detective*," she muttered, and he attempted to ignore the offense that filtered into her expression. He couldn't allow himself to care about that at the moment. This was his job. His reputation, his livelihood were on the line.

Davis followed Cassidy down the hallway, through the bedroom, and to the closet. He stopped at the door while she walked inside and moved to a drawer built into custom shelving, where she removed a gun safe. She carried it toward Davis, who stepped out of the way as she placed it on the nearby credenza and keyed the code, which opened the safe—gasping when she found it void of a firearm.

"It should be here," she said with a disappointed look on her face.

Davis refused to allow himself to be affected.

"Should be but isn't. You want to explain that?"

"I can't. I didn't take the gun out of here. I assumed it was in there. I've never used it. Never had a reason to . . ." Her eyes met Davis's, and he knew the minute she realized what his thoughts were.

Until now.

"You can't believe that I would be stupid enough to use a gun that I own to kill my husband."

"Stupid or smart? No one would ever accuse you of being stupid, Evans. You're a brilliant woman who knows how these things work. You've been intimately involved in hundreds of cases. You know how incredibly insane it would be to shoot your husband with a gun that was registered to you. It would be a gross error in judgment that might lean in your favor."

"*Or* someone else took that gun."

"Who, Evans? I watched you open the case. I couldn't have done it. No one else could either without that code. I'm assuming it was only shared with you and your husband."

"I assume you're asking all this because it has been brought to your attention by someone else that the gun even exists."

She purposely avoided answering my question.

"Yeah, it has. I need to take you in."

"You're arresting me?" Her eyes widened, and he gauged her reaction, noting that she was genuinely surprised. Possibly because she'd gotten caught and not because she was innocent.

"Don't have much of a choice at this point."

"Okay." She extended her wrists toward him, and Davis felt the gut punch from such a simple but logical reaction. Things were changing faster than he liked.

"I'm not going to cuff you, Cass. I assumed you'd go willingly."

"I will, but I don't want there to be any reason for your character to be in question." The accusation was there, and it felt like another gut punch.

I'm no longer sure if you're truly innocent.

"You let me worry about that," he said lowly. "Let's go."

20.

Cassidy sat in the holding cell, staring at her hands. She occasionally glanced around, feeling her world again spiraling out of control. Her gun was missing. Did that mean they found it? Was it the one used to murder Niles? If so, that meant she was going to be arrested.

Arrested for a crime she did not commit. The one ally she had no longer trusted that she was innocent because he refused to tell her anything. No one said a word about what was going on with the case. No one communicated with her at all, and Cassidy was fearful of what that meant.

They're not telling me anything because they're going to officially charge me.

Davis had arrested her, bringing her in like an official suspect and politely asking her to get in the holding cell. Once she had, he locked her in and walked away, giving one last glance that didn't offer much hope.

She exhaled a shuddering breath as she lowered her eyes to her hands yet again. There was so much nervous energy, and she couldn't do anything about it. If Davis was no longer in her corner, no one was there.

"This can't be happening. *How* is this happening?"

"I've been wondering the same thing myself, Cass."

She lifted her eyes to find Captain Allen Jones, an old friend and colleague, staring pensively at her. His arms were locked across his chest.

"I'm sure you have," she uttered sarcastically.

"You think I'm happy about this?"

"I *think* you have a job to do, and emotions aren't really a necessity."

"Funny you say that . . ."

The look he gave had Cassidy squaring her shoulders. She felt what was coming next.

"What's the deal with you and Davis?"

"There is no deal."

"You sure about that? Because from where I'm sitting, it looks to be very much like something is going on between the two of you."

"Maybe you should find another seat then, Captain, or another source. I'm sure Harper's been telling his version of what he thinks is between Nathaniel and I."

Captain angled his head to the side. "So you admit there's something between you and Detective Davis?"

She noted that he used his official title because of her slip addressing Davis by his first name. "I'm admitting that Harper is using false accusations to paint a narrative that doesn't exist."

It was a lie, or at least had been before Davis dragged her in here. She couldn't imagine he'd risk his career for her or anyone, for that matter. The avoidance of compromising his career had brought him to Atlanta in the first place.

"He's been spending time with you at your home, Cass. The two of you took off for New York together. He got you here in record time, which leads me to believe you two were already together when I called him. That seems like something to me."

She opened her mouth to respond but was cut off by someone else.

"Results are back."

Cassidy lifted her eyes to Davis, who'd suddenly appeared. Captain Jones turned to Davis and shook his head in annoyance. He paid Cassidy one last glance and then left, leaving the two of them.

"Well?"

Davis moved closer to the cell but didn't make a move to let her out, which only had Cassidy's stomach twisting.

"We found a partial print on the gun."

"It was my gun. Makes sense that my prints were on it."

"It does, which is also interesting, considering that the partial didn't match you. In fact, it completely excludes you as the one who handled the weapon."

Cassidy frowned but watched his expression closely. She sensed that Davis was not happy about the news.

"Did you *want* it to be a match?"

He released a sigh, staring at her intently. "Of course not. Why would you think I'd want solid evidence attaching you to this?"

"Because you seem disappointed that it's not."

"I'm disappointed that I'm at a dead end yet again."

"So I assume that means you're not booking me."

Davis didn't speak. He only stepped away and held his hand out, requesting the keys from a uniformed officer who was close by. She handed them over, and then Davis moved back toward the holding cell to let Cassidy out. She shivered, brushing her hands over her arms to settle her nerves.

"So, did you run the partial?"

Davis shook his head, staring at Cassidy. "I can't tell you that."

"Right. Boundaries. *Boundaries* we should have had and maintained from the beginning. If I'm free to go . . ."

"You are. Give me a minute, and I'll drive you home. You can wait for me—"

"No. That won't be necessary. I can get myself home, Nate."

"Cass . . ."

She held her hand up. "Please. Things are already more complicated than they should be. Let's not make it worse. I'll be fine."

Davis offered a tight nod. They shared another awkward moment of silence before Cassidy turned to leave. She hadn't bothered bringing a purse; she only shoved her wallet-sized card holder into her pocket along with keys and cell phone before leaving the house. They hadn't taken either from her when she was escorted into the cell, so she left without another word to anyone, least of all to the man who had her mind and emotions all over the place.

❖───❖───❖

An hour later, Cassidy was stepping out of the ride share, feeling a wave of annoyance when she noticed Tia's car pulling into her driveway moments later. She didn't bother forcing a smile or extending pleasantries after the day she had. She couldn't care enough to, so when Tia approached the yard where Cassidy was waiting, she decided to get right to it.

"Hey, Cass, I was coming by to check on you. I called a few times and came by yesterday, and you weren't home."

"Yeah, I've been busy."

"Oh . . ."

Cassidy noticed that Tia seemed offended, but if she was waiting for clarity or an explanation about how she'd been busy, that wouldn't come.

"It's really not a good time. I've had an extremely long day—"

"You want to talk about it?"

"No, actually, I don't. What I'd like to do right now is take a long, hot bath, drink some wine, and try to remember who I was before all of this ... this ... I don't even know what *this* is."

"Cass ..." Tia's face shifted into a sympathetic expression.

Sympathy was the last thing that Cassidy needed. However, what she wanted most wasn't possible. For her life to go back to what it had been before Niles was murdered—hell—before she'd met him would be just as great.

"Tia, I'm fine, I assure you. Just tired and a bit overwhelmed at the moment."

"That's understandable. Is there anything I can do to help? Maybe I can order you dinner. It can be here by the time you finish your bath."

Cassidy smiled weakly. "No, I appreciate it, but I don't have much appetite. I'll give you a call, okay?"

"Sure."

Tia smiled softly before turning to leave, but Cassidy thought of something. "Wait. There is something you can help me with."

Tia perked up, and Cassidy watched her intently. She trusted Tia, always had. But did she really have the luxury of truly being that confident about anyone in her life? There had never been a reason not to, but now, she had to protect herself, which meant not leaving anything to chance. Maybe she was being naïve. Tia never had access to her home when Cassidy wasn't there. She didn't have access to multiple aspects of Cassidy's life, but that didn't mean there weren't possibilities.

"I was looking at the schedule, trying to make sense of some dates. On April nineteenth, I was scheduled to speak at Duke. My mind is a little frazzled. I'm pretty sure we were there, but I'm wondering if the date had possibly been moved or rescheduled. Do you mind checking for me?"

"No, I don't mind at all. I can check right now. I remember that date. We ate at Sin-full and stayed at the Diamond Elite Hotel. Their spa was top tier."

Cassidy nodded, offering another forced smile. "I could definitely use that right now."

"I could book you an appointment." Tia peeked up from swiping through her phone. "Local, that is. Doesn't have to be there. Might do you some good."

"I might take you up on that. I'll keep it in mind."

"Duke was on April nineteenth, and that's the original date. No rescheduling." Cassidy watched her intently, hopeful to see something—anything—and came up empty.

Do I really want her to be guilty?

If it means clearing my name, yes.

"Are you sure?"

Tia nodded. "Yes. If there's a change of any kind, I make a note. I also link all the dates to the original email request for easy access, just in case there are any complications or I need to reference something about the event."

When Tia's eyes met with Cassidy's for a final time, Cassidy smiled softly. "Thank you."

"You're welcome. Is there a problem? Did Duke reach out to you with an issue?"

"No, just piecing things together. Trying to make sure everything is adding up."

"Cass, with everything going on, it might do you some good to let me take on a few things."

"I appreciate it, but I've got it all covered."

Tia nodded. "And what about the case? They figured out anything yet?"

"No, nothing solid."

"I'm sure that's not helping much, either."

"No, it's not. I'm going to head inside. If I need anything, I'll reach out."

"Right, sorry."

"No need to apologize. I appreciate you checking in."

While Tia walked back to her car, Cassidy stepped inside and locked the door behind her before leaning against it. Her head rested against the cool, sleek surface, and she closed her eyes, feeling the weight of the world settling onto her shoulders.

There wouldn't be any answers tonight. Her only plan was to get lost in several bottles of wine while trying to forget that she was now dealing with two losses. One of a husband who'd turned her life upside down and one of a man who temporarily made that same life feel less suffocating.

Davis.

21.

Thirty-two matches to the partial print. All at least a six-point match. Three from minors. All excluding Cassidy. Someone else handled her gun, but who?

Davis glanced at the list of partial matches one last time before flipping the list over out of frustration. A beer landed on the table seconds later, and he lifted his eyes to find Reese settling into the chair across from him.

Reese motioned to the beer with the one he held before turning it up. "My treat. Figured after the day you had, you could use that."

"Yeah, I could. Thanks."

"You're welcome."

"So, you two fucking or what?"

Davis paused only seconds before the rim of his beer met his lips, delivering a hard stare to Reese. "What the hell?"

"It's a valid question," Reese smirked. "Maybe not appropriate, but valid."

"Damn sure isn't appropriate."

"I agree, and if you want to punch me ..." Davis leaned across the table, and his fist made contact with the left side of Reese's face.

"What the hell, man?" Reese growled, glaring at Davis, who shrugged nonchalantly.

"You said if I wanted to hit you . . ."

"But I didn't fucking finish." Reese nursed his face, flexing his jaw, and Davis shrugged again lazily.

"Figured you were going to tell me to go ahead and do it."

Reese smirked, shaking his head as he carefully lifted his beer to his lips and swallowed a few gulps. "I was, but shit. Didn't think you'd do it."

"Your fault, not mine," Davis mumbled, lifting his beer again.

"So, since you hit me, I deserve an honest answer at least." Davis glared his way, and Reese held up his hand in surrender.

"Easy, slugger. You don't have to hit me again. I get it. Not my business." He motioned to the paper facedown in front of Davis. "Find anything?"

Davis glared at Reese, who smiled wider. "I thought I already proved I'm a friend, not a foe."

"Right."

"Just offering help if you want it."

"The kind of help that ends up on the captain's desk?"

Reese barked a laugh. "Fuck no, and I'm offended you'd insinuate that I'd be whispering anything at all to the captain."

Davis grinned. "I have to ask. Seems that's how things work around here."

"With Harper, maybe. Not with the rest of us. We stand together, but we also don't respect cops being pussies."

Davis offered a nod. "I think I got it covered. I've already started working my way through the list. Got it down to twenty. Shouldn't be hard to weed out a few more."

"If I can help . . ."

"I let you know."

"Hey, stranger . . ." They both looked up to find that a third person had joined them. Davis was already familiar with Sam, and Reese wanted to be, based on how he checked her out.

"I assume by the greeting, you two already know each other," Reese said smoothly. Sam flashed him a smile before her eyes lowered to Davis.

"We're familiar."

Reese stood, pointing to the chair he was previously occupying. "Here, you can take my seat. I was about to head out."

"You sure? Don't want to interrupt." She kept her eyes on Davis, waiting for his approval, but he kept quiet while Reese spoke up.

"I'm sure, sweetheart. Have a seat, but be careful about what you ask him. He's in a bit of a mood, and it might grant you a mean left hook if you pry where he doesn't want you."

Davis laughed arrogantly, and Sam's eyes bounced between the two men with her brows furrowed.

"See you around, Davis. The offer stands. Enjoy your evening, sweetheart." He winked at Sam and walked away. She eased into the seat across from Davis.

"You don't mind, do you?"

He shook his head. Regardless of what was going on, he liked Sam. He wouldn't be an asshole just because he was frustrated by things he couldn't seem to get a handle on . . . the case, but more importantly, his feelings for Cassidy.

"What are you drinking?"

"Nothing, actually. I placed an order to go, saw you over here, and decided to say hi."

He watched her face, trying to decide if she was telling the truth. When he was satisfied she was, he nodded.

"You work with him?"

Before he could speak, she added, "Cheap shoes and typical detective attire—dead giveaway. You're about the only detective I know who doesn't look like one. If I didn't know you personally, I'd swear you were an underwear model or something."

Davis belted out a laugh. "Underwear model?"

"I mean, it's possible. You have the body for it. Definitely not bad on the eyes. Just don't have the diva personality. That's the only noticeable contradiction."

"What type of personality do I have, Sam?"

"One of a man who punches his coworkers for asking the wrong questions."

He grinned behind the neck of his beer before the rim met his lips. "It wasn't unprovoked. He was being a dick."

"Didn't say it wasn't. I don't take you as the type to go around punching people unprovoked."

He chuckled lightly.

"How have you been, Nate? Haven't heard from you in a little while. I texted, but you didn't respond."

"Yeah, been a little busy with a case. Sorry, I—"

She shook her head. "Don't explain. That's not us. I get it. You busy tonight?"

Davis considered the offer on the table and found his mind drifting to the reason why he wouldn't accept.

Cassidy.

"Maybe another time." It wasn't a lie. For now, anyway. "Got some work to catch up on."

Sam smiled softly and stood. "Maybe another time then," she repeated and stared at him. When he lifted his eyes, hers offered concern.

"You okay? Seem a little *distant*."

"According to you, I'm always distant."

"Yeah, you are, but this feels different."

It was because of her . . .

Cassidy.

"I'm good, Sam. Just work stuff."

"Well, take care, and I'm around, you know. For whatever. Even just to talk." She stepped around the table and pressed a kiss to his cheek. Before she could walk off, he caught her hand and gave a gentle squeeze.

"Thanks, Sam. I appreciate you."

He let her go, and she left. They both knew there wouldn't be another time or anything more than what they'd already shared. Sam wasn't privy to why, while Davis couldn't get the woman who'd completely changed the direction of his life out of his head.

⟨⋯⋯❧⋯⋯⟩

Sitting in his living room reviewing the names on the list, Davis managed to exclude most of them with a gut feeling and simple internet searches. He then focused on those who were local and came up empty. He'd circled back to those that were out of state when one name, in particular, stood out in a way that he couldn't seem to bypass. Something about it felt eerily familiar and had Davis flipping through the case flies to find the list of people who had immediate access to Cassidy when he realized why the name felt familiar.

Laura T. Murphy.

Tia Murphy.

"Cassidy's assistant." The partial print matched a school identification print of a child in San Diego. It was possible that Cassidy's assistant having a fingerprint on record that matched the partial on the gun was merely coincidental, but those types of coincidences rarely ever existed. Davis's gut told him that he needed to dig a little deeper.

He found social media for Tia Murphy and began navigating through her page. There hadn't been any posts prior to her freshman year of college, and only a handful back then. She sporadically posted typical pictures of food, vacations, and selfies, hardly anything personal. The most important thing that stood out to Davis was that her life before working with Cassidy was pretty mundane. She was a typical college kid, but there wasn't anything significant about her life. Not one post of friends or family. The year she began working with Cassidy, everything about the young woman's world shifted. She started wearing expensive clothing, carrying high-end bags, and posting pictures of herself at chic restaurants and hotels.

Davis remembered Cassidy mentioning how Tia traveled with her and was at all of the speaking engagements, so he referenced the photos and locations Tia posted with the ones that Cassidy posted on her own social media sites. Although Cassidy's page was more on the professional side, with very little about her personal life, he realized that many of the travel dates that Tia posted matched those Cassidy had posted. The two spent quite a bit of time together, but Cassidy had already mentioned that.

"Tia Murphy. Who are you?" Davis mumbled to himself.

It was late, and his eyes felt the strain from all the hours of staring at his laptop, so he decided to call it and start fresh the next day. His first task would be contacting Tia to ask her questions about her life with Cassidy. There was something there, and he needed to figure out what that something was. Cassidy seemed to be trusting of the young woman, but Davis had no personal connection, allowing him to view things from all angles. At this point, he needed a win.

⋯⋯⋆⋅⋯⋯

The following day, Davis found himself following closely behind Tia Murphy as she navigated from her duplex in midtown to Buckhead Village District, where she parked and grabbed a coffee, then proceeded to peruse in and out of several shops. He kept his distance, watching as she purchased items from high-end stores, swiping her card like she didn't have a care in the world. After an hour of watching the same thing and realizing there wasn't much to gain, Davis decided to make an introduction, catching the young woman as she chose to break for a bite to eat at a local café.

He caught her by surprise when he eased into the seat across from hers at the corner patio table she'd selected. Davis smiled when the young woman scowled at his presence initially, then something flashed behind her eyes before a smile followed, and she completely took him in. "Nice to meet you, Ms. Murphy. Mind if I join you?"

"You're already seated, so asking if you can join me is redundant."

He smiled charmingly. "You're right."

"Do I know you?"

"No, but I know you, and I think it's time you and I had a chat."

"You know me?"

"Know of you, I should say. I'm Detective Davis. I'm working the Williams case." Davis watched her intently, searching for a reaction. There wasn't one that held any significance.

"Am I supposed to know what you're referring to?"

Davis smiled again. "Maybe not. Jerrod Williams, who you know as Niles Anderson, Cassidy's husband. You are Tia Murphy, her assistant, correct?"

She smiled smugly. "You're here, so you already know the answer to that, Detective."

He nodded. "I do."

"So what can I do for you?"

"I was hoping to ask you a few questions. There are several things I need clarification on, and I was hoping you could help me out."

"I'll answer whatever I can, but I'm not sure there's much I can help with. Most of what I do for Cassidy is handled by way of working remotely."

"But you have spent time with Cassidy and Niles in their home. You've seen them together. You have been privy to how they interacted with each other."

"Well, yes. But not often. I've had very little access to Cassidy's home or her personal life. She's a very private person."

"She is. But from the time you've spent around them, what would you say their relationship was like?"

She frowned slightly. "They were happy. She loved him, he loved her. I envied them, if I'm being honest."

"Why so?"

She shrugged. "When you were around them, you just sensed that they loved each other. You know how you see couples, and they just vibe. That was Cass and Niles. They felt right together. The way he looked at her, you could see in his eyes that she was special to him, which is why it's so devastating to find out their entire marriage was a lie. I still can't believe that. It felt so real."

"People are good and make you believe what they want you to."

"Yeah. Guess that's what he did because Cass loved the guy. She had no clue who he really was."

"Did you?"

Her composure faltered. Davis caught it. There was something there. "Did I what?"

"Did you know that Niles Anderson was not who he claimed to be?"

"No." She made a face. "How would I know?"

"You worked intimately with Cassidy. You were around them. Maybe you saw or noticed something about her husband—"

"I wouldn't have *noticed* anything about him. I worked for Cassidy, and like I said before, I didn't spend much time around them."

"But you did spend enough time around them to note that they loved each other. That they vibed."

Davis remained calm while he noticed Tia growing defensive. Her body language shifted—shoulders tensed, eyes narrowed. "When people are truly in love, you don't have to be around them daily to sense that love. Simple interactions are enough."

He nodded. "I agree. If that's what they truly want you to believe. But nothing's perfect, and everyone has secrets. Every marriage has cracks on the surface. Wouldn't you agree?"

"That everyone has secrets, yes. As for marriage, I couldn't say. I've never been married before, so I'm not an expert on the matter."

Davis had gotten her riled up and decided to shift things a little. "Working for Cassidy meant having access to her and her life, correct?"

"Yes, but only specific things."

"How much access did you have to her home?"

"I've been to her home only while Cassidy was there. Never alone."

Defensive. Interesting.

"What about when she traveled on vacation with her husband? Did she rely on you to collect the mail, water the plants, feed the pets?"

"Cassidy didn't have pets, and her plants are fake. As for mail, she's never been gone for more than a few days at a time. No need to worry about an overflow in that short span, so no."

"Have you ever had keys to her home? You know, just in case of an emergency or to run by and pick up something, drop something off?"

"No. Again, Cassidy was a very private person and also very responsible. Not the type to have emergencies that would require me to have access to her home while she wasn't there."

"And how was your relationship with Niles? The two of you close?"

"Close, no. We communicated sometimes when he wanted to surprise Cassidy and needed to align his schedule with hers. I'd been enlisted to make dinner reservations and even suggested a few gift items for him, but that was the extent of our dealings. I worked for Cassidy, *not* her husband."

"But you occasionally dealt with him outside of your communications with Cassidy."

"If you're asking if I spent time with the man, the answer is no. If your next question is, was I sleeping with him, the answer is also no. I respect Cassidy far too much for that, and I respect my paycheck even more."

"Why would you assume I would ask if you were having an affair with Cassidy's husband?"

"I watch enough TV to know that speculation of the pretty assistant sleeping with the husband is always in the back of everyone's minds."

Davis smirked. "I'm sure you understand why that is. You are quite beautiful, Ms. Murphy," he said ironically. He wasn't flirting, only noting that she'd referenced herself as the *pretty* assistant. She glowered at his compliment, so Davis continued. "So she pays you well?"

"Very. Better than I can expect to be paid as an assistant anywhere else, which is why I wouldn't risk my job by sleeping with her husband."

"Noted."

"Is that all, Detective? I have a busy day and would love to grab a bite to eat in *peace* before I get to it."

Davis nodded and rose from his chair. "That's all I have for now, but I may reach out if I think of anything else. Would that be okay?"

"Do I have a choice?"

His smile expanded. "No, actually, you don't, but it makes the process a lot smoother if you cooperate, and I don't have to go through alternative methods to question you, Ms. Murphy."

"I have no issue cooperating. I'll do anything I can to help Cassidy. She didn't do this. You have to know that."

"What I know is that someone killed Jerrod Williams, and it's my job to figure out who that person is, regardless of what I think or feel I know. I'll be relying on the facts to make my case."

"Then I do not doubt that those *facts* will lead to you figuring out that person is *not* Cassidy."

He held her stare for a moment longer. "Enjoy the rest of your day, Ms. Murphy. I'll be in touch."

"I assume you have my number and know how to find me."

"I do."

Davis turned to leave, stopping after only a few steps before he turned to face Tia again. "I do have one more question, Ms. Murphy."

"Yes?"

"You're adamant that Cassidy didn't kill her husband. Do you have any idea who did and why?"

And there it was. The lack of ability to maintain eye contact. The small tell that she knew something. Maybe not who killed Williams, but there was something she was holding back, confirming that gut feeling that Davis had yet again.

"No. I haven't got a clue. Like I said, I didn't know much about the guy outside of his relationship with Cass. There's no way I could know who he pissed off enough to shoot him."

Shoot him?

"Right. Again, enjoy the rest of your day, Ms. Murphy. I hope I didn't cause too much of a disruption."

Her eyes swept his body lustfully. "Not at all. You enjoy your day as well, Detective."

22.

"Detective." Despite how her body reacted to the sight of Davis on her doorstep, Cassidy's greeting was less than welcoming. She was unsure about where she stood with him and still trying to process why she cared so much about the man who had proven he lacked consistency with how he felt about her.

"You busy?" When Davis's eyes moved past her, searching what little of her home he could see from the doorway, she exhaled a sigh and forced her arms across her chest.

"What are you doing here, Nate?"

She softened her demeanor, unable to stick with the frustration she felt from his unannounced visit. Regardless of everything that transpired between the two, she was logical enough to understand his position and hers. Davis had a job to do. One that was complicated by the connection they both undoubtedly felt. She could lie all she wanted, but Cassidy truly missed his presence.

"Had a few questions. You mind if I come in for a minute?"

Cassidy angled her head to the side, peering at Davis. "You sure that's a good idea? Maybe we should head to the station instead."

"I deserve that. Not gonna say it doesn't sting a little bit, but I had it coming."

"Yes, you did," she huffed but stepped out aside, allowing him enough space to enter her home. Davis made himself comfortable in the living room while Cassidy continued to the kitchen. She noticed the ease with which he settled onto the sofa in her home like he belonged there. "Can I get you anything to drink? Water, juice, a beer?"

She waited, and when Davis lifted his eyes to her, delivering an insanely unfair smile, she did her best to keep her own hidden. "No coffee this time?"

"No . . ." She reached for the bottle of wine she'd opened right before he arrived. "I googled it. Might not be a good idea to offer you coffee, Detective."

Davis chuckled and nodded. "Might not be a good idea for you to have that either." She glanced his way and caught his eye just in time to see him motion toward the glass of wine she poured. Her body flushed with warmth from memories of New York when a few glasses of wine had ended with Davis in her bed.

"I think I can handle myself. You want one?"

"I'll take a beer if you have any." He offered a lazy smile, and she enjoyed how his eyes leisurely crawled over her body. The oversized sweatshirt concealed her physique, but the midthigh yoga shorts left her legs exposed. Either way, it didn't matter. Davis had already seen every inch of her body.

After grabbing his beer, she carried it and the glass of wine to the living room, handing it to Davis before she tucked herself into the corner of the sofa opposite where he sat. Cassidy lifted her legs and folded them beneath her before cradling her wineglass and taking a sip as she peered at Davis over the rim. "You had questions?"

Davis cleared his throat, balancing the beer on his knee. "Yeah, I wanted to ask about the day your bank stated they called to verify the transfers."

"What about it?" Cassidy's nose wrinkled slightly before she lifted the glass of wine.

"They were adamant about contacting you. Said they used your number, correct?"

"Yes."

"And it was noted they spoke with you?"

"According to the associate, yes."

"But you said you had a speaking engagement that day."

"I did."

"Tia, your assistant, travels with you. Is it possible that she's the one they reached? Maybe she had your phone while you were speaking, and they reached her, not you."

Cassidy gently shook her head. "No, it's not possible. I always keep my phone with me. There's never a time when Tia would have had it."

"What about when you were speaking?"

"Not even then." Cassidy swallowed a large gulp, hesitant about the confession she was about to make, unsure why it would have mattered. "I have an aversion to speaking in front of larger crowds. After my parents left, I rarely communicated. According to Clara, I withdrew into myself. Books were my escape. I'd read just about anything." She smiled softly before her eyes met with Davis's.

"Anyway, I didn't have many friends. I felt awkward and out of place most of the time. My therapist said it came from being abandoned. My parents leaving me with a neighbor was a part of the reason why. Although I was familiar with Clara and had been to her home enough times to feel comfortable, my parents' leaving shifted something in me. Keeping to myself didn't change over the years, I suppose. Being in front of large crowds made me anxious, fearing people were analyzing me. I know that's weird, considering it's what I do. For each speaking engagement, Tia was there, right up front, as a focal point for me, to keep me grounded. I kept my phone to use my notes to stay on task. She was there that day, just like all the others. The bank didn't contact me or her. It wasn't possible."

Davis nodded. She could see him processing. "So you hate speaking in front of large crowds?"

"Pretty much."

"Psychology fits. It's typically one-on-one, but the direction in which your career shifted is not so much. Knowing you're uncomfortable in that space, why would you take on such a task?"

Cassidy smiled and shrugged. "I hadn't really planned on the book becoming a bestseller and people wanting me for speaking engagements. That was never the plan. It just kind of happened."

He laughed. "It didn't 'just happen,' Cass. It was destined. You're great at what you do, and you've had a stellar career."

She frowned, staring at him pensively. "You still believe that, after everything you know about me?"

Her eyes remained affixed on him, waiting, hoping. Her stomach twisted at the thought of how much she wanted— *needed*—his approval. "Yeah, I do. Why wouldn't I?"

"You know why," she said quietly.

"You have to let that go. You did nothing wrong . . ."

"I hid the truth, which might not be classified as 'wrong,' but it certainly wasn't the right decision."

"Do you truly believe that? If you did, then we wouldn't be having this discussion right now. You believed you made the best decision possible, given the circumstances. You didn't lie, Cass. You made an ethical choice to prevent other women from falling victim to a very sick and morally corrupt man. There's no way in hell I could hold that against you. I *don't* hold that against you."

His firm stance on the matter allowed her to relax. "Thank you."

Davis offered a tight nod before he asked his next question. "Has Tia ever been here alone?"

"No, never. You're asking an awful lot of questions about Tia. What is it that you're not telling me? Did you find something that makes you think she's somehow connected to this?"

"Yes and no."

"I don't like the way that sounds."

"Neither do I, but this is where we are."

"And where exactly *are* we, Nate? Are you accusing Tia of something?"

Cassidy would be crushed if she had yet again fallen victim to someone abusing her trust. First, Niles, and now, Tia. How had she allowed that to happen twice?

"The partial print we found on the gun matched thirty-two people. It's how we were able to exclude you completely. It's evident someone wiped the gun to conceal their identity, but they messed up and left something behind."

"The partial . . ."

Davis nodded. "Neither of the six points matched your print. But it did match that of one we found in the database of a child. There was a record listed from Ident-A-Kid."

"For Tia?"

"The name listed was *Laura* Tia Murphy."

Cassidy grimaced quickly before her face expressed the thoughts of surprise and curiosity she was experiencing. Davis added, "So, you see why my focus has shifted to her. Too much of a coincidence for me not to dig a little deeper."

"And this Laura Tia Murphy is Tia, my assistant?"

"I'm pretty sure it is."

Cassidy shook her head. "But how is that possible? I did a background check before I hired her. Nothing came up. I've been around her, and nothing felt off."

"I'm sure you used Tia Murphy, and there wasn't anything on Tia Murphy. While she was working for you, there likely wasn't anything to hide, which meant nothing would have felt off. I did some research and found out that when she turned eighteen, Tia went to the Social Security office and requested a name change, dropping her first name. Since she wasn't completely altering her name, they would have approved the request without questions and issued a new card. Nothing before then would have shown up, only school records. It's perfectly legal."

"How is this possible? How do I keep missing such important things?"

"Trust."

Cassidy tensed.

"You said it yourself. You were tired of being alone. That's how you let your husband in. You also dropped your guard with Tia, but it's not like you didn't at least try to protect yourself with her."

"So what now? There's a partial print that matches hers. If it's not a twelve-point match, even a paralegal could prove reasonable doubt. What else do you have?"

"Nothing yet."

"Then we're right back where we started."

"Not exactly. At least now we have a solid lead. Someone other than you. Is it possible that Tia was sleeping with Niles?" Cassidy's face tensed, and Davis quickly added, "We have to consider the obvious. You didn't kill him, but someone did. The guy was a piece of shit, Cass. Considering what he did to you, is it that much of a stretch to believe that he might have been—"

"Fucking my assistant?" she hissed in anger. "No, it's not. But it *is* hard to believe that she would let him. But then again, who the hell am I to make that type of assertion? I married the guy and hired his potential mistress."

Davis set his beer down and moved closer, confiscating Cassidy's wineglass and placing it on the coffee table beside his beer. His hand ended up on her thigh. "Cass, you're human."

"I'm a gotdamn fool, is what I am. My assistant was sleeping with my husband, possibly in my house or at *his* apartment, that I wasn't aware he had. Like the naïve woman I am, who everyone thinks has it all together, I don't know shit," she yelled, leaning toward him so that their faces were close, eyes aligned. "The great Cassidy Evans, the expert on reading people and solving crimes, couldn't even notice that her husband was a gotdamn fraud. I should have known."

She sucked in a deep breath to balance her emotions but failed miserably. The weight of Davis's stare only made matters worse, so she tried to pull away, but he caught her arm and pulled Cassidy into him. His lips met hers, and she didn't resist. Her emotions were all over the place, making her feel as if she were drowning. Giving into the kiss felt *right*. It felt *safe*. More than anything, it felt *real*, so she allowed herself to kiss him back.

Cassidy lifted her hands to his face, trapping his bottom lip between her teeth. She felt him tense before pulling back enough to show the narrow stare that landed on her face.

Please, don't shut me down.

Desperate for the connection, she arched her back and lifted her mouth to his neck, kissing up the curve of his jaw. The intense silence made the mood a heady mix of weighted expectations. When he kissed her back, she exhaled a sigh of relief and watched as he moved down her body. His hands hooked into the band of her spandex shorts, dragging them slowly down her thighs.

A chaotic mix of her clothes and his went tumbling to the floor until he was situated between her legs again. Strong hands gripped her thighs, spreading them apart. Unlike their first encounter in New York, Davis showed no signs of taking things slow. Maybe he sensed that was what she needed, or perhaps he was simply being selfish. Both were acceptable at the moment. He thrust forward hard until he was completely seated in her depths. The fullness of him had Cassidy's teeth sinking into her lip when he jerked back, only to return with just as much intensity. Cassidy placed her hands at his waist while he leaned into her knees, pressing them upward toward her stomach.

She met him thrust for thrust as they rode out the frustrations and desires that had been simmering between them since returning from New York. Cassidy got what she needed—an escape. To feel worthy, desired. Davis hammered into her with purposeful plunges guaranteed to relieve the tensions she refused to allow to take her under. The euphoria of her body clinging to his while he rode her hard was precisely what she needed. The moment was also a pleasurable reminder that whatever was between them would never be a "temporary" connection.

23.

Davis walked into the precinct that following day with a newfound motivation. The night he spent with Cassidy further confirmed his previous feelings. Whatever was between them wouldn't be temporary. He wanted more, and based on the way she'd given in last night and the disappointment in her eyes when he left her bed this morning, Cassidy's feelings weren't all that different from his.

Until he cleared her name and convicted the person who killed her husband, they couldn't be more than they were. Davis was grateful for the lead pointing toward Tia as a suspect, but he still had to prove the case. He needed evidence as well as the how and why, which led to him doing the one thing he swore he would never do—ask for help.

Reese.

Davis cringed when he heard the sleep-laced tenor of his colleague's voice. "You off today?"

"No, why?"

"You sound like you're still in bed, and if not, then you haven't rolled out of one too long."

"*One* would be accurate. I met a friend last night, and we decided to get further acquainted at her place. Can't say I'm disappointed either."

Davis groaned and then chuckled lightly. "Spare me the details. I need a favor if the offer still stands?"

"I don't know, Davis. My jaw is still a little tender." Reese's tone was light, so Davis smirked.

"That's on you. You can't blame me for you being a dick."

"No, I can't, can I? I guess I'll hold up my end of the deal. What do you need?"

"A warrant." He paused, thinking about accessing Tia's phone records, before another thought entered his head. "Two, actually. Was going to see if you could help expedite them."

"Finally got something solid with the Williams case?"

"That's what I'm hoping, but I need to do a little more digging before I know for sure. That's going to require access to phone and bank statements."

"Got it. Let me head home, shower, and change. Then I'll be on my way. You at the precinct now?"

"I am, but I was kinda hoping to get this done a little quicker than that. You think you could swing by here first?"

"Well, shit. Not only are you cashing in, but you're preventing me from washing my ass in the process."

Davis tensed again. "Wait, never mind. Maybe you should head home first."

Reese chuckled amusedly. "You guys are safe. I took a quick shower at her place before I left, which may or may not have continued last night's activities. For the most part, I'm decent. Just in yesterday's clothes, so I'm a little wrinkled."

"I don't think that will matter all that much."

"I damn sure hope not if you want those warrants sooner rather than later. It's best to catch DA Greene before her day starts, or you might not get them for a few days. If you can force her hand now, I'd be willing to bet you'll have them before lunch." He paused. "With my help, that is. I'm kind of her favorite."

Davis was more than willing to take the ribbing if it meant getting those warrants in hand. There was no telling how long it would take for the cell companies to hand over their records, but he felt confident he could get her banking information today as long as the banks were local. He would reach out to Cassidy to find that out. She had a record of what banks Tia used if she paid Tia.

"You slept with Greene, didn't you?"

"I won't say yes because that would be incriminating myself, but I won't say no, either, because that would be, well, you know ..."

Davis shook his head, smiling. "Well, maybe you *should* go home to change because if that's what it takes to get those warrants, I want you to be presentable ..."

"What the hell, Davis! Are you seriously considering pimping me out for warrants?"

"I won't say yes because I might not get what I need, but I won't say no, either."

Reese laughed hard and loud. "Who the hell would have guessed the office asshole has a sense of humor. You might fit it in around here, after all. ETA twenty. Meet me at her office."

"Done, and thanks for this."

"Oh, don't thank me just yet, Davis. You're gonna owe me big for this."

Davis groaned under his breath as he ended the call. Either way, he couldn't really complain. He was getting what he needed out of the deal, and if that meant being indebted to Reese, he'd still consider it a win.

"Here you go, Detective Davis. Copies of all Ms. Murphy's transactions for the past six months. Is there anything else I can help you with?"

Davis accepted the stack of papers from the associate and quickly scanned them to make sure it was what he needed. Once he felt sure, he lifted his eyes to her. "Can you check to see if she also has a safe deposit box?"

He'd only requested the transactions from any savings and checking accounts from the bank Cassidy used to pay Tia monthly. There had been two. One when she first began working for Cassidy and a second that she switched to a little over a year ago. Davis served warrants to both banks, hopeful that he could find anything connecting Tia to Niles or Jerrod outside of the interactions she'd admitted to.

"No problem. Let me check for you real quick." The associate walked toward the door with Davis in tow. She paused at a podium with a computer atop it and began pecking on the keyboard. After a few minutes, she shook her head.

"No safe deposit boxes. Only the checking and savings accounts. Is there anything else?"

"No, that will be all. Thanks for this." He lifted the papers. She nodded and walked away. Davis headed to his car, too anxious to wait to check the statements when he returned to the station. Repeating his actions from leaving the first bank, he sat in the parking lot scouring through the paperwork, hoping to find something useful. He had come up empty the first time and felt sure he would again . . . until he made it to the last statement.

"Son of a bitch," he muttered, eyes focusing on transactions from the current month. Four deposits of $5,000, each made two days apart, with the first one occurring two days after Williams's death. The tricky part was that they were transfers made from an account that didn't belong to Williams.

Who the hell is Benjamin Clark, and why would he have paid Tia $20,000?

"Hey, Cass, come on in." Davis brushed a hand over his head as he stepped out of the way to allow Cassidy access to his home. It wasn't *his* because he was renting, but it was close enough. After he locked them in, he watched Cassidy move around his space, running her fingers over the few items of furniture he had. The two-piece leather sofa set, rug, and tables could have easily been purchased as a showroom model set. The stand that held the TV and the small, poorly built bookshelf adjacent to it housed a handful of books he read a time or two. Cassidy's open hand brushed the back of the sofa as she moved behind it, ending her tour. He couldn't curb the satisfying feeling of seeing her moving around the room, exploring, no doubt trying to gain insight into things she didn't know about him. At that moment, he realized Cassidy could have all of his secrets. He would gladly hand over those she discovered and the ones she couldn't.

"So, this is you."

Davis smirked, shoving his hands into the pocket of his sweats. He was dressed casually, having rushed home to shower and change before her arrival. He'd also grabbed dinner on the way since he wasn't much of a cook. Since they were spending the evening in, he saw nothing wrong with dressing in his usual lounging attire of a T-shirt and sweats.

Cassidy must have felt similarly, considering she wore track pants, a matching jacket, and running shoes.

"Yep, all me. Well, in furniture form, that is."

Cassidy turned his way, offering a soft smile that she paired with an arched brow. "There's not much to you if we're making the comparison to you in furniture form."

Davis chuckled and lifted one shoulder in a lazy shrug. "Consider me a minimalist, at least when it comes to all this."

He removed one hand from his pocket and motioned toward the room. "I'm a pretty simple guy. I don't need much."

"Interesting."

"How so?"

"Just simple observation. I might have overlooked my fraud of a husband and his potential mistress, but I didn't miss that your ex-fiancée didn't seem like the type to be okay with a minimalist kind of guy."

"And you'd be right because she wasn't. I simply didn't care. I will only ever be who I am."

He noticed the flicker of recognition in Cassidy's eyes before he added. "And if we're going by honest, you don't seem like the type of woman who would be okay with a minimalist kind of guy, either."

She arched a brow again. "Because of my lifestyle?"

"That, amongst other things. You're a brilliant woman, Cass. Accomplished, decorated career. I'm a detective with no plans of being anything other than a detective. I'm comfortable here."

"So, no aspiration of landing an office at Police Palace?"

He shook his head. "No, not for me. Not that I couldn't or don't feel I'm good enough because, I assure you, I am." His heated gaze crawled over her body, and he enjoyed the way her muscles tensed with recognition. "But like I said, I'm simple. I don't like the politics of it all. I'm good right here. Probably would have stayed a uniform if the hours and shift weren't shit. Detective gives me a little more flexibility with my schedule and pays a little better. As you can tell, I'm living the good life." He grinned, and hers matched his.

"I like your version of 'the good life,'" she said quietly, eyes roaming again. "Feels comfortable. *Real*. Feels like *you*. Reminds me of living with Clara."

"Well, damn. Not sure how I feel about that. You said her house was a piece of shit."

Cassidy rolled her eyes. "I never said it was that bad. It was small, yes, and maybe not in the best shape, but it was home, and I miss having the security of a real home. This reminds me of that time in my life."

And you remind me of what I want in mine.

Davis cleared his throat. "So . . ."

"Right." She rolled her shoulders back. "You said you found something?"

"I did. Come take a look." He pointed to the kitchen. "I ordered some pizzas. One meat lovers, and the other's a veggie. Wasn't sure what you'd like."

"Both are okay, but I'm more partial to the meat lovers, so I hope you're okay with veggie."

"I've eaten a vegetable a time or two in my life." The teasing granted him a genuine smile from Cassidy.

After they ate, Cassidy sat at the table across from Davis. He would have preferred to have her closer, but the table was small, so she was still within reach. Close enough for him to smell the light scent of vanilla on her skin. A scent that he had begun to enjoy a little more whenever they spent time together.

He watched Cassidy as she stared at the bank statements he handed over after they settled at the table. She focused on them for a long moment, and Davis was about to ask if she knew what she was looking at until she finally lifted her head, features tight, eyes full of questions.

"Are you thinking . . ."

"That money might be connected to the money from Williams's account?"

She nodded, and Davis spoke once more. "Yeah, I am. Not sure how just yet. Got a couple of theories, considering the deposits from that Benjamin Clark account, but I'm not big on coincidences. Those deposits total twenty grand."

"Yeah, but who is this Benjamin Clark? Do you know who he is?"

"No, haven't done a deep dive on him yet. Figured I'd see if you could help me with that first."

"I don't know who he is. Name doesn't sound familiar."

"Well, we can check that out. One thing I learned is always to follow the money."

Cassidy took a bite of pizza, chewed, and swallowed it down before Davis had her eyes again. "You said you had a few theories. Mind if I share mine first?"

Davis shook his head and lifted a slice. "Not at all. Please do . . ." He motioned for her to say what was on her mind, curious to know what she was thinking. Despite the blind spots Cassidy had with Niles and possibly Tia, she was still a brilliant woman and had years of investigating skills under her belt.

"If Tia was sleeping with Niles, it could have possibly been motivated by money."

"You said he didn't have access to a lot of cash. Based on what I've seen of his accounts, other than what he transferred from yours, he had more credit than accessible cash."

Cassidy shook her head. "No, that's not what I mean. Think outside the box. It's possible she wasn't sleeping with Niles for selfish reasons. What if she was sleeping with him for access? Access that she planned on giving to someone else. Someone who *did* have access to large amounts of cash. Someone willing to pay her for access to Niles."

Davis smiled, watching Cassidy, who frowned at him. "What?"

"Great minds think alike. Maybe this Benjamin guy paid Tia to help with access to Niles. She might not be the killer, but she could very well be an accessory to the crime."

"It's what I was thinking. We need to figure out who Benjamin Clark is."

"Yes, we do. But we can't weed out that she got the money from Williams, either."

"No, we can't, but there's no proof. You've already looked at his banking information."

"The statements, yes. But when I went to the bank, I focused on the safe deposit box. I never requested copies of all his transactions like I did for Tia. Pending when his statements cycled, there might be some missed transactions that happened after the cutoff date, showing proof that connects him to Tia. There might be something connecting all three."

"But we won't find that out tonight," Cassidy huffed. Much like himself, he assumed she was just as annoyed with all the lingering questions.

"No, not tonight. I can work on it first thing in the morning, though."

"God, this is stressful." She turned up her beer, finishing about three-quarters of it before the bottle landed hard on the table.

"I won't pretend to understand—"

"Good, because you have no idea what this feels like," Cassidy hissed; then seconds later, her eyes met his. "I'm sorry . . ."

"Don't be. I've told you plenty of times you're allowed to own your feelings. No matter what they are."

"But that doesn't mean I have to take those feelings out on you."

Davis smiled arrogantly. "That depends on what those feelings are. I might not be opposed to you taking them out on me."

He loved how she blushed because it let him know she knew exactly where his thoughts had gone. "Just an all-around good Samaritan, aren't you, Detective Davis?"

"I'm selective about who I'm a good Samaritan for, Cass." He winked, and she laughed lightly.

"Noted. So, was that all, the bank statement? It's not much. In fact, it's just as circumstantial as what you had on me."

"I have one more thing."

"Oh yeah? What's that?" she asked as she perked up and lifted another slice of pizza, consuming a healthy bite.

"A gut feeling."

"A gut feeling?" She spoke with a full mouth, frowning at Davis.

"Yeah, a gut feeling. My instincts are pretty spot-on with those things. I trust my gut, and my gut is telling me that Tia's guilty."

Cassidy narrowed her eyes. "Your gut also told you I was guilty, so forgive me if I'm not over-the-moon excited about you counting that in the positive category."

Davis nodded with a cocky smirk. "I never once believed that you were guilty of killing your husband, Cass. I did have moments where I allowed the evidence to challenge that feeling."

"So, you don't *always* trust your gut?"

"I do, but my job is to follow the facts, allowing them to create the narrative. The facts are sometimes misleading. In your case, they were completely wrong. Well, what little facts I did have."

"And what if the facts challenging your gut feeling about Tia end up completely wrong about her too? Then what? She's our *only* lead. I can't imagine Captain Jones is happy with how long this is taking. They're going to want an arrest."

"I don't give a damn about stats, Cass. If I don't have a solid case, I'll never rush to judgment just to meet metrics. What I feel about Tia and the evidence we have so far aligns. She may not have pulled the trigger, but she knows who did."

"I hope so," she said quietly.

"Enough about that for tonight. There's not much else we can do, so how about we focus on something else."

Cassidy smiled softly. "You're not about to offer me coffee, are you?"

Davis threw his head back and laughed, lifting a slice of pizza. "No, I wasn't going to offer you coffee. At least, not right now. I figured we could watch a movie or something, then, maybe, if I get lucky, we can have *coffee* in the morning when we wake up."

His eyes met hers, and Cassidy's smile grew. "I think I like the sound of that."

"Do you?"

"Yeah, I do."

24.

Cassidy awakened the next morning, snuggling into the warmth of the bedding that cocooned her body. The weight of the arm that had been draped over her waist and the press of a chest against her back were no longer there, but she felt completely at peace for a brief moment. She welcomed the momentary escape because her life was in total chaos. Although she could have stayed in the moment for a few more hours, she was anxious to find out where the missing element was.

Davis.

Cassidy padded into the bathroom to find that Davis had already prepared for her. There was a towel with a washcloth folded neatly on top of it and a single packaged toothbrush sitting on top of them. Just off to the side was a sweatshirt that belonged to him, which she couldn't wait to snuggle into. She smiled at the items before taking in her reflection in the mirror. Her smile expanded when she noticed how happy she appeared. It had been a few weeks since she'd felt a genuine reason to smile.

What am I doing?

This feels right, but shouldn't because . . .

Shaking the thought, Cassidy turned on the water, waiting for a warm flow before washing her face and then brushing her teeth. She and Davis had showered together after their final session, so she tugged on the sweatshirt he'd left her next to the stack of towels and nothing else before leaving the bathroom to find her gracious host.

Her thoughts drifted to the evening before with just how gracious he had been. Her body still ached with a pleasurable memory of how he handled her, and her smile expanded again.

The house was quiet, void of anything other than the creak of the wooden floors beneath her feet as she moved through the living room, frowning at the empty space. There was no sign of Davis, but the minute she reached the kitchen, she heard the muffled repetition of something coming from outdoors. She continued to the door that led out of the back of the house and peeked through the plastic blinds to find a screened-in porch with a heavy bag hanging in one corner and Davis pounding his fists into it. He was only wearing sweat bottoms, which hung low on his waist. His feet and upper body were bare, allowing Cassidy to admire every line and contour of his lean, toned physique.

This man is an anomaly.

A very sexy and complex one that I'm mildly addicted to.

She watched with a honed focus, enjoying how his body moved with precision as he switched up his movement. When she could no longer handle the distance between them, Cassidy turned the doorknob and pulled open the door, leaning against the door frame with one shoulder, folding her arms over her chest.

Davis glanced over his shoulder long enough to offer a sexy smirk before his fists dug into the heavy bag again. Several combinations landed with precision and skill while occasionally shifting his stance and dipping low, sending jabs upright into the bag.

"Great sex and a morning performance. Keep this up, and I might never leave. At the very least, I might make this a regular thing."

She was granted another cocky smirk over a muscled shoulder before Davis pounded the bag again. He picked up the pace, and her smile expanded, noticing that he was truly performing.

"Now, you're just showing off," she chided.

Two more combinations, then he dropped his arms and fully turned to face her. Cassidy's body heated as his eyes moved from her face, down her body to her exposed legs, and then back up. The sweatshirt she wore stopped at her upper thighs, and based on the look he delivered when his eyes lingered at the apex of her thighs, he knew that she was bare beneath the soft, worn cotton.

"Maybe I was showing off. I might like the idea of you never leaving, and this . . ." He paused and moved to Cassidy, placing a hand at her waist and moving it down her hip. "Being a regular thing."

With a sharp tug, her body collided with his, and Davis's hand was at the back of her neck. The pressure of his fingers against her skin, along with the smooth, warm feel of his tongue gliding across her lips before his landed hard against hers, sent jolts of pleasure through her body, landing right between her thighs. The kiss was sweet but intense as his tongue explored, stroking hers with memories of the way it'd stroked other parts of her body the night before. His eyes remained lustfully intense when he pulled away, but a smile curved his lips. "I see you found the stuff I left for you."

Cassidy nodded after pulling her lip between her teeth to hide her own smile before responding. "I did, thank you."

"Come on. I'll make you breakfast." Instead of allowing her to walk, Davis's hands were at her waist, and he easily lifted Cassidy from the floor. She locked her legs around him, and he groaned.

"Fuck. You are naked under here."

"Is that a problem?"

"For me. No. For you, maybe."

He entered the house carrying Cassidy, kicking the door closed before he moved them to the sofa, bypassing the kitchen.

"Wait, what about breakfast?"

"I get mine now, then you get yours."

Cassidy landed with a thud on the sofa, and he settled between her thighs like it was the only place he belonged. Soft kisses met her pussy as a warning before his tongue skillfully explored. He devoured her like his life was hanging in uncertainty had he not done his job correctly.

Ravenous fingers met her clit, keeping time with the thrusts of his tongue. Cassidy's climax rose at a blinding speed until she startled. Her core tensed to a painful degree while her body elevated to a magical place. Everything was lost except the intense orgasm that aggressively laid claim to her body. She allowed it to take flight, rendering her helpless until she was a trembling, quivering mess of nothingness.

"So perfect. So beautiful." His low, sultry voice sent another round of tremors through her, and she settled into the pleasure because what else was there?

Nothing. Absolutely nothing but him.

After they cleaned up, Cassidy sat at the table, watching Davis move about his kitchen. He was in jeans and a T-shirt, while Cassidy wore her pants from the night paired with his sweatshirt. They both thought the safest option was to be fully dressed, or neither of them would be very productive.

He plated breakfast and sat beside Cassidy, dragging her chair insanely close to his. She lifted a fork and peeked at the food.

"This actually looks good."

He chuckled. "I have a handful of things I'm good at. This is one of them. Not much to it. Eggs, cheese, and a little salt and pepper."

"Omelets aren't really simple. The whole flipping and folding part never works for me."

"It's timing. You have to let the bottom fully cook before you get to that part. I'll teach you."

"Detective. Boxer. Chef. You're interesting."

"You left off the most important one."

"Which is?" His eyes lowered to her lap, and her cheeks flushed.

"I'm sure you know."

Cassidy schooled her thoughts and rolled her eyes. "So, boxing. You've done that professionally? What you were doing out there didn't seem like just a hobby. You're good. You've trained?"

His face tensed. "As a kid, yeah, but I never fought professionally. Had a handful of amateur fights, but that's it."

"Why not professionally?"

"It was never a passion of mine. Just something to do." She noticed his tone was clipped and decided to let it go.

"Oh." When she felt his hand on her thigh, thumb moving across the fabric of her track pants, her eyes lifted to his.

"It's not really something I talk about."

"You don't have to explain."

"Wasn't it you who said I needed to level the playing field?"

She remembered commenting on him knowing more about her than she knew about him and nodded.

"Then I don't have to, but I want to."

She kept her eyes on his, watching how he moved thoughts around in his head, struggling for the words he wanted to offer or was willing to share. She could feel the push and pull.

"My parents didn't have a great marriage. They loved each other dysfunctionally, and that wasn't ever really enough, but they stayed together. My dad was careless with life. He did a lot of dumb shit. More or less a career criminal. My mother was the optimist who believed that one day he would get his shit together."

"Did he?"

Davis laughed bitterly. "No, he was shot and killed by a cop after pulling a gun on him while robbing a convenience store."

Cassidy gasped while shock settled into her expression. "He ... wow ..."

"Yeah."

"Is that why you became a cop? Because of what happened to your father?"

The way he laughed arrogantly had Cassidy confused. "If you're asking if I joined the force to satisfy some injustice because my father was wronged, then no. He made choices that held permanent consequences. He robbed a man at gunpoint and was given multiple opportunities to prevent losing his life. He shot at that cop, and the cop shot back."

"You two weren't close?"

"No. But that has nothing to do with my feelings about what happened to him. We weren't close, but I loved him as much as I possibly could."

"I guess we have that in common. I loved my parents as much as I could, given how little they loved me."

The pressure of his hand on her leg increased, settling her anxiety. When their eyes met again, she sensed he understood, so she looked away.

"I'm not him, Cass."

Her eyes shot up to his, and she realized he had somehow managed to read her thoughts. Relating to Niles had cost her in the worst way, and here she was yet again, allowing herself to be vulnerable.

"I wasn't—"

He leaned in and gripped her chin, placing a reassuring kiss on her lips. "You were, and it's okay. I just need you to know that you can trust yourself with me. It will take time, and I'll never rush you, but you're safe with me, Cass."

"Thank you. So . . ." She needed to shift the direction of their conversation. "The boxing thing . . ."

His eyes were on his plate until he had a forkful of his omelet. "What about it?"

"You trained but never fought professionally. Why?"

"My mom put me in classes to train my focus on something other than being angry with my dad. It was also a way to keep me out of the house when he was going through his rants about what a disappointment I was as a son and how inadequate my mother was as a wife."

"He was abusive."

"Verbally, occasionally. I got more insults than compliments from the guy, but he never put his hands on either of us. Eat before that gets cold."

She realized he was no longer interested in sharing his background, which was okay. He'd given enough, and she realized that life wasn't always perfect, but there was always something worth finding solace in. Boxing had been Davis's outlet. Cassidy decided she needed to find hers because, for now, it seemed to be him, and that was a disaster in the making, especially since history had a way of repeating itself in her life.

25.

Davis walked into the precinct with thoughts of Cassidy lingering. Things were getting deep between them, which only further convinced him that he needed to put an end to the search for her husband's killer.

As soon as he was settled at his desk, he had company. His eyes lifted to his captain, who stood over him with a stern expression in place. "I got a call today from my boss."

"And?"

"And I've been doing the best I can to keep them off your ass, but if you don't close this case soon, there's not much more I can do for you."

"Do for *me*? I wasn't aware I asked for your help or protection."

"Don't act indignant, Davis. Regardless of what you think, I'm on your side. You can't fight everybody."

"I'm not fighting anyone. Why don't you understand that wanting to keep to myself doesn't have to translate to me being against everyone here."

"Because that's not how things work. We are one unit, and if we aren't, then it fucks up the vibe. You don't have to have Sunday dinners with the guys here, but you at least need to offer them respect. Offer *me* respect."

"It's not given, Captain. Respect is earned, and when they understand that, I won't fuck up the *vibe* around here."

Captain Jones released a sigh, relaxing his shoulders. "I get your point, and I agree. It should be earned, not given, but haven't I done that?"

"You have."

"Then why not show a little gratitude? You're good at your job—definitely an asset. You have a different way of seeing things, and I admit the fresh way of thinking works in our favor. I'm glad you're here. I hope you hang around for a while, but you must start finding a way to fit in a little in the process. Starting with Harper."

Davis nodded, smiling arrogantly. "Can't say I give a damn what he thinks of me, and I can promise I won't piss him off intentionally, but that doesn't mean I won't piss him off at all."

"I guess that's going to have to be good enough," Captain mumbled. "So, where are you on the case?"

"I have a few solid things. Working on one now."

When the captain leaned over his desk, Davis groaned his disapproval and decided to let it go and extend an olive branch. "Followed the money, and it led me to this guy." He pointed at the screen to a social media profile belonging to Benjamin Clark.

"Who's he?"

"Boyfriend of Cassidy's assistant."

"Which one you looking at, him or her?"

"Both right now. He made several deposits into her account that totaled twenty grand."

"You think that's the money Williams stole from Cass."

"Possibly. I don't believe in coincidences. Twenty grand is a very specific number, and even though he made the deposits in small amounts, they were all days apart and a few days after Williams was killed."

"So, what are you thinking? The two are connected?"

"The three. Williams, the assistant, and the boyfriend. It's very possible the assistant was sleeping with Williams to gain access for the boyfriend. He might have been the one who killed Williams, and if that's the case, then Clark paying her money would make sense."

"But how does that tie back to Williams making twenty grand transfers from Cass?"

"Not sure yet. Only a theory at this point, but I'm about to pay the boyfriend a visit to see what he can tell me."

"Good. Keep me posted. I'd really like to get this case closed. I've asked for leniency with making an arrest, but they won't keep glazing over this. Cass makes for the potential of this being high profile."

So would I.

After Captain Jones left, Davis pulled the address listed for Clark and decided to check him out. Hopefully, he could catch him alone. Davis wasn't quite ready for Tia to realize he was investigating her to the degree of labeling the woman an active suspect, so his moves had to be calculated for now.

<hr />

When Davis pulled into the apartment complex where Clark lived, he shut off his engine and stared at the building that housed Clark's unit. He thought carefully about going up to the door but decided to sit on the place for a minute. While in his car, he leaned back, watching the entrance, until a notification from his phone temporarily distracted him.

How's it going?

He smiled at Cassidy's text, knowing it wasn't as simple as wanting case details. She was thinking about him, possibly missing him. Or, at least, he wanted that to be why she'd reached out.

Found Clark. Sitting on his place now.

You going to talk to him?

If he's alone, yes.

Where are you?

At his place.

The dots came up, danced, then stopped several times before Davis smirked and sent another text.

No, you can't join me. Let me do my job.
I got this part covered.

Never said you didn't.

He grinned.

No, but you want to be here.
Your thoughts are loud.

I'm restless.

I can help you with that later.

Promises, promises.

He sensed both the joke and the silent plea.

One thing I can promise you is that you
can always count on my promises, Cass.

When the text was sent, he noticed a car pull into the spot two over from him. He watched a man exit a navy blue sedan, lock the doors, then walk up to the two steps. He disappeared under the awning of the building. Davis had managed to get a good look at the guy's profile, along with the leather jacket that Clark had worn in several photos on his social media page. The signature locs were also a dead giveaway: shoulder length, tips dyed honey blond.

Definitely Clark.

Davis exited his vehicle and headed under the same awning until he located the unit that belonged to Clark and knocked on the door. With his hand on his gun as a precaution, he waited.

"Yeah?" He heard through the door before Davis hollered back, slightly lifting the weapon. The guy was potentially a killer, so he thought it best to be proactive.

"Benjamin Clark."

"Who's asking?"

"Detective Davis. APD."

The door opened cautiously, and Clark came into view. He was a big guy, at least six feet, with a solid frame, which he expanded to make himself appear larger as he scowled at Davis. Davis did a once-over to ensure that Clark wasn't armed.

"Detective?"

Clark's eyes swept Davis, who tapped his badge.

"I'd like to ask you a few questions."

"About?"

"Do you mind if I come in?"

"Yeah, actually, I do. What the fuck you want to ask me questions about?"

"Tia Murphy." Davis watched his face and noticed awareness flash in his eyes. The two definitely knew each other.

"I don't know who that is."

Davis smiled. "Do you really believe I would be here if I didn't already know you know Ms. Murphy? Now, let's try this again . . ."

"I ain't trying shit. Fuck you and your questions. You got a warrant?"

"No."

Clark shrugged nonchalantly. "Then you damn sure ain't coming in my place, and I ain't answering shit." He moved to close the door, but Davis placed his hand on the faded wood and shoved it back. Clark, in turn, pushed forward, and the door hit Davis's shoulder.

"Looks like you are going to answer my questions after all. You just assaulted a detective, which is a crime. Now, put your hands behind your back, and don't fucking move. You're going with me."

"Nah, fuck that. I ain't do shit."

It was true. He hadn't "technically" assaulted Davis, but if it came down to it, Davis saying he did wouldn't actually be a lie since Clark had hit him with the door.

"Your word against mine. Hands, now."

"If I don't, you gonna shoot me?"

"Yes, but I won't kill you. I'll only hit a leg or a shoulder. Nothing major," Davis warned with a stern look. He noticed the moment Clark struggled internally, weighing his next move, and decided to help him out.

"Whatever you're thinking—don't. I have a feeling that she's not worth what it will cost you to do something stupid like fighting me on this."

"Who the fuck is she?"

"Tia."

"This about me or her?"

"Her—for now. Depends on what you can tell me."

"Look, I don't know shit. I'm not even with the crazy-ass broad anymore. She ended things, saying she was about to dip."

"Dip, as in leaving town?"

"Yeah." Clark was hopeful, but it didn't change Davis's mind.

"Good, then you won't have any issues telling me what you *do* know about her since you just established you know who she is. Now, hands."

"Fine, but you really gotta cuff me? If this isn't about me, I'll tell you whatever I need to. *Willingly.*"

Davis let him go, and Clark adjusted his stance, yanking the hem of his shirt.

"Let's go."

"We can't just do that shit here?"

"Could have, but now you've pissed me off, so the offer no longer stands. Station. Move. Now."

"How long you gonna make him wait?" Captain Jones asked as he and Davis stood outside the one-way mirror, watching Clark shift uncomfortably. Every so often, his head would turn toward the door. His body language was tense, and his constant fidgeting expressed his nervousness.

"Not much longer. I'm about to go in now. The longer I make him wait, the more cooperative I know he'll be, hoping to get this over with so he can go home."

"Is he going home?"

"Not sure, but my gut tells me he might be able to tell me something useful. He's not the one who killed Williams. If he had anything to do with it, I won't credit him being the one who actually pulled the trigger."

"You and your damn gut. You better hope it's right. In a way, I wish it wasn't. I'd love to throw some cuffs on that guy and mark this case officially closed."

Not happening.

He's not our guy.

"Maybe I'm wrong. Not likely, but if it makes you feel better to wish I was . . ." Davis smiled arrogantly.

"Right," Captain murmured as Davis left him there, heading toward the door to the interrogation room.

He entered and bypassed the table, electing to lean against the wall and stare at Clark. He watched him with a trained focus for a long moment in silence. Just staring. He wanted him to be as uncomfortable as possible, and it worked.

"I thought you brought me here to ask questions, not sit on my ass all day staring at the walls. I got shit to do."

Davis smirked and nodded. "What's your relationship to Tia?"

"We don't have one."

"Humor me, and let me determine how to classify the two of you."

Clark shrugged. "We met. We had sex a few times. She ended things."

"That's all?"

"What else is there? I'm not the commitment kind of guy. We had a little fun. The arrangement worked out for both of us."

Davis nodded. "You seemed annoyed that she ended things."

"Nah. Not really."

"What do you do for a living, *Benji*?" Davis got the intended result when Clark scowled at the nickname.

"Why?"

"Because I fucking asked. You want to go home? Answer the questions and stop asking them."

"Maybe I'll ask for a lawyer."

Davis smirked. "Is that what you're doing?"

"Don't know yet. Do I need to?"

"That's not for me to say. If you are, however, be specific. If that's what you want, you're more than welcome to one, but then I reserve the right to treat you like a suspect and not just someone who willingly cooperates by answering a few questions."

"Suspect for what?"

"Murder."

Davis noted that Clark's eyes widened slightly in surprise, but he did his best to seem unbothered. "Murder? I didn't kill anybody."

"I don't think you did, but I do believe you can help me figure out if your girlfriend did."

"You think Tia murdered someone?" He laughed, amused by the thought. "She's a little irrational at times, and I like that about her, but damn, sure not the type who could kill someone."

You'd be surprised.

"The first mistake in crime is underestimating people, but I will say, I believe she's involved in a murder. I haven't decided how involved. So, do you want to talk, or do you want a lawyer? Make up your mind. I too have *shit to do*."

"I'll talk for now, but the minute I feel like this isn't going the way it needs to, like shifting from her to me, I'm done and requesting a lawyer."

"Good, now tell me about the twenty grand you transferred into Tia's account."

"How the fuck you know about that?"

"You might want to rethink your focus by being more concerned with *explaining* why you did it. Not *how* I know. Let's prioritize, *Benji*. Why did you give her that money?"

"I didn't give her shit. She gave the money to me and asked if I would deposit it into my account, then transfer it to hers. Some shit about avoiding paying taxes. It could be considered a gift if I gave it to her."

"And you believed her?"

"Didn't have a reason not to, and it's not like I really cared. She made it worth my while and gave me an extra five to keep for helping her out."

"So she gave you five hundred to deposit twenty thousand into her account?"

"Five *grand*. Come on, Detective. I'm a businessman and much smarter than that. A little over 20 percent seemed fair." He smiled arrogantly.

"And as a businessman, you didn't ask where the money came from?"

"Nah, didn't need to, but I assumed she got it from her boss, maybe a bonus or something. She always has money like that. Works for some rich lady who pays her way more than she should, considering she don't do shit but check emails, post on social media, and occasionally make a dinner reservation."

"What do you know about the woman she works for?"

Davis felt instantly protective of Cassidy, and the thought of ensuring she wasn't a target hadn't surfaced.

"Nothing other than she has money. Had to if she was paying Tia just to check her emails and shit like that. I never really knew much about it, though. Tia was closed off. We didn't do a lot of talking. She wasn't the sharing type or the relationship type. Said it was because her old man wasn't shit. Cheated on her mother all the time. Now that I think about it, everything about her made sense. Tia didn't do emotional shit either, which made us work even better."

"So what did the two of you do?"

"You've seen her, right? I'm sure you can figure that out."

"The nature of your relationship was strictly sexual?"

"It damn sure wasn't a meet-the-family type of deal. Not that either of us wanted that anyway. We hooked up and had fun. Did our own thing when we weren't together, and no one caught feelings."

"So you never met her boss *or* her family?"

"Nah, neither."

"She talk about her family a lot?"

"Not really. Nothing other than what I told you about her pops being a cheater, but I also didn't ask. Like I said, she wasn't the sharing kind, and I wasn't the need-to-ask kind."

"Just the deposit-money-into-her-account-without-asking-questions kind."

"It wasn't illegal."

"If she acquired the money illegally, then your handling it makes you an accessory to whatever that illegal activity is."

"Not if she didn't disclose where she got the money. No knowledge, no accountability, right? Isn't that some shit y'all say, Detective?"

"Maybe, but you already said she intended to avoid paying taxes. That's a federal offense, and you were willing to help. That is a crime, *Benji.*"

His face tensed. "Stop fucking calling me Benji. Look, I don't know why I'm here or what you want me to tell you, but if it means you forget I said that, I'll say whatever you want."

"September sixth. Can you tell me if the two of you were together on that date?"

"How the fuck am I supposed to remember that?"

"Don't care, but I suggest you try because if not . . ."

"Man . . ." Clark moved, and Davis pushed away from the wall before he held a hand up. "Phone. You already patted me down, so you know I don't have shit on me."

Davis nodded for him to continue, and Clark leaned back, removing his phone and unlocking it as he scanned the messages.

"What date was that again?"

"September sixth."

Clark smiled and massaged his chin. "Yeah, we were together. All night, actually."

"Are you sure?"

"Hell yeah, I'm sure." He slid his phone across the table. Davis walked over and picked up the device, reading the texts on the screen.

You serious, shorty?

Yeah, I'm serious. Unless you're not with it.

Nah, I'm definitely with it. Just didn't think you
meant it when you put it out there. We can do that
shit tonight if you're game.

I'll see you tonight then at my place.

Bet, what time?

Ten.

"What's this about?"

"She kept talking shit about making a movie of us. The day you're asking about was the night we did it. Wanna see it?"

"You made a sex tape with Tia?"

"Yeah, she recorded it on her phone. We fucked for hours doing a bunch of wild shit. We both passed out at like three that morning. She recorded the entire night on some freaky shit. You sure you don't want to see it," Clark taunted.

"No, I don't want to see it, but I do need you to send it to me as evidence."

"Evidence, yeah, right." Clark chuckled smugly, and Davis wanted to punch him in the face to mellow the guy's arrogance.

He wasn't opposed to porn, but Davis had no interest in watching a homemade recording of the woman who could potentially be a key factor in keeping the woman he was falling for innocent. *Had* fallen for. Tia was the key to preventing Cassidy from being convicted of a crime Davis felt sure she hadn't committed.

"What's your number? I can send it now."

Davis removed his wallet, slid out a business card, and tossed it on the table. "Send it to that email."

He watched Clark navigate through his phone, attach the video, and then send it after a few swipes and taps. Once he was done, Clark tossed his phone on the table and leaned back. "Done. Can I go now?"

Davis did a quick mental sweep of everything he thought Clark could help with, which wasn't much at this point, and one thing bothered him. Tia hadn't existed before college. If he could find out more about her family, then he could potentially find out more about *her*. Any assistance pointing in the right direction would save time.

"One more thing . . ." Davis moved to the table again, peering down at Clark. "You never met her parents, but do you know if they were close? She talk to either of them or visit on a regular basis that you know of?"

Clark quickly shook his head. "Her mom's dead, and her father's in prison. I remember she went to see him once and was in a fucked-up mood after. She got drunk as shit that night and passed out, but that's all I can tell you."

Davis offered a nod and turned to walk toward the door.

"Ay, is that it? Can I leave now?"

Davis faced Clark with a smug grin, moving back to the table and swiping the phone, which he slipped into his pocket. The last thing he needed was for Clark reaching out to Tia and tip her off. "Unfortunately, no. I can't guarantee you won't tip off your girlfriend about our little chat or anything we've discussed, so you'll be here for the next forty-eight hours. I'll make sure they take good care of you while you're my guest."

"What the fuck, man? You can't do that!"

"Actually, I can. I can keep you here to build a case against you for forty-eight hours. If I don't, I have to let you go, but by then, I'll have what I need, and you'll be free to leave—if you didn't lie to me, that is. If I find out you did know what Tia was up to and that you were a part of it, I will bury your ass, understood?"

"Man, fuck you and her. I told you I didn't murder anyone. I don't even know what you're talking about. I want a lawyer, *now*."

"Sure, but I hope you have one on retainer because, if not, there's nothing I can do for you."

"You're supposed to give me one of those court-appointed ones if I can't afford one. Ain't nobody got that kind of money."

Davis grinned and stepped toward the table. "See, that's where you're wrong. Too many TV crime shows. You only get a public defender if we charge you. As of now, I'm not. You're simply a person of interest. I'll have someone take you to our holding cell. I appreciate your cooperation, Mr. Clark."

"Fuck you."

Davis walked out, closing the door behind him to several more threats and promises that wouldn't help Clark's current predicament. If he weren't careful, he would be charged, just not with murder or accessory to the murder of Williams. Davis was sure he could come up with something.

Captain Jones met Davis just outside the door. "So, I take it we're losing him in the system for the next forty-eight hours?"

"I need time to verify what he told me. She's guilty, Captain. All I have to do is tie it all together."

"Go. I'll take care of this. You've got two days, Davis. That's it because I have a feeling the minute he walks out of here, he's going straight to her."

"Agreed." Davis removed Clark's phone from his pocket. "I need to get this upstairs to the tech guys. I have to verify his alibi, which means I need to know what towers his phone and the assistant's were pinging off of the night Williams was murdered."

"You don't have a warrant for this."

"No, but this will be off the record."

"Keep it clean, Davis," Captain warned.

"Always."

26.

"**A**re you fucking kidding me?"

He read the name on the list multiple times, and as angry as he was at the discovery, he was grateful to have a lead that would undoubtedly get them closer to finding out who actually killed Williams—the how and why would eventually follow.

"You found something."

"Yes, and it's not exactly going to help. It gives Tia an alibi, but let's start with the money."

"What about it?" Cassidy's face scrunched, and Davis pointed to the sofa. She sat, and he sat next to her.

"Clark is Tia's boyfriend. Did you know she was dating anyone?"

"Not until recently. Over the years, she's had a few men in her life, nothing serious." Davis scowled, and she immediately felt concerned.

"What's that look?"

"Nothing. Clark said the same thing. Apparently, her father was a cheater, and she didn't have much faith in men."

Cassidy recalled conversations they'd had over the years about Tia's lack of trust in men.

"Shit, so she didn't do this. What about the boyfriend?" Cassidy began to panic. She was hopeful that what they'd discovered about the money would get them closer to the murderer, but evidently, it was proving both of their theories might have been wrong.

"What I have provides an alibi for both of them. Here, let me show you something."

Davis removed his phone and began shifting through the device. Moments later, he pulled up a video he'd forwarded to his email and handed the device to Cassidy.

"Why are you showing me a sex tape?" She frowned at him, confused about what he wanted her to watch, but the stern look on his face had Cassidy conceding.

"Just take a look. You don't have to watch the entire thing."

She nodded, hit play, and the bodies began moving on the screen. She immediately noticed Tia and some man in a bedroom. The room was dark, but the video was clear, and she easily identified the woman she'd trusted with her life and personal information for the past few years.

"You watched this?"

"Some, not all. I wasn't given much of a choice. This is part of the job, Cass; you know that."

"I don't give a damn about you watching porn, Nate. I'm more concerned with how watching this will find anything that might help clear my name."

"There wasn't much. According to the boyfriend, they were there all night. She recorded the whole thing, and it went on for hours . . ."

"His phone or hers?"

"Hers. She took the original and made that." Davis motioned to the phone in Cassidy's hand. Her eyes lowered to it briefly before they narrowed, and she tapped the screen. She did it several times, feeling Davis move closer.

"What's wrong? You see something?"

Cassidy's pulse thrummed at an expedited rate and not from the sexual content on the screen. Her reaction was from something else. Something that shouldn't have been possible. She had to be imagining it.

"Look at this. Did you see this?"

"See what?"

Cassidy rewound the video and pressed play until the frame she needed was visible, then took a screenshot of the image. She rewound the video once more and hit play for Davis to watch. "Pay close attention to her wrist."

"Why? What am I looking for?"

"Just watch. You'll see exactly what I'm talking about."

She pressed play and kept her eyes on Davis while he watched the replay. When his jaw tensed at the exact moment Tia's wrist came into view, she spoke up. "You saw it, didn't you?"

"Son of a bitch."

Davis took the phone from Cassidy's hands, rewound the clip, and played it again. He fast-forwarded and then watched a few more frames, pausing at another section. He extended the phone to Cassidy, allowing her to see what he just watched.

His tone was low. "Either that's two different people, or I'm crazy."

"No, you're not crazy. I believe it's two different people, and I recognize one of them."

"You do?"

"Well, maybe not her, but I know that mark." She reached for the phone and navigated to Davis's photos, where she pulled up the screenshot of the frame she'd captured.

"It's a birthmark. A very unique one that I've only seen once in my life. It belongs to Kami Arnold."

The surprise from what she was saying slowly filtered onto Davis's face. "What the hell, Cass? Are you sure?"

"Yes, I'm sure. This birthmark belongs to Kami Arnold. But it doesn't make sense. There are frames where it's not there. And Tia doesn't have that birthmark."

"Are you sure?"

Cassidy nodded assuredly. "Yes, I'm sure. I would have noticed something as unique as that. When I spoke with Kami, she was a total mess. She didn't trust anyone, least of all me. I did everything I could to gain her trust, to make her feel comfortable. At one point, we discussed her birthmark. Even as a child, she hated it. Said kids picked on her because she was 'dirty.' I told her it was unique and beautiful, like her. The similarity of her mark to the shape of a heart was God's way of making sure she always knew she was loved."

"Cass . . ." Davis moved closer and wiped a tear from her cheek. All the emotions she had held onto for years since the trial came flooding back. Sure, Arnold was a horrible man, but he was still Kami's father, and a child rarely understood the weight of most adult situations. Cassidy had been yet another adult who'd let Kami down. "You okay?"

"I'm fine." She rounded her shoulders and refocused. "Tia didn't have that mark. That means . . ."

"Either the women are working together, or she covered it when she was around you."

"This is insane."

"Crazier things have happened. That very well could be Kami Arnold. What do you know about her life after the case?"

"Not much. A few months after sentencing, the mother committed suicide. Kami was adopted. The caseworker who was assigned Kami after what happened to the mother took a special interest in her and handled things personally. It was a private adoption, filed through the courts but not *handled* by the courts."

"Do you know who adopted her?"

"No, I thought it was best that I left it alone. I assumed things would get better for Kami. I couldn't handle finding out they didn't."

"I understand. Then that's where we start. We need to find out who adopted her."

"It was a closed adoption. That's going to take some time."

She watched Davis, seeing his thoughts spiraling before he stated, "I have an idea. It's a long shot, but with how things are playing out, I feel it will give us exactly what we need."

When he stood, she did as well. "You're leaving?"

"Yeah, I need to check something."

"Check what?"

She could sense he wasn't willing to share. "I just need a few hours. Can you trust me?"

His pleading eyes met hers, and she nodded hesitantly. "Yes."

"Good, thank you. We're close, Cass. I promise. I want this over with as much as you. Sooner rather than later, so that we can move past it."

He kissed her on the forehead and headed to the door. "Do not call or contact her until we know for sure. If she calls or contacts you, ignore it. If what I'm thinking is right, that's her. I have to get my hands on the original footage because either she covered that birthmark, or that's two different people. If that's two different people, then Tia no longer has an alibi."

"Which means she could have killed Niles."

Davis nodded harshly. "And I need you to promise not to do anything until I return. Don't go digging, and do *not* contact her."

"I won't."

Cassidy pulled up her phone as soon as Davis was gone and began pacing. She was hopeful, but if Tia was Kami Arnold, so many questions needed to be answered. For now, she was stuck at Davis's house, her mind spinning out of control with another round of guilt from how she'd ended up in this position in the first place.

27.

"This way, Detective." Davis followed the guard through the last gate into the visitation area. He had requested private access, which put him in a room alone with Arnold. He thought it was better to have a one-on-one since their visit wouldn't be conventional or very friendly. The warden agreed and granted Davis's request.

After he was inside, Davis settled into a seat and waited for the guest of honor. Not long after, two guards escorted Arnold inside. His ankles and wrists were chained and cuffed, causing him to shuffle toward the table separating him from Davis. Once he was seated and cuffed to the table, one of the guards tossed out demands about Arnold's expected behavior before nodding at Davis.

"He's all yours, Detective."

Arnold kept quiet until the guards were out of the room, and it was just the two of them. "Detective? What the hell I do to get you out here to see me? I've been keeping my nose clean."

Prison had hardened him. His head was now shaved bald, and his features were those of a man who had seen better days. There were healed scars, battle wounds that hadn't been present in the photos Davis came across of Arnold before or after the trial, likely from getting his ass handed to him while inside. Nobody liked rapists and murderers, but they especially didn't like them when their crimes victimized innocent women. A guarantee to a hard time on the inside was to make it known that you were there for harming women, children, or the elderly.

"You look like shit," Davis droned.

"I'm not sure what you expect. This isn't exactly a spa retreat."

Davis searched his face again. Arnold got antsy under his critical gaze.

"You gonna tell me why the fuck they dragged me out of my cell to come see you, or should I demand to leave?"

"Got better things to do?" Davis arched a brow, and Arnold scowled.

"Maybe. Now, what the fuck do you want?"

"Tia Murphy."

Arnold's expression mirrored confusion, as if the name didn't register, and Davis added, "She visited you a few months ago. She's the only person who's visited you in years."

A flicker of recognition flashed in Arnold's eyes. "Yeah, what about her?"

"You know who she is?"

"I've been here too damn long, Detective. She's the only visitor I've ever had. Of course, I know who she is. Just didn't remember her name."

"Because it's not the one you and your wife gave her?"

Arnold stared at Davis. Neither spoke for a long moment, and Davis was the first to break the silence.

"Why did your daughter come to visit you? After all this time, you've had no contact. Why now?"

He scoffed his annoyance. "You'd have to ask her. I never denied the girl, even when I should have. She's always had access. She's my kid. Guess there wasn't much appeal about visiting your old man in prison when he's been accused of killing and raping women."

"*Convicted.* You were found guilty."

Arnold smiled. "Seems that way, doesn't it."

Davis felt his anger rising. The smug bastard wasn't in the least bit accepting of the things he'd done. What he'd learned of the man reading articles from throughout the trial was that he always maintained his innocence. He insisted the sex had been consensual, and not once had he murdered any of the women he slept with. Since his conviction, he'd stuck to that same story. Occasionally, he'd been quoted in articles and interviews stating how the women wanted everything he gave them. He bragged about sleeping with the women, and it occasionally getting a little rough, but that it had always been a willing exchange on both sides. Never rape.

"I don't give a shit about any of that and damn sure don't give a damn about you admitting to crimes I'm certain you committed . . ."

"Then what do you give a damn about, Detective? My baby girl? You here to ask for her hand in marriage, to see if I care whether you have your way with her? She's grown up quite nicely. I can see why you might want a piece of her. Hell, if she wasn't my kid, *I* would want a piece of her."

The insinuation made Davis feel sick to his stomach. Arnold was more or less admitting to considering a sexual encounter with his own child. However, coming from a man as morally corrupt as Arnold was known to be, Davis shouldn't have been surprised, but he was still appalled.

Sick son of a bitch.

"I want to know why she was here. What did she say to you?"

"What's it worth to you?"

Davis flooded with rage and leaned across the table. "You should be asking what cooperating with me is worth to *you*, asshole."

Arnold smiled again, seemingly unbothered. "I'm in hell, Detective." Arnold's eyes traveled around their room before landing on Davis again. "Have been since the day they put me in this cage of death. What the fuck can you do for me that can change my current position? Your threats don't mean a gotdamn thing."

"This place might be hell, but you haven't felt the type of hell I can bring into your life with a few promises to some of the people in here with you. If you don't cooperate, I'm sure they will. From what I hear, they already don't like you very much around here. Can't imagine that would get any better if they got a green light to make your hell more of a gotdamn nightmare than you're already living. Now, what did she say?"

He watched Arnold consider what he said, and eventually, he caved. "I got enough enemies in here as it is. Not looking to gain more. You want to know what the crazy bitch said? Fine, I'll tell you."

Davis expanded his chest and leaned back, waiting.

"For the first ten minutes, she just stared at me like a gotdamn lunatic. Wouldn't talk, just sat there, staring. By the third time I yelled at her to open her mouth, she told me how she really felt about me. Not that I was surprised. That girl loved her mother. Never really gave a shit about me."

"That happens when you beat on a woman and yell at her child," Davis growled.

Arnold laughed bitterly. "You don't know about me."

"I know enough. What did she say?"

"Said I ruined her life. That she lost her mother because of me. That not being able to keep my dick in my pants was the beginning of the end. I told her she didn't know shit. She was a kid. Couldn't begin to understand what went on between her mother and me. She yelled some shit about me being a fucking cheat and a liar. That all men were cheaters and not worthy of being loved by women. I told her that her mother was a weak disappointment who didn't know shit about pleasing a man. Told her to make sure she did, or she'd end up just like the bitch. Broken, useless, swallowing a bottle of pills, and slitting her own wrists like my sorry-ass wife."

Davis was floored. It took everything in him not to lunge across the table and smash the guy's face into it. How could any man, any father, say such horrible things to their own kid? If Tia was as messed up as Davis believed her to be, Arnold had played a significant role in why she was. It didn't have a damn thing to do with Cassidy.

"You really are a sick son of a bitch. You deserve exactly what you got."

"So did Kami and her mother."

Davis felt his fists curl into a ball but needed to get whatever else he could from Arnold first. "What else did she say?"

"That's about all. Just wanted me to know what a piece of shit I was. How I ruined her life, and that I was the reason she lost her mother. I don't see what the fuck she's complaining about. They told me she was adopted. Came here not long after her mother killed herself and forced me to sign over my parental rights. With them fancy-ass clothes she wore in here, it looks like she got the better deal. From what I can tell, she did good for herself."

"And you did it?"

"Did what?"

"Signed over your parental rights?"

"Why the fuck wouldn't I? The day I landed here, nothing out there mattered anymore. Not her or her mother. No one else but me. I had to worry about myself . . . deciding how to stay alive because the people in here believed all the shit they heard about me and weren't going to make my stay any easier."

"Good, because everything they've heard is true, and you need to pay for your sins every minute of every day while you're still breathing."

Arnold smiled. "You sound just like that crazy-ass daughter of mine. She said the same thing. They brainwashed her just like they brainwashed that gotdamn jury."

Davis pushed away from the table and stared down at Arnold. "They got it right this last time. You're where you need to be. You're gonna die in here. Sooner rather than later, I hope. Maybe I'll see what I can do to expedite the matter."

After a hard stare, Davis turned to walk away. Arnold spoke up once he got to the door and knocked so the guards could let him out.

"You never told me why you were here, Detective. Why are you asking questions about my girl? She finally make good on that promise?"

Davis frowned, turning to face Arnold again. "What promise?"

"That the bitch who lied to her would get what was coming to her too. Seems the apple doesn't fall too far from the tree."

"Who was she referring to?"

"That shrink lady she talked to. She testified that Kami lied, and it pissed her off. Apparently, the woman promised to make sure everything worked out like it should have. Kami believed her. So did my wife because right before she slit her wrists, she told my girl that she was to blame for me being in here and the reason why she downed that bottle of pills. Said Kami let her down and tore our family apart. One thing I can say about my wife is that she was a sorry excuse of a woman, but she loved me more than anything. Would do anything I told her to. Even killed her damn self because I made sure she knew she didn't deserve to live if I was in here."

His smile was devious. Davis turned and left the room, knowing that with a family like the one she had been given, Tia was cursed from the day she took her first breath.

As soon as he was in the car, he dialed the precinct.

"Jones."

"I need a bolo out on Tia Murphy. I'll send over her picture, and I need you to send uniforms to sit on my house."

"What's going on, Davis?"

"I'm pretty sure Tia Murphy is the one who killed Cass's husband."

"Pretty sure isn't good enough. You're gonna have to do better than that if I make that call, and why the hell do you need officers to sit on your house?"

"Cassidy's there."

"What the . . . You know what? Never mind. I'll take care of it, and you better be sure about this because if I pull the resources, we cannot keep this quiet. Someone's getting arrested before the night's up."

"I know. Send a couple of uniforms over to Murphy's house as well. I'm about to pick her up, but I can't be sure I can take her quietly. If she was the one who killed Williams—"

"Got it. Send the address. I'll make sure our guys meet you there. But what makes you so sure it's her?"

"She's Arnold's daughter. I went to see him, and he confirmed it. He also mentioned she was holding a grudge against not just him but Cassidy as well for tearing up her family."

"Cass? Why the fuck would she hold anything against Cassidy and not Trent, or hell, even the prosecution?"

"Long story, which I don't have time to explain right now. You'll just have to trust me."

"You get *one*, Davis. You better damn sure make good use of it, or you won't get another."

"I'm sure."

As soon as he pulled up to Tia's townhouse, Davis removed his radio from the charger inside his vehicle, got out, and rounded to the rear to get his vest. Once he had the radio affixed, he walked to the cruiser sitting on the Tia's place, and both uniforms stepped out of the vehicle. Davis greeted them both with a nod and got to business.

"One of you move to the back, one at the side of the building. I'm heading inside. What frequency you on?"

"Two," the officer closest to him answered. Davis adjusted his radio, and both the uniforms were en route to their designated areas.

Davis unholstered his gun, removed the safety, and looked around before cautiously going to Tia's door. There was one window with closed blinds, and he didn't notice anyone peeking through them, so he pressed one shoulder into the door, his fist landing hard against it.

"Tia Murphy. Detective Davis, APD. I'm coming in."

He waited, and there was nothing, so he banged again as an added precaution. "Tia, if you're in there, this is my last warning. I'm coming in."

When there still wasn't a response, Davis moved in one fluid motion from the side of the door, lifted his foot, and allowed it to land against the wooden surface just beside the doorknob and the lock. One solid kick was enough force to get him inside, where he quickly scanned the place.

The space was damn near spotless, with nothing out of the ordinary aside from the two rolling suitcases a few feet away from the door. A purse sat on top of one with a passport tucked in the side pocket.

Looks like I'm just in time.

Davis didn't have a chance to get his hands on it because Tia appeared in the hallway. "I guess I should have decided on that earlier flight."

Her voice held a smugness that had Davis's finger easing back on the trigger as he aimed the gun at her head. When she continued advancing on him, he made it clear that wasn't a good idea.

"Stop right there. Hands up where I can see them, or this ends badly, Tia."

She paused and lifted her hands but smiled arrogantly. "You gonna shoot me, Detective? Without cause?"

"With everything I now know about you, I'm considering it, and I have a feeling my captain would back me if I did."

With his gun still aimed at her head, he used his free hand to remove his cuffs. Once they were detached, he moved slowly toward Tia, never lowering his gun until he grabbed her wrist, yanking it behind her back and spinning her in the process. He holstered his gun and repeated the motion until both arms were locked behind her back.

"Tia Murphy, you're under the arrest for the murder of the victim identified as Jerrod Williams. You have the right to remain silent. Anything you say can and will be used against you in a court of law. You have the right to speak to an attorney and to have an attorney present during any questioning. If you cannot afford a lawyer, one will be provided for you at government expense."

"You sure that's the name you want to use, Detective. Don't want to risk throwing the case away on a technicality."

"It's the name you legally changed yours to. I'm more than covered."

She shrugged lightly as Davis spoke through his radio. "Suspect apprehended. I'm coming out."

"Ten-four, Detective."

He jerked Tia toward the door and motioned to the suitcases. "Cass didn't mention you were leaving. Considering you killed her husband and tried to frame her for it, the least you could have done is said goodbye."

"Who said I did any of that?"

"The evidence. Now, let's go. You and I need to have a nice long talk."

"I have nothing to say to you, Detective. If you want answers, you can have them, but there's only one person I'm giving them to. As sexy as you are, it won't be you."

He knew the answer before he asked but decided to inquire anyway.

"And who would you like to talk to?"

She smiled, angling her head to the side. "I'm sure you know the answer to that."

"Unfortunately, I do. Let's go."

He jerked her arm and shoved her forward, grabbing the purse from atop the suitcases as they left the apartment.

28.

"What are you doing here?"

Harper stared at Cassidy with a dry yet accusatory expression in place. "I should be asking you that question. Last I checked, this was Davis's place."

Cassidy placed her hands on her hips and scowled at Harper. "It is, and he's not here, so you can leave and drop by another time when he's home."

"Would, but I can't. Not here for him. I'm here for *you*."

"Me? Why? And how did you know I was here?"

"I know where you are because your boyfriend told Captain this is where you were, and Captain asked me to retrieve you."

"I don't have a boyfriend. I'm married."

"*Widowed*. And does the marriage even count since you have no idea who the guy really was?" Harper mumbled and pushed past Cassidy, entering Davis's house. She closed her eyes briefly, hating how easily she still made that mistake of claiming her old life.

Married.

After closing the door, she turned to find Harper examining things the same as she had done the first time she had been invited into Davis's home, only she had been invited. Harper hadn't.

"You can have a seat while you explain why you're here."

He glanced her way before doing as she asked and sat on the sofa after unbuttoning his sports coat. "I just told you why. I'm here on Captain's orders."

She moved closer, folding her arms over her chest as she peered down at Harper. "I know he sent you here, but you still haven't explained why, and don't you dare say because Nate asked him to. That part I get as well."

"Nate." Harper chuckled bitterly. "Your boyfriend decided to finally stop wasting the taxpayers' money and do his damn job. He's en route to get a suspect. Whoever that suspect is, he felt as if they might end up here looking for you. Not sure how unless you guys are really being that careless with whatever this is. I'm guessing Captain is still trying to cover his ass. If he sent uniforms, it would go on record."

"A suspect?"

"You and the boyfriend keeping secrets from each other already? Figure you would have been the first to know."

"What is your problem with Nate, Harper? Or is it not about him, and instead, you have a problem with me or us? I'm over this indignant, condescending streak you've been on lately."

"My problem is that I was accused of compromising a case for taking you to a crime scene to do what you've done a million times before—what you're trained to do. Davis is everyone's hero when he's crossed so many damn lines compromising this same case by getting involved with the main and only suspect. If that's not enough reason for me to have a problem with the two of you, then I don't know what to tell you."

"I think it's more than that. You don't have a problem with us. You have a problem with *him*. It doesn't take much to see that you're annoyed that he hasn't fallen under your watch and gotten in line . . ."

Harper stood. "You're damn right I'm annoyed. He's an arrogant son of a bitch who doesn't give a damn about the chain of command."

"With you, you mean. From what I've seen, he respects Jones."

"*I'm* the senior detective. That's *my* house. *I* built it."

"That's Jones's house. He built that precinct. He's your boss, and you're not Davis's. If you want respect, try giving it instead of expecting everyone that walks in there to fall at your feet and kiss your ass, Harper. You want it—earn it. I'm sure Nate will be more than willing to show you respect if you show the same in return."

"Doubtful, and for the record, it's not just me he doesn't respect. Did you know he barged into Trent's office asking questions about your old case? About your relationship with him?"

"Yes, I know."

It was a lie, but she wouldn't address that with Harper. She and Davis had discussed Trent. How he knew of their past was no longer relevant in her eyes.

"Right. I'm sure that came up during those cozy moments while you shared a bed with him."

"I'm an adult, and so is he. What we do in our private time is no concern of yours or anyone else's. The sooner you understand that the better off we'll all be. We've been friends for a long time, Greg. I hope that means something to you. If not, fine, but our friendship—past or present—in no way gives you the right to be judgmental about my choices, understood?" She stepped closer to make her point, and Harper nodded.

"Got it."

Before Cassidy could respond, Harper lifted his phone, rattling off a greeting. "Harper. Yeah, Captain. I'm with her now." Cassidy kept her eyes on him while she listened. "No, all good here. Sure, I can do that. We're on our way now."

After he ended the call, Cassidy arched a brow, requesting details since she had been the topic of discussion.

"Suspect is secured. They want you down at the precinct."

Her heart was racing.

"Who's the suspect?"

"Not for me to say. Not my case, and you're not my business. Let's go. Captain or Davis can tell you if they want you to know."

She knew further questioning Harper wouldn't gain her more details than she already had. Instead, she gathered her purse, phone, and keys and locked up Davis's house with the spare key he'd left before joining Harper in the car. At this point, Harper's thoughts and opinions were no longer a priority. She had to think about what she would find once they reached the precinct.

⚜

"Captain?" Cassidy met him outside the interrogation room. She glanced at the one-way mirror and then stepped closer, not believing what she was witnessing on the other side.

Tia was cuffed and sitting at the table with Davis propped on the edge, one foot resting on the floor, both hands resting on his thighs. His back was to the mirror, but Tia faced it. Cassidy's eyes lowered to Tia's wrist, which was turned slightly upward, just enough for her to catch a glimpse of the birthmark there.

It's really her.

"Is she the suspect? Is that why I'm here? *She's* the one that murdered Niles?"

"Don't have our smoking gun yet, but from what we just uncovered, I have a good feeling that's our woman."

Cassidy cringed. "What did you uncover?"

"That's Arnold's daughter, but I guess you already know that."

She nodded. "Assumed but didn't know for sure."

"We do now."

"How?"

"The boyfriend mentioned that Tia's father was in prison and that she visited him there."

"The boyfriend?" Cassidy stated mindlessly, still trying to process what was happening.

"Benjamin Clark. Davis brought him in for questioning. We've still got him on a forty-eight-hour hold. Needed to make sure he didn't tip her off." He motioned to the interrogation room, and Cassidy's eyes followed, only rounding back to him when he continued. "Davis pulled visitor logs for Arnold, and guess who was on there."

"Tia."

Captain nodded. "Davis went to see him several hours ago, and Arnold had a lot to say about his daughter wanting revenge . . ." His eyes narrowed, landing hard on Cassidy. "With you. Not the prosecutors or Trent. She's placing all the blame on you, Cass. I assume that means the rumors are true."

"What rumors, Captain?"

"Come on, Cass. Do me the honor of at least respecting our history. People talk. You already know that. I'm asking you. Should I be worried about backlash from the Arnold case?"

"I didn't do anything wrong."

"Then why does that woman in there hate you so much that she potentially killed your husband and tried to frame you for it?"

Cassidy glanced at the mirror. "I made her a promise that I didn't keep. Sometimes, it's the little things that break people. You never know at the time, but when it all falls down, the small details are the only ones that matter."

"Cass, I need to know what we're dealing with. If something that might hurt this department—hell, the city for that matter—will come out, then tell me now. I don't want to be blindsided."

"There's nothing you should be worried about, Captain. I give you my word. The worst of what I did was have an inappropriate relationship with my superior. That's all. I never lied about the details of the case. I wouldn't have done that."

"Then what promise did you make and not keep?"

"That her voice mattered and that everything would be okay." Cassidy's eyes left him and landed on the one-way mirror. "She lost her father and her mother within weeks of each other. Her entire family was torn apart, and she was left alone."

Something I can relate to.

"Because the psycho bastard raped and murdered innocent women."

"As true as that may be, as a child, all she ever knew was that she lost her parents and somehow decided to blame me. She fixated on it. Even if I don't understand how or why, I know what that's like. I know how the mind works. How it tricks us into believing things make sense when they really don't. In her reality, she lost her parents because of me, and her mind has allowed her to believe that all these years."

"Well, truth or not, we still have to prove that she was the one who actually pulled the trigger. The guys upstairs are digging through her cloud storage, searching for the original video to kill her alibi, but it will help to get a confession."

"Which isn't happening without your help." Davis's voice had both Cassidy and Captain Jones looking in his direction.

"What's that supposed to mean?"

"She refuses to talk. To me, at least. Said if I want to know all the details, then I had to get Cassidy in the room. She'll only talk to her."

"Not happening," Captain drilled out.

Cassidy's eyes were on him in a matter of seconds. "Why not? I know how to handle myself in there."

"Given the nature of things, I'm not so sure you can—"

"Please let me go in there. You want a confession, I can get one."

"And then she gets a lawyer who gets the confession thrown out because of your history. The only way you go in the box with her is with the DA present to ensure it's all on the up and up."

Davis finally spoke up. "Then get her here."

Captain Jones looked between them before he shook his head in defeat, knowing he wouldn't win the argument with them teamed up. "Fine, but don't you dare enter that room until DA Greene arrives. In fact, head to my office now so that I can keep an eye on you."

Cassidy nodded and delivered a tight smile to Davis before following Jones. While he initiated the call with the Greene, Davis stopped Cassidy outside of the captain's door.

"You sure you want to do this?"

"I feel like I need to. Especially if I'm the only way she'll confess. I need my life back."

Davis moved closer, placing a hand at her hip. Cassidy looked down where they were connected, then lifted her eyes, looking around before he gripped her chin and brought her eyes to his. "Hey, it doesn't matter."

"It does."

"Not to me, so if you haven't changed your mind, let them see. I don't care."

She smiled and leaned into his touch. "Neither do I."

She should, but at this point, what she felt for Davis felt right. And not in the way it had with Niles. With him, it was a connection of need. She wanted something or someone, and he checked all the boxes. Davis was the complete opposite. He was everything she shouldn't have wanted, but she felt more alive than she had in years or ever, honestly.

"You sure about this. If you go in there, you'll be completely exposed with everything."

The case. Tia might bring things up that could have people second-guessing my character.

"Maybe it's time for that. If people want to judge, then let them. I need this to end so I can move forward with my life."

"With me?" His eyes lowered to hers while he silently waited. When she nodded her confirmation, he leaned in and brushed his lips against hers. "Good, because I want that too."

The clearing of a throat had Davis and Cassidy turning to find Captain Jones staring awkwardly at the two of them.

"Greene's on her way." He pointed at Cassidy. "You in here with me until she gets here."

Davis grinned and kissed her on the cheek. "Go ahead. I have a few things I need to take care of while we wait."

She smiled, lowering her eyes briefly, then watching him walk away, knowing that regardless of how things ended, he had given her something she hadn't felt since she'd lost Clara.

The opportunity to be accepted and loved without judgment.

⊷———❧———⊶

"This is risky." DA Greene glanced at Cassidy, Davis, and Captain Jones before she swung her eyes toward the one-way mirror.

"You want a confession that will hold up for a solid conviction, then she needs to go in there." Cassidy's eyes shot up to Davis when he stepped forward to make his point.

"I was under the impression that you were good at your job, Detective. Why can't you go in there to do the same thing instead of relying on her to do your job for you?"

DA Greene arched a brow in Davis's direction, and Cassidy naturally assumed his reaction would be typical of what she'd seen when someone challenged him about his capabilities. She was shocked when he glanced over his shoulder at her and then smiled at Greene.

"This needs to be her show. It's what she wants . . ." He tossed his chin toward the interrogation room, then reached back, took hold of Cassidy's hand, and pulled her to his side. "And it's what Cass needs."

Cassidy heard Jones mumble something under his breath, and apparently, Davis did as well because he squeezed her hand. Her cheeks flamed with heat as she looked up to find Greene staring right at her.

"Should I be concerned about whatever *this* is?" Her tone was professional and sharp as her eyes bounced between Cassidy and Davis.

"Not unless you simply have a thing for minding people's personal business—"

"Davis . . ." Captain warned.

"Cass and I haven't crossed any lines that could compromise this case."

"I damn sure hope not. Whatever you two have going on better not find its way into what's happening in there, understood?" Greene glanced at Davis, but her words were for Cassidy, so she nodded stiffly.

"Understood."

"From my understanding, you know how this works. Don't get in there and forget the rules. If she says anything that sets you off and you can't keep your shit together, you're out of there. If I feel like things are getting out of control, I will step in and end this. A confession would be great, but we have enough evidence to get a conviction."

Cassidy glanced at Davis, who turned to face her. "We have the original video from the night of the murder. It's what we were thinking. There was another young woman there that night. For most of the recording, it wasn't Tia on that video. The boyfriend was evidently so high that he didn't notice or care. We caught them taking pills on camera just before they got started in the bedroom."

"Are you charging him too?"

"We might. If he truly knew what she was up to that night, it would make him an accessory," Greene answered instead of Davis.

"Now, are we doing this or not?" Cassidy glanced at Davis, who stepped closer and spoke quietly.

"It's up to you, Cass." His hand cuffed the side of her face, and she leaned into his touch and nodded.

"I need this."

"All right then, let's go. Let her do most of the talking." Greene motioned to the one-way, and Cassidy inhaled a deep breath, releasing it slowly before she walked away from the group and stepped to the door. Moments later, she was inside, facing her past.

"I didn't think you'd be bold enough to come in here." Tia smiled, and Cassidy kept her emotions schooled as she took the seat across from her, bracing herself for what she would find out and fully prepared to get this over with.

29.

"Where would you like to start?" Cassidy kept her eyes on Tia, waiting. She didn't have to wait for long.

"With your husband ..."

Tia's eyes were devious and taunting when they met with Cassidy's.

"What about Niles?"

"Niles?" Tia laughed amusedly. "That's not his name. Neither is Jerrod, but you know that, don't you, Cass? What you don't know is who he *really* is."

"I'm assuming you do?" Cassidy tensed at the reality of discovering a little more about the man she obviously had no clue about.

"I know who he is. He and I spent quite a bit of time getting cozy."

"So this whole thing was the two of you working together?"

"No. I knew nothing about the guy before I started working for you. Once you hired me, he and I got to know each other *very well*. If I wasn't convinced that all men were full of shit and not worth the trouble beyond providing orgasms, I would have considered keeping him around for a while."

"Keeping him around?" Cassidy questioned calmly when she felt her insides raging.

"Not there yet, Cass. This is *my* show, *not* yours."

Still playing games.

"So, you are admitting that you were having an affair with my husband?"

"Husband?" Tia laughed lightly. "He wasn't much of a husband, now, was he? The guy had been fucking other women from the start of your marriage. You do realize he only married you for one reason?"

She hadn't in the beginning, but she did now.

"And you were one of those women?"

"Yes, but I mean, can you blame me? He was too damn sexy to pass on, and damn, he really knew how to fuck. But I don't have to tell you that, right?" Tia winked at Cassidy, attempting to taunt her more.

Cassidy's face flamed with the awareness that she and Tia weren't alone. Others were watching, but she couldn't allow herself to get sidetracked. There was an intended goal, and she fully intended to reach the finish line. She wanted the confession.

And you're going to give it to me.

"How long were you sleeping with him?"

"A little over a year."

"And you didn't know him before you began working with me?"

"Fucking your husband was an added bonus. It had nothing to do with my original plan, but it did sweeten the deal. Kept me around a little longer than I intended to stay."

"And what was that plan?"

"You owed me. I decided to cash in." Tia smiled, and Cassidy noticed how her confidence shifted.

"Cashing in by killing Niles and framing me for it?"

"No. Actually, that wasn't the plan, and still not there yet. Follow my lead, or we're done here."

Cassidy nodded tightly but felt her patience quickly waning. She wasn't sure how long she could keep this up.

"Your show. Please, proceed."

"Your fraud-ass husband wasn't important to me until I realized his importance to *you*. It's a shame you never really meant as much to him until it was too late. All he originally wanted was your money. The guy wasn't shit, truthfully, and I almost felt sorry for you. *Almost*."

"I'm assuming that he admitted to marrying me for money." Cassidy tensed, almost holding her breath as she waited.

"You and about ten other women. Well, that's a bit of a lie. He never married any of the ones before you. Not sure why you got a ring and they didn't, but I guess maybe you did mean something to him in a twisted sort of way. He fessed up about the others after I found out who he really was. Dexter Calvin Taylor. Thirty-eight. Born and raised in Austin, Texas, where he married his high school sweetheart, Dana Taylor, then woke up one day and decided he was done with her and tired of being Dexter. Can't say I blame him. Who the fuck wants to be named Dexter?" Tia smirked before continuing. "He completely walked away. Just disappeared. I didn't believe him until I did a little digging. He got cocky about it too. That's how I found out about the other women. He'd meet them, fuck them really good, steal their money, and disappear. I'm still amazed that he could do that so many times without getting caught. But I suppose he had a type." Tia glanced at Cassidy, sending a silent message. "You do realize that's why he never wanted kids with you. Children complicate things. Makes it a little bit harder to make a clean break."

Cassidy cringed at the reminder that Niles never did want children. He had been adamant about making sure they didn't.

"The guy was pretty damn smart. I have to give him that."

"When?" Cassidy's jaw clenched.

"When did it start?"

"Yes."

"Eight years ago is as far back as I know, but I'm sure it's longer. Eight years ago is when he became Jerrod Williams."

"He told you this?"

"Not at first. I found out right after I started sleeping with him. That's when he tried to convince me that I needed to leave you alone. Take the money and go. I guess it wasn't a good idea to have two cons working the same hustle."

"He offered you money?"

"Yes, the money he was stealing from you. He had an entire life you didn't know about. He could have easily paid me off; you would have never known. There was a little over half a million in one of his accounts. Part of that he stole from you. I assume you know about that by now?"

"I do." It was a struggle to remain calm, but Cassidy managed, which wasn't what Tia wanted. "Did you help him steal that money from me?"

Cassidy still hadn't figured out how he'd gotten access to the money. Someone had to help. She felt it could have been Tia after everything she just confessed.

"No, but like I said, he was smart and had plenty of other women he was dealing with. It wouldn't take much to transfer your calls to another phone. He knew we were out of town. He knew what time you were scheduled to speak and also knew you kept your phone with you. I'm sure he had it all planned out."

"So, when I asked about the dates, you knew why?"

"Assumed, yes."

"I guess I should be surprised, but I'm not," Cassidy said calmly.

"Come on, Cass. You have to give me more than that. You're a little too composed," Tia taunted. "I just told you I was fucking your husband, who married you intending to clear out your bank accounts and then disappearing like he had done to his *wife* and multiple other women without a second thought. That's got to be worth something."

Cassidy could tell that Tia's goal was to hurt her, and it was upsetting that Cassidy was taking this all in stride.

"Why would I react? Niles obviously played me, lied to me, stole from me, cheated on me, but he got what he deserved, didn't he? You killed him. No reason for me to react—"

Tia's eyes flickered with amusement. "Who says I killed him?"

Cassidy's smile mirrored Tia's but for a completely different reason. "Not *who*. More like *what* proves you killed him? The evidence is pretty convincing."

"There is no evidence, and even if there was, I have an alibi."

"Do you?"

Tia nodded. "Yes, I do. I can show you if you want. Ask them to get my phone. We have an audience, right?" Tia smiled and waved at the one-way, but Cassidy kept her eyes straight ahead so they were waiting when she had Tia's again.

"They've already seen the video."

"Then you know I couldn't have killed him."

"If you had been more careful, then possibly, but they've seen both—the one you made and the original recording. I know you weren't the only female performing on that video. You missed a few things. Criminals often get too confident. Your father was pretty damn confident, wasn't he, Tia?"

Cassidy's eyes lowered to the birthmark on Tia's wrist. When she realized what Cassidy was doing, she pulled her arms back and pushed them under the table. She watched Tia's expression falter briefly. It was only a second or two that Cassidy would have missed had she blinked at that exact moment.

"One small detail. One you didn't think about. You went through all that trouble for nothing."

"Took you long enough to get here."

"A lot has changed," Cassidy said calmly.

"Yeah, I suppose it has. At first, I was offended that you didn't recognize me, but then again, why would you? I was just a kid and a minor hiccup in your pursuit to lock up my father and throw away the key. Get a promotion, a career, fame, and a bank account to match. Fuck who you destroy in the process."

"Is that what this is about? Your father? My money?"

Tia smiled widely. "I don't give a damn about my father. He should have gotten the death penalty, and even that wouldn't be enough. I guess I should at least thank you for making sure he's never getting out of there. As much as I hate how you used me to make that happen, I'm glad the world knows the man he truly is, a rapist and murderer."

"And what about your mother?" Cassidy kept her eyes on Tia, whose eyes narrowed into thin slits.

"She made her choice. She could have lived a happy life without him, but she was too much of a coward."

"So then, it was all about money? I can't believe that you killed for money. You could have asked. I would have given it to you."

Tia smirked but remained silent. By this time, Cassidy was over it and decided she wouldn't get the answers she needed. Tia's only intention had been to throw the fact that her husband was a liar and a cheat in her face. Things Cassidy already knew about him. The information wasn't needed or wouldn't change anything, so she pushed back from the table and stood.

"Giving up so soon?"

"You're wasting my time. There's nothing you can tell me that I don't already know. *Unless* you want to fess up about why you killed Niles other than to frame me for it."

Tia laughed, shaking her head. "You were right about one thing."

"Which is?"

"I fabricated an alibi, but not to kill Niles. It was so that I wouldn't become a suspect when *he* killed *you*."

"When he . . ." Cassidy's words fumbled before she managed to get her thought out. "Niles planned to kill me?" Cassidy rushed the words out in disbelief. Of all the blows she'd taken since the day Niles had been shot, this had to be the hardest to accept. It wasn't enough to pretend to be someone he wasn't, to fake being in love, but he'd also planned on taking her life. How? And why was he the one who ended up on the wrong end of a gun if she had been the target?

"Sure did. Or at least, that was the plan. Something changed the night he was supposed to do it. I don't know what. He never told me, or maybe I didn't give him a chance to. I called to make sure things were set up. It was around eight or nine. He started rambling about not going through with it."

Cassidy swallowed thickly, remembering the call that came through. Right after they had sex, Niles insisted he had to leave to follow up on a lead on one of his missing person cases.

"And?"

"He asked me to meet him at his apartment. I knew something was off."

"But you went anyway."

"I did. Already had the alibi in place, and Ben was too fucking wasted to notice, or he didn't care that I wasn't the one in bed with him that night. I slipped out to meet Niles. We got there around the same time because as I passed the garage just as he was pulling in, guess who was behind him."

Me.

Tia smiled.

"I called him again. Asked where he was. He confirmed he'd just got there. I parked on the street because I knew about the cameras in the garage. When I made it to his apartment, he was acting crazy. Talking about how he couldn't do it. He wanted to figure things out with you but couldn't if I stayed around."

"So, how did you end up with *my* gun?"

"He brought it with him. I really don't think he ever planned on going through with killing you. He showed up that night to get rid of me. Permanently if I refused to take the money. He had a new plan. Stay married to you and have his happily ever after. I wasn't feeling it, so I also decided on a new plan. When he asked me if I would agree to take the money and go, I said yes. He walked into the bedroom, left the gun on the table, so I picked it up and shot him."

"Why shoot him? Why not just take the money?"

"Are you *really* asking me that? The man showed up with a gun, silencer affixed, to talk me into taking money as a payoff not to tell you who he really was. Too many loose ends. For all I knew, he left that gun there to make me feel comfortable while he got another from the bedroom to shoot me with. It was me or him. I chose me. I'm sure you can understand that."

"But he didn't have another gun?"

"No, he didn't. He had twenty grand, which he planned on giving me as a sign of good faith that he would pay me the rest of the money if I let this go." She shrugged.

That explains the twenty grand she gave Clark to deposit into her account.

"And then what?"

"At the time, I had no idea. If you hadn't followed him that night, then I never would have needed to frame you for killing him. So, technically, that was your fault."

Cassidy laughed, shaking her head. "It's *my* fault you killed *my* husband and tried to frame *me* for it."

"I didn't want you to die or be framed for murder. All I wanted was what you owed. How much have you made over the years because you lied to me? New York Times bestseller, speaking engagements, interviews. I deserved some of that—all of it, really."

"And you're not getting any of it. The only thing you're walking away with is permanent residency in a cell where you'll be stuck for a very long time. Like father like daughter, I suppose."

"You sound so sure, but I would be inclined to disagree."

"You just confessed *everything*. Why on earth would you believe you can walk away from this?"

Tia leaned back, smiling assuredly. "I confessed to you. I've learned a few things from being around you, Cass. Everything I said here to you is off the record. Not admissible in court. None of what I said in here matters."

"That's where you're wrong. It does matter."

Cassidy and Tia both turned their focus to the door when DA Greene stepped into the room. Cassidy understood what was happening, but Tia did not. There was no way in hell she would walk away from this. The confession she'd just given wouldn't be admissible, but the DA had everything she needed to get a conviction.

"Who are you?"

"District Attorney Greene. I'll be the one bringing charges against you. The burning question is … What those charges will be."

"Definitely won't be murder," Tia said confidently.

Greene smiled casually and approached the table, placing a legal pad and pen in front of Tia.

"What's this?"

"Where you're going to write your confession."

"Why would I do that?"

"Because although confessing to Cassidy won't make it to court, premeditated murder will."

"Premeditated means planned. I never *planned* to kill anyone. I'm sure you heard everything I said and know my decision was more of a reaction to my circumstances."

"Possibly, but what I will present is that you *planned* to kill him, which is why you orchestrated an entire production under the guise of creating an alibi, met him at his apartment, and shot him. You then proceeded to plant evidence that would convince the police into thinking that Cassidy was the one who shot her husband."

"I never did that."

"You did, Ms. Murphy. You were the one who made sure her gun ended up in our custody. Only you hadn't planned on your print being what we found when we had it."

Tia's eyes nervously moved from Cassidy back to DA Greene. "That's not what happened."

"Says who? Because that's how I'll be presenting the case against you. You're more than welcome to try your luck in front of a jury, but that might not be the smartest decision. You purposely sought out Cassidy with predatory intentions, had an affair with Niles, and plotted to steal her money because you felt she owed you something. When that didn't work out as planned, you murdered her husband. I'm pretty sure I can convince a jury of your peers to convict you without breaking a sweat. You can take your chances, or you can take the deal I'm offering you."

Tia didn't speak until Greene made sure she understood she meant business. "I'm going to take your silence to mean you're declining my offer." Before she could take her first step, Tia spoke up. "What's the deal?"

"Man one. Ten years. Eight if you can keep your nose clean while you're in there. That's the best you'll get, but at least you'll have a chance to salvage some of what's left of your life."

"That's the best you can do?"

"I can take the offer off the table and just go with what you deserve. First-degree murder, which means you'll die in prison. Decide now."

Cassidy didn't bother waiting for her response. She walked out of the interrogation room feeling confident that she had her life back, which meant she could finally breathe.

30.

The first thought that came to mind after ending the call with the district attorney was a sense of calm. So much had changed in such a short time.

Cassidy closed her eyes and exhaled a slow, shaky breath after receiving the update that had been promised once the case was officially closed. Tia Murphy had been sentenced to ten years for manslaughter one.

It's finally over.

She looked around the bedroom she'd been sharing with Davis since the day Tia confessed. After everything she'd learned, she couldn't bring herself to spend another night in the house she shared with Niles.

Jerrod Williams.

Dexter Taylor.

After their own research, Cassidy and Davis confirmed everything that Tia revealed. Niles had a wife he'd walked away from and several other women who knew him by various aliases. Thanks to Cassidy, the ones she could locate now had closure. They hadn't gotten back what Niles had stolen from them, but they got a sense of justice knowing that he paid for his indiscretions.

With his life.

When Cassidy mentioned to Davis that she wanted to sell her house because she couldn't fathom living there any longer, he offered up his as a temporary solution while she put hers on the market. She almost declined, but he had been very convincing. Now, here they were, her things taking up one side of his closet while his took up the other.

After inhaling one more cleansing breath, Cassidy navigated through the house, taking in the subtle changes that had happened in the short time she'd moved in. Her presence was in the light scent of cinnamon and vanilla, stacks of psychology books, a handful of photos, and a wire wine rack on the counter in one corner of the kitchen.

Davis never complained about her things taking over his space. If anything, he went out of his way to make her feel welcome by adding small touches that acknowledged her presence.

The wine rack had been a gift from him, along with an electric wine opener and coffee pod machine. That one had been an inside joke which made Cassidy smile each time she used it. Davis's house was slowly becoming their house.

She had his attention as soon as she stepped through the back door. A quick glance over his shoulder before his fists pounded out a combination on the heavy bag.

"Everything okay?"

"You would know if you had stayed in there with me instead of coming out here."

She had a good visual of his profile and caught the sexy grin he offered before he dipped and landed another combination.

"Thought you could use the privacy."

"Privacy, why? You already know the details. We were both waiting on that call."

When Davis finished the last combination, he dropped his arms, allowing them to hang loosely at his side, and closed the space between them. While he moved, Cassidy took her time, allowing her eyes to move down his chest to the black shorts covering his lower half, sitting just beneath his narrow waist.

By the time her eyes were on his face again, that cocky grin was back in place. "You done?"

"For *now*, yes."

He chuckled and moved closer, delivering a ghost of a kiss. "What did Greene say?"

"Done deal. Ten years, but she can be out in eight, which means I have at least eight years of peace before I have to worry about her again."

His expression shifted to one of irritation. "You really think I'm going to let you worry about her ever again?"

"It's not like you can prevent it."

"I can if you're with me." His statement left no room for rebuttal, but still, Cassidy pushed for clarity.

"*With* you?"

"Yeah, *with* me."

"Define *with you*." The slow smile that eased onto his face had Cassidy regretting the request.

Almost.

The heated gaze that fastened with hers had her body reacting to the recollection of being *with* Davis.

"*With me* means me going to sleep beside you every night, waking up to you every morning, subbing a few of my workouts with ones that involve you getting worked out." His hands landed on her hips, fingers pressing into her skin as he pulled her body flush against his.

"*With me* translates to me being in you several times a day whenever time permits, and I plan on making sure I have the time."

Cassidy grinned, looping her arms around his neck and leaning deeper into his hold. "I might be okay with ensuring my time also permits that to happen."

"I thought you would. But just in case, I thought maybe I'd give you a preview of what it feels like to be *with m*e."

"Don't last night and this morning count?"

"They do, but I would have put a little something extra on it if I had known I was pleading my case of convincing you to stay."

"What makes you think you needed something extra? Maybe you've already done enough convincing."

"Have I?" He leaned his face toward hers.

Her smile expanded in a matter of seconds. "You can't expect me to say yes, knowing there's another offer on the table."

Davis laughed, brushing his lips over her mouth. "No, wouldn't expect you to pass that up. In fact, I have to insist that you don't."

She yelped when he lifted her but didn't hesitate to lock her legs around his waist, feeling a sense of nostalgia for how many times the two of them had repeated the scene over the past couple of weeks.

"Well then, I guess it's decided."

"Damn sure is," he murmured, navigating them through the house and back to the bedroom, which meant it would be another late-night meal for them. Another thing that had become the norm. Mainly because they spent so much time working up an appetite.

Cassidy would never complain. She didn't have it all figured out, but this time around, she decided she didn't have to. What she *did* know for certain was that she was in control and would never again settle for anyone being a part of her life simply because she was tired of being alone. Being alone was a far better option than accepting less than she deserved. For the first time in her life, she felt she deserved real happiness. That meant putting herself first and making anyone who wanted to be a part of her life earn it. So far, Davis was off to a good start, and for now, she focused on letting him prove just how much he wanted it.

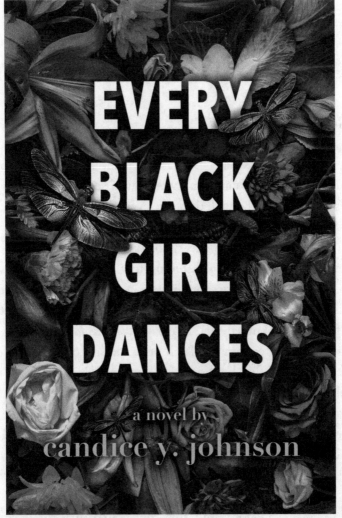

ONE

"GIRL, YOU ARE *black as hell."*

That's not exactly what the woman perched in the aisle seat says to me, but it's what I hear as our plane hits a second round of turbulence in half an hour. Even heaven seems annoyed by her incessant yapping about all things relevant to only her. Thank God, this flight only has a little more than two hours to go.

My row-mate is too cheery for six in the morning. I should be taking my first pee, not listening to a complete stranger with zero sense of boundaries or discretion, chattering about social media and current events while casually tossing in how pretty I am for a dark-skinned girl. Make that *extra dark*, as if I'm not already aware. Her thin lips latch onto the rim of her Styrofoam coffee cup as she flips her bright red curls, utterly oblivious of how insulting her backhanded compliment really is. Somehow, my blatant snub and wide-eyed silence isn't the effective deterrent I'd hoped it would be. Now, she's circling from waxing about visiting her elderly grandfather for a spell in Frisco, Texas, back to her fascination with my skin.

God, I don't have the strength to speak laymen's right now.

"I hope you don't find this rude, but your skin is simply luminous to be so ..."

"Dark?" There. I finish for her. She knows it's rude before she alludes to it. My submissive face takes over as I lean against the window, observing her green eyes grow into saucers and soak up all this darkness in awe. "Makes you want a Snickers, huh?"

Her paltry giggle in response to my direct jab is a staunch reminder of the harsh scrutiny my particular shade of black forces me to deal with every day: she just doesn't get it. She chirps her name as if I care enough to register the pointless syllables in my memory bank. Sandy. Penny. Chrysanthemum. Hell, who knows what she just rattled off? For the rest of this flight from Los Angeles to Dallas, all I want to hear is my playlist while I catch a few zzz's.

What's-her-name blinks, taking a brief respite from her irrelevant musings to breathe. Facing me, she rests an elbow on the armrest and perches her head on top of her hand, curiosity etched across her heart-shaped face. Seriously, if she doesn't stop staring, I will invoice her for a counseling session. Sis acts like my skin's giving her third-world healing.

"Your braids are so . . . unique," she sings loud enough to provoke the passengers occupying the rows in front of and behind us to indiscreetly investigate for themselves as if I can't see them squirming in their seats just enough to judge whether her assessment's on point.

"So different," she mutters, intent on eliciting the response she didn't squeeze out of me the first time. One of her wiry hands gestures as if to reach across the empty middle seat between us to fondle my tailbone-length braids, regarding them with the wonder of a mythical creature she's discovered is actually real. A scowl replacing the excruciating smile I've managed to maintain this long prompts her to draw it back quickly. She darts an index finger toward them instead. "The colors weaved across the middle—I've never seen that before."

"Jamaica," I eek out as pleasantly as I can on the strength of the sigh which carries it.

"Your name's Jamaica?"

I giggle. Not because there's humor in the situation, but because I'm tired. These types of cultural interrogations are seemingly barren but never easy to birth. I'm a realist: no response I give this woman will make her see anything other than my skin. Her creepy gaze almost makes it impossible for me to restrain my snarky attitude, which is two seconds from reaching: *I wish you would.*

"No, ma'am, my name's not Jamaica. The color in my hair represents the Jamaican flag. Where my dead father's from."

"Oh."

She's uncomfortable now. One, because the bitter taste of ignorance isn't so tasty on her tongue. And two, I have yet to give up any useful intel on myself. Not even my name, which sis has been patiently waiting for since we strapped in for takeoff. But as long as I've mastered the resting "B" face—which I'm about to switch on effective immediately—silence shall ever be her portion.

"What did you say your name is? What is it that you do?" *See how intrusive she is?* When I saw our flight wasn't crowded, I expected to snooze all the way home to Texas. But instead, I got stuck with . . . her.

Maybe if I respond, she'll back down and stop leering at me like a puppy begging for a treat. Keeping my cool, I flash the smile the dental hygienist I hired to fix my teeth with my first Hollywood check and blurt, "I write and direct films."

"Oh yeah?" She perks up under the false impression that a bond is forming between us. "What kind of movies do you make? Anything I've seen?"

"Probably not," I hark a laugh as insipid as our wordy transaction. Obviously, there's no way this suburban duchess, who's probably never tasted a swear word, has been exposed to my gritty dramas. If she had, this conversation would've already detoured to mute.

"I make films exploiting Black trauma," I go on to explain. "You know, pimps, domestic violence, drug trafficking, crack babies. Real entertainment." I pull my denim jacket closed and lean closer to her, mimicking her pose on the other side of the armrest. "I write the real rough stuff. Families killing each other, men who can't keep their junk in their pants, silly, trifling baby mamas, and female doormats. Hood stuff like that. But I'm flying to escape the set of my latest film, *Crack Dreams*, because I'm sick of profiting off my brothers' and sisters' pain for the appeasement of people like you."

And just like that, sis turns away with a 'tude, reclines her seat, and pushes out a fake yawn. When she squeezes her eyes shut, I jam my earbuds in and press play on the first song in my playlist. Guess our meet and greet is over.

You've only got one reason not to love me,
But I can give you a thousand more
It's amazing how you hate me
Because my future's far from yours . . .

The jazzy tune by my best friend, Tati Ko, blares through the earpieces, and I recline my seat. Tati's being positioned to be the next queen of R&B music, but I'm flying back home to Parable to help celebrate her million-dollar win on *Battle Exes*, a wilderness-style reality competition show pairing ex-lovers and pitting them against their rivals from past seasons. Even though her ex helped secure Tati the win, she kept the entire bounty for herself. The Twitter crowd and I couldn't be happier that she got her revenge against the narcissist who's still threatening her and her family with violence over her selfish decision.

I peer out the window. The skies seem friendlier than the universe has been to me lately. Not that I'm anything close to a singer, but I can hum a mean tune, so I do it along with "Redeemed by Me," the song Tati wrote for my debut film, *Flogged*. *Flogged* chronicles the life of 16-year-old Nas, who was sold by her mother into the sex trade for drugs, and later convicted of murdering both her kidnapper and her mama. Like I told sis earlier, warm fuzzies.

Hard to believe, but a week ago, the same tune I'm jamming to now almost got me killed. Okay, maybe I'm being dramatic. But the incident was enough to make me come close to soiling the yellow sundress I planned on returning after sporting it at my girl Olivia's bachelorette party. Just because I have a few dollars tucked away in savings doesn't mean I'm not cheap.

Olivia's party was so lit, I stayed way longer than I originally intended. In my defense, *pole dance karaoke* far exceeded my expectations, killing my self-imposed curfew. But when the bride's mother slides from the top of the pole to the bottom in slow motion while killing the best of Whitney Houston in mezzo-soprano, you don't move. If nothing else, it helped me forget the crap day I had in preproduction for my next movie.

Anyway, I was zooming down the side streets on the way back to my loft, belching the remnants of the mini-mountain of mimosas I drank, feeling too good to notice I was pushing my red convertible Lexus well over the speed limit by 20 miles an hour. Didn't even see the police car waiting to catch an unsuspecting lawbreaker like me slipping until I flew by him, and the lights started chasing me.

"Great, just great. Hudson, I'll have to call you back," I told my boyfriend, who'd been on speaker the entire hour-long ride, to help keep me awake.

"What's wrong? Everything okay?" The slight panic in his voice did nothing to ease the fear swirling in the pit of my stomach as I eyed the wailing lights behind me. The way the flashes of blue and red intermingled with each other felt like a threat and made my stomach sink. Immediately, I wished I hadn't guzzled so many drinks.

"I'm not okay. I just got pulled over," I explained as I pulled to the side of the road and put the car in park. My trembling hands outshook my quaking voice. Minutes ago, the air was so cool; now, a trail of sweat immediately formed around my edges.

"Is that all?" Hudson chuckled. "Just comply with whatever they say, and you'll be fine." The amusement in my man's voice shook off any buzz threatening to keep me from walking a straight line if I was issued a sobriety test. Not to mention the one word that would ban my ovaries to him for the rest of our tenure together: *comply*.

What the entire hell?

"I have to go. I'll call you back." Ignoring Hudson's unsolicited advice, I reached to the dash where the phone was mounted and hung up. Then I started my video recorder and rested my hands on the steering wheel like my father taught me.

Breathe, girl, breathe. You're going to be fine.

Spying the officer creeping toward my car in the rearview, I was suddenly aware that my braids were secured in a bun at the nape of my neck. What if he mistook me for a man? Would it make a difference? Was there just a matter of minutes before I became a hashtag swimming in a pool of my own blood? Would there be protests in my name, or would I be quickly forgotten by the next day's news?

Would I be awarded a posthumous Oscar?

I won't lie. The officer's brown skin was a relief when he appeared at my window. After chronicling some pretty damning scenarios involving the boys in blue in my films, at least I was being stopped by a cop who looked like me . . . right?

"Good evening, ma'am. Do you know why I pulled you over?" His baritone thundered through my spirit. His broad chest heaved, and his badge issued a silent dare. *Try me.*

"I guess I was speeding," I said, not that my misdemeanor needed confirming.

"You were." His head tilted to the side, then quickly upright. "Hey, aren't you Hudson Pyke's girlfriend?"

No, I'm JC Burke, the dummy who let my blue-eyed lover get famous off my scripts while I literally became his shadow. But yeah, I'm her.

Eyes ahead, hands on the wheel. "Yes, Officer. That's me: JC Burke."

"Uh-huh."

I hesitantly allowed my head to inch left, scanning for the officer's name in case I needed receipts later. In the meantime, Officer Riggins's eyes darted past my face to the phone mounted on the dash.

Smile . . . You're this close to becoming viral.

"That last movie of yours - the cop was acquitted of attempted murder for shooting the kid in the back, right?"

I knew it. "Yes, he was, sir. I mean, the girl was running away after being suspected of shoplifting a T-shirt. And there was no excuse for swinging at the boutique owner when he tackled her, even though no stolen goods or weapons were found on her. At least she was only paralyzed, right?" I pressed my lips closed, bottling the rest of my opinion inside.

"Right. What was the name of it again? The movie?"

"*First-Degree Melanin.*"

His brows pinched together, broad shoulders hunched. "Yeah. The wife didn't care for that one too much." His low voice dodged my cell's audio as his fingers tapped against his ticket pad, which I preferred instead of on his holster. "She said the plot was unrealistic."

. . . in spite of the real Wisconsin news story I based it on?

"Look, it's hard to see out here. We don't want you having an accident, do we?"

You mean by car or bullet?

Without relaxing my tightened jaws, I peeled my stoic glare away from the badge, staring ahead. "No, sir, we don't."

"Good. Slow down," he warned. Taking a quick second to assess my threat level, he must've determined my 135-pound frame wasn't too menacing because he jammed the pad back into his pocket and exhaled the tension from his body. "Be safe out here."

The lump obstructing my throat didn't dislodge until Officer Riggins hopped back into his patrol car and left me reeling on the side of the road. How long had I held my breath? I slumped over the steering wheel in tears, trying to coerce my spirit to climb back into my mortified flesh, all while Hudson's instructions burned my chest.

Comply.

I slammed my hands against the dash until I swore I'd drawn blood. Without a shred of empathy, the rearview mirror gave me a glimpse of my runny mascara and snotty nose. *Comply* rang in my ears, breaking me down worse than the actual traffic stop.

After a few minutes, I turned the key in the ignition and pulled back onto the main road at a much-slower pace. Without bothering to call Hudson to give him an update, I powered off the phone. Let him worry whether I had *complied* for the rest of the night while I tried getting some sleep.

Once I got home and climbed in bed, I slept better than during the six weeks we'd been working on *Crack Dreams*. The next day, I powered through Olivia's wedding, then hit the reception with Hudson at my side. It was a grand affair of excesses and sparkle, so I didn't need to bring up his prior night's infraction until after the bride and groom's first dance. I think I did a pretty good job presenting the thousand other ways Hudson could've handled things better when I told him I got stopped; however, he made a conscious effort to misunderstand while *white-splaining* me instead.

"What's the big deal, JC? The drinks are flowing, and everybody's happy. There's no reason to walk around here with your face all twisted up." Hudson spun me as the other couples slow danced around us. His eyes were hidden behind his signature red frames. Tousled brown hair mussed from yanking it every two seconds while I patiently walked him through the source of our latest fight.

Hudson dipped me, but I locked my back to protect my breasts from spilling out of the strapless eggplant bridesmaid dress barely containing them. When he pulled me up, I pushed into his chest, hoping to feel the same security in his arms that I felt on our first date.

Nothing.

"At least you didn't get a ticket." Hudson's nonchalant assertion harbored dangerously close to amusement.

I backed away, dishing a death glare. "Have you heard *anything* I've said? I could've had my head blown off last night."

"Sure, in an imaginary scenario, which has absolutely no bearing on here and now." He smoothed a hand over my braids. "All I'm saying is don't waste your energy on something that didn't even happen. You've had 26 years to understand how traffic stops work. All you have to do is—"

"Don't you *dare* say, 'comply'!"

That word transported me back to the playground in elementary school when my bullies forced me to eat dirt pies.

Know what my teachers said when they gave me a spit cup to rinse the dirt out of my mouth in the bathroom? *"No one likes a tattler. Next time, walk away."*

What kind of a gutless waste of skin says that to a child who soiled her panties because she got jumped? *Code: comply.* Same disrespect, different recipe. And every time the man who rarely says he loves me outside of the bed brushes off my concerns with the standard refrain that I'm "just being emotional," it tastes like one of those disgusting dirt pies.

Hudson gently tugged me by the rhinestone belt cinched around my waist, pulling me closer. "Can we have one day without you swiping your black card?" As soon as the question dropped, his pale skin turned crimson when he noticed my lips pulled in a tight line. "I'm sorry."

"I am too."

Two minutes later, it wasn't hard convincing Olivia I wasn't feeling well and had to exit the celebration early. Hudson didn't call my name when I walked away from him. Didn't reach for my arm to hold me back or match my steps so I couldn't lose him on the way out of the gargantuan hall. By my estimation, he had at least 20 steps from where we were dancing to the parking lot to right his wrong.

But he didn't.

"Oh my, I didn't realize I'd fallen asleep." Sis is awake now, blowing stale air up my nostrils, which I quickly cover with a hand. Judging by her restored cheery demeanor despite our earlier exchange, she's still not woke, though.

"Just in time for landing." I grant her a smile, my fleeting apology for getting fly when she's only trying to make this trip pleasant for us. That's one thing I've hated about myself since I was a little girl. Being bold enough to buck, then too quick to nurse the wound when 'ish gets uncomfortable. I'm brazen on film, but I'm scared of being muted if I hit the wrong note.

Once we've landed and been given the go-ahead to exit the plane, sis stretches, then peels herself from the seat to retrieve her bag from the overhead. She grins and maneuvers into the aisle, pushing her way through the other passengers, all trying to get off the plane at once. "Enjoy your trip."

"You too." I don't follow behind her.

My backpack seems heavier when I hoist it over my shoulder, waiting for row after row of passengers to empty the plane. When there is finally nothing but empty seats in front of me, a kind gentleman allows me to squeeze into the aisle ahead of him. I'm praying the nice gesture will be indicative of my week at home.

Maybe.

People scurry past me as I slowly make my way to the baggage claim. By the time I get there, sis has already grabbed her stuff and is heading off. We lock eyes for a moment, and she waves like we'll see each other again in this lifetime. I wave back, thinking how at some point in our lives, every Black girl dances to someone else's expectations. It's about time I choreograph for myself.